"Things could get really complicated really fast..."

Jaime handed Emmett the shovel. "Then we uncomplicate it. I think I've already proven I'm a much better planner than actual renovator. I'm turning in my shovel and hammer."

He flicked the brim of her ball cap with his thumb and index finger. "That will definitely speed things up."

She batted her eyelashes at him. "And here I thought you wanted to take things slowly."

"Well, there is twenty-first century slow and then there is 1920s slow." A twinkle lit his blue eyes. There was still something he wasn't telling her— something she didn't know—but Jaime pushed that thought out of her head. There was time to figure all of it out.

And maybe, just this once, it would be okay if she didn't examine things so closely.

Maybe, it would be okay to just see where this took them. She leaned forward and brushed her lips across his.

"I definitely think twenty-first century slow is the way to go..."

Dear Reader,

I have a love affair with second-chance love stories. There is something about two people who are willing to take another swing at love after it's kicked them in the teeth that just makes me root for them.

Jaime and Emmett have that kind of story. High school sweethearts, neither expected their romance to end with a class trip to Pennsylvania...and neither is quite ready for what it means when that spark of attraction ignites once more. I adore both of these characters, but Jaime holds a special place in my heart because of her willingness to look into the darkness and still see light.

Happy reading!

Kristina Knight
KristinaKnightAuthor.com

Kristina Knight decided she wanted to be a writer, like her favorite soap opera heroine, Felicia Gallant, one cold day when she was home sick from school. She took a detour into radio and television journalism but never forgot her first love of romance novels, or her favorite character from her favorite soap. In 2012 she got The Call from an editor who wanted to buy her book. Kristina lives in Ohio with her handsome husband, incredibly cute daughter and two dogs.

Books by Kristina Knight

HARLEQUIN SUPERROMANCE

The Daughter He Wanted

For Kyle, because you find a way
to make me laugh, you hold me
when I need a good cry and you're
always ready to go on an adventure.
I love you.

CHAPTER ONE

"BUT IT ISN'T FINISHED."

Jaime Brown pushed a lock of curly blond hair behind her ear, but it was so muggy on this May afternoon that the lock sprang right back to the side of her face to tickle the sensitive skin along her jaw.

"Isn't like your little party is tomorrow. There's time." The grizzled head of the renovation project scratched dirty hands over his scruffy chin.

Luther Thomas had sounded fatherly over the phone when she'd hired him. Competent. He might be good at his job, but after five days on the island he and his "crew" had put a few holes in the room walls downstairs and that was it. She'd found them drinking at the tavern, fishing on the docks and sitting under the big maple trees in the parking lot, but as far as actual work went she hadn't seen much.

Plenty of time. No, there wasn't. The reunion might still be six weeks off, but there were two complete stories of the old school building to renovate. Having the ground floor demo'd was a huge step in the whole process.

"We're knocking down walls, rebuilding a staircase and replacing old windows. That isn't just slapping up a new coat of paint." She pushed the long sleeves of her gray T-shirt up her arms, hoping for a little relief from the heat.

Damn the month of May, anyway. When she'd left her cottage on Gulliver's Island this morning it was a comfortable sixty-five degrees with a light breeze blowing in from the west. Perfect weather for lightweight-but-long-sleeved. But the crazy weather along this part of Ohio's Lake Erie struck and the breeze changed to a full-on wind, bringing in muggy air that didn't usually hit until after Memorial Day.

What she wouldn't give to pull the shirt over her head. The ribs on her left side twinged, as if the scars covering them were still raw, brown with dried blood and ugly. No chance she'd pull the shirt off, even if her sports bra covered more than the bikinis she used to wear on hot summer days.

"Don't worry about it," Luther said, beginning to sound like a broken record. Every time she asked about the teardown, the shape of the staircase and the windows she got either a "don't worry about it" or a "plenty of time" answer. Well, she wasn't taking that answer this time. The project might not be important to Luther, but it was important to her.

To the whole island community.

She folded her arms beneath her breasts. Through the fabric, her fingers instinctively sought out the scars that were now faint pink lines crisscrossing her ribs and one ugly, jagged mark that reached over her left breast. She'd rebuilt her life over the past ten years; she could deal with a lousy construction foreman.

"When we spoke on the phone you assured me this section of the building would be finished this week."

"The reunion isn't tomorrow or even next week." Luther didn't bother to look at her when he spoke and Jaime gritted her teeth. "We've got six more weeks to finish." He kept walking toward the door.

Jaime followed the tall, foul-smelling, dirty-jeans-wearing lunker of a man she would never have hired if she'd met him in person. But people could hide all manner of things over video chat, although it had never failed her before. Like breath that reeked of stale beer at nine-thirty in the morning. She wrinkled her nose and then swallowed. He picked up the hammer he'd left at the bottom of the staircase leading to the second floor of the run-down school house.

She had convinced her father and the rest of Gulliver Township's trustees that she would have it restored by July, in time for her high school class to host the annual Gulliver School Reunion.

"Six weeks to finish the job, yes, but you've been here nearly a week and aside from a couple of holes in a couple of walls nothing has been done." The man kept walking and Jaime hurried to keep up.

She waved her arms at the main floor, walls still dividing what were once the main office, cafeteria and gymnasium, broken window-panes hung at odd angles and—she tripped over her feet—the warped hardwood floor that might indicate a foundation problem. "This room was to be completely demolished by Friday. It's Thursday and you've barely made any progress since arriving on Monday. Your crew didn't even show up yesterday."

Luther tossed the hammer toward his tool-box where it clanged against other metal tools. "My crew handles jobs like this all the time," he said, a patronizing lilt to his voice. At least his words were no longer slurred like they had been yesterday morning when he'd insisted his guys would be back from the mainland by lunchtime. They hadn't returned by lunch or even been on the evening ferry. "The walls will be down next week. We'll take a look at the floor. It's Thursday. I need to catch the ferry so I can go home."

"The ferry doesn't arrive for another hour. And it's *Thursday*. One more day in the work-week."

"Not much I can do here on my own, any-way."

"All the more reason for your crew to show up for work on time."

They stepped into the warm sunshine and Jaime breathed a sigh of relief. Out here the air felt ten degrees cooler than inside. Most of the downstairs windows were so warped they didn't open, and the windows upstairs had been installed as solid panes. Leaving the front and back doors open created a slight cross breeze but not enough to keep the interior of the ancient school building cool. Maybe she should consider investing part of the budget in an air-conditioning system, after all.

The goal for the school renovation was to create a tourist attraction on the island and at the same time to provide the island with a space for events like the upcoming reunion.

Technically it was her class's ten-year so they were in charge of food, drinks and party planning, but everyone who graduated from Gulliver's Island School was invited and most of them would come.

Gulliver needed this space. She wanted a project that would keep everyone focused on the present and not the past. No way would she allow this jerk of a construction worker to ruin everything just because he'd thought working on the island would be a breeze. She might not have a degree in construction, if there was such a thing, but she knew how contracts worked.

"You assured me the walls on the main floor will be down today and that the replacement windows will have been ordered. Have either of those things been completed?"

Luther opened the door of his dusty red truck and slid in behind the wheel. "Lady, I know how to run a construction project, and I know what my obligations are. I've been on this damned island for four days straight and I need a break from no cable television, watered-down beer and AM-only radio, okay?"

Jaime caught the door before Luther could slam it shut. "You're here to work, not have a vacation."

Luther narrowed his eyes before pulling

the door out of Jaime's grasp. It slammed shut and she winced. "The school will be ready by July one, until then I'll run the project as I see fit. And, today, I'm running it to the dock so I can catch the morning ferry and go home." He twisted the key between his grimy fingers and the truck engine roared to life. Before Jaime could demand he stay to at least order the new windows, he tore out of the parking lot, leaving her in a cloud of dust.

Jaime coughed and sputtered, waving her hands before her face until the dust cleared. Jerk.

Her cell phone blared out a hit from Florida Georgia Line; the song a favorite of her best friend and cochair of the reunion committee, Maureen Ergstrom.

"Mo, if one more thing has gone wrong I'm going to light a match and burn this damn building down."

"Calm down, there, Firebug. No need to commit arson before eleven. Luther strikes again?" Laughter filled Maureen's voice.

Jaime sat on the concrete step leading into the school. As with everything else about the old building it was off, leaning crookedly against the building with one side a full two inches lower than the other. She felt like she was sitting on a warped teeter-totter.

"Luther just walked out. Says he's tired of our boring little island and wants to go home."

Something banged over the phone line. Probably Maureen's kitchen chair pounding into the counter. "He can't do that." She sounded panicked so Jaime kept her voice calm.

"From our walk-through yesterday morning I don't think any new work has been done since his crew left on Wednesday." Jaime shoved her hand into her hair. What was she going to do? All the local firms were already booked for the summer. Getting the Cleveland crew had been a miracle so late in the season. "And before you ask again, I don't know where we would find another crew. I think we're stuck with Luther and the no-shows."

"Maybe it's a sign."

"Of my complete ineptitude? Thanks."

Maureen made a shushing sound over the phone. "A sign that this year we skip the reunion. Our class is so scattered no one will mind—"

"We're not skipping it. The reunion is a tradition."

"A stupid tradition. Clara dumped the planning in your lap at the last minute and after everything that happened before graduation… I think everyone would be happy with a fish fry on the beach."

"We are not turning the annual reunion into a fish fry, Mo." Her stomach tightened just thinking about dropping this particular ball. Yes, Clara had dumped the reunion on her with no notice. Yes, the past couple of months of their senior year had been horrific for Jaime.

She gripped the phone more tightly in her hand.

"Come on, what town needs an island-wide reunion every summer? Our class was never big on these kinds of things, anyway."

Jaime cleared her throat, pushing the panicked butterflies out of her stomach. She would not be the victim. Not again. Not when she had worked so hard to put her life back together. "We aren't skipping. It's our turn to host and that's final."

The reunion would not be canceled; not because Jaime hired a shoddy construction firm. She would not give the islanders another reason to act as if she was…wounded.

"I'll meet you at the diner in fifteen and we'll go over the early RSVPs and start thinking about the actual planning," she said and hung up before Maureen could really get going on the cancellation conversation. If Luther and his crew were going to milk this job until the last minute, she would be prepared to use each of those final seconds to make sure the reunion went off without a hitch.

Her ribs twinged again.

It was ten years ago, for Pete's sake. She was over it. Six more weeks and she could completely put it out of her mind and in the meantime she had the school to renovate, the reunion party to plan and her job at the winery. Plenty of work to keep her mind occupied and fully in the present, where she preferred to be. There was no reason to keep living in the past. Wasn't that what her therapist told her? She was still cured.

Two years before she'd been a borderline agoraphobic afraid to leave the island. Sometimes afraid to leave her cute little cottage on the west side of town. The first two sessions with Dr. Laurer were held via video chat. For the following four months Dr. Laurer brought the ferry to Gulliver twice a week to meet with her at the cottage or at the diner. The day she took the ferry to his office for a session he'd declared her cured. She'd celebrated with her parents at a nice restaurant on the waterfront.

The fact that she hadn't been off the island

since that day was beside the point. She was over the past. Over the attack. No need to keep bringing it up.

Maybe if she'd gone to the mainland with Maureen for a girl's day, or even to go to the movies with her mom once or twice she would not have thought twice about driving to Cleveland to meet with Luther before hiring him. There were always reasons to skip an impromptu shopping or movie trip, though. After a while people stopped asking her to do things off the island and until the excitement about the upcoming reunion started she didn't think twice about all the ways she had become complacent about her life.

That stopped now.

Canceling the reunion, letting the school project founder, would bring the past up in a big way. Would stress out her parents, who deserved so much more than constantly worrying their daughter would freak out and never leave her house again. The whispered conversations would start. The pitying looks. She loved the island and she loved the people on it, but they had to stop treating her like she was broken.

She wasn't.

She was healed. Maybe if she kept telling herself that it would actually be true.

Fifteen minutes later Jaime sat in her favorite corner booth at the Gulliver Diner watching out the big plate-glass window and stealing glances at a booth in the back to a stranger with broad shoulders and a tight T. His black hair that was short enough to look tidy but long enough to look just a little bit dangerous. He looked…interesting. At least from the back.

But Jaime didn't leave her bench seat to covertly check him out on her way to the bathroom. It was enough to watch the economical movements he used to cut into his eggs Benedict.

She shifted in her seat and the cracked purple vinyl sighed with the movement. The Formica-topped tables were chipped, and the black-and-white-tiled floor was scuffed and scarred beyond repair, but the Gulliver Diner was a mainstay on the island. Funny, though, Anna, the diner's only waitress for as long as she could remember, usually paid a lot more attention to tourists, and she'd barely flirted with the hot guy in the corner. Maybe the view from the front negated the pulse-pounding view from behind, she thought.

Finally, Maureen pulled up in her little blue golf cart and hurried inside. She wore skinny jeans and Converse sneakers with a striped sailor top in navy and white. Her hair in a ponytail, quilted backpack slung across her torso, she looked pulled together. Jaime shrank back against the seat as her outfit would never be mistaken for fashionable.

Anna brought over a tall, frosted glass and a pitcher of iced tea. She topped off Jaime's glass, filled Maureen's and set the pitcher on the table for them. "You girls want a sandwich?" She waved her hand toward the kitchen. "Hank's making triple-decker clubs for lunch today. I just served the last of the Benedicts to him," she said, pointing to the corner booth. Jaime's gaze came to rest on the back of the stranger with broad shoulders and dark, dark hair. She couldn't see his face but her tummy did a little flip-flop.

Which was silly. She didn't do the flip-flop thing any longer. Especially not in grubby work clothes. She should have taken the time to change before meeting Maureen for lunch.

They each ordered sandwiches and Anna disappeared behind the counter.

"Listen to this one." Jaime tucked the strand of blond hair behind her ear, determined to ignore the discomfort weighing on her narrow shoulders. Before she could begin reading from the questionnaire in her hand Maureen interrupted.

"I think we need to seriously consider *not* having an island-wide reunion this summer." She held up her hand and Jaime bit back the protest that immediately sprang to her lips. "The school reno is a huge project, and it's more important than the reunion. The reno will bring tourists back here year after year. Having all our old classmates come in and seeing the old-timers who moved off-island years ago is great. What the island needs, though, is a steady stream of tourists. Newcomers. Old residents."

"And they'll come, but the reno doesn't trump the reunion."

"Maybe it should." Maureen reached across the table to pat Jaime's hand. As she and so many others had so many times over the past decade. She was sick to death of their patronizing. "The reno was a last-minute fix to the location problem when the winery said no to hosting the main reunion events. That is on our class. The pranks we pulled still make people see us as a bunch of bored kids—"

"All the more reason to prove to them that we've all moved on from the idiots we were in high school. We can do both and put all the gossiping to rest."

"I just think we should seriously consider

pulling back. Finish the reno in style and do a big opening for the reunion next summer."

Jaime blinked. Waited another moment. "Is that all?"

Maureen nodded.

"Good. Motion denied."

"You didn't bring it before the committee." Maureen beetled her brows.

"The reunion 'committee' consists of you, me and Clara. Clara dropped all of her responsibilities in my lap a month ago, so her vote goes to me. That makes it two to one for the reunion."

Maureen made a face. "You always have an angle."

"Only when it really matters. So, on with the RSVPs. Who wrote this?" Jaime rattled the paper in her hands and read, "'Since leaving Gulliver I've completed my law degree and now work for one of the leading defense firms in Cleveland...'" she pitched her voice higher, trying to mimic the Minnie Mouse tone Pam Andrews had used through three speech classes and in her valedictory address on graduation day. She rolled her eyes and made up the next part. "'But if I don't make partner by the time I'm thirty, I'll just move to the Magic Kingdom to reunite with Mickey.'"

Maureen laughed. "You've got Pam down pat, Jai."

The tension between them dissipated as they read the latest batch of reunion mail to hit Jaime's mailbox.

Jaime breathed a sigh of relief. Usually their close-knit community made her feel safe but lately... Lately all she felt was annoyed. Annoyed that, because the attack had happened ten years before and she was now planning her class's ten-year reunion, everyone seemed to think she needed extra care. Her mom kept calling at odd hours... Maureen had come up with every reason possible to cancel the reunion... Anna had sent home leftovers from the diner at least twice each week... Even Tom, her boss at Gulliver Wines, had suggested she bring in a couple of interns to help with summertime events.

Her father and a few of his cronies came in for lunch, laughing with Anna as they ordered club sandwiches and thick-cut fries. The men started talking, about township business or maybe last night's baseball game, Jaime couldn't be certain. Anna kept the tables bused and the coffee cups filled. Jaime knew every single person inside the restaurant. This was just the way she liked it. Quiet. Normal.

Tourists were a necessary part of island life, even though the crush of them made her skin itch. A solo stranger sitting across the room? No big deal. She glanced at the stranger who had pushed his empty plate to the edge of the table. A welcome distraction, really. But a mass of humanity exiting one of the ferries? She shivered. Of course without the tourists the three main islands—Kelly's, South Bass and Gulliver's—wouldn't survive.

From her vantage point, she could see the Marblehead Lighthouse across the bay and, if she craned her neck, just make out the top of Perry's Monument. In late May, the trees were budding and colorful flowers splashed along the Lake Erie shore. In another week or so Cedar Point, a huge amusement park, would be open and the ferries would increase their trips to the islands.

"Mine is worse." Maureen cleared her throat, dragging Jaime's attention back to the table, and then speaking in a deep baritone. "'I left Gulliver to play football, and I did.'" She shook her head and then spoke in her normal voice. "Jason never did learn how to string more than a few words together, did he?"

Jaime focused on her friend. "He lost a little too much oxygen to those half nelson's in wrestling meets. He's done well for himself, though. I hear next fall he'll be the main anchor for one of those college football shows on cable."

Maureen's jaw dropped. "Jason the Jerk you defend when he was a bully all through school but Pam the Perfect you throw to the wolves?"

"Jason wasn't so much a bully as a kid who didn't know his own strength. He didn't, and probably still doesn't, have a mean-hearted bone is his whole body."

Jaime checked off the last two names on the list for the reunion. Nearly all the invitations had been accepted. Not bad considering she and Maureen had only taken over Project Reunion and had sent out the invitations two weeks before. One name without a checkmark stood out. Emmett Deal. Who'd disappeared on prom night, never to be heard from again.

Except in her dreams. Well, usually only when she stayed up too late watching cable and saw him on one of those home renovations shows. On those nights his muscular, tanned form seemed to sink straight into her brain like a weighted hook sank to the bottom of Lake Erie. Her stomach would do that flip-flopping thing it kept doing when she looked at the broad shoulders of the stranger in the corner. So she was a sucker for a pair of broad shoulders, was that so bad?

She was definitely not obsessed with how he looked, shirtless and buff, with a tool belt around his lean hips. Nope, she hardly ever pictured that at all, and she definitely had not done a little comparison shopping between the hunk on cable TV and the hairy guys Luther had brought with him to the island.

"Anna mentioned the diner would host the meet and greet on Friday night, if we wanted." Jaime closed the folder and slid it into her satchel.

"Love that idea, and we could stagger the times so the place isn't overrun all at once. Everyone wants to eat here when they come back home, anyway."

Maureen checked her watch and slid out of the booth. "I've got that volunteer thing at the elementary this afternoon. God, I can't wait for summer break. Want to hash out the party details tomorrow over breakfast? The kiddo will be knee-deep in kindergarten fun by eight-thirty, so I could be here by eight-forty-five." Maureen emptied the pitcher into a travel cup while they made plans and then hustled out the door. Jaime signaled Anna for a refill and watched out the window as the first ferry pulled into the dock.

She looked around. If the school reno went well, there would be few quiet mornings like this at the diner. Still, it would be good for the locals if more tourists hit their shore instead of the other islands.

"Now that Thomas has canceled the contract, we should cancel the reno, gut it and tear it down." Mason Brown's voice was quiet in the restaurant, but she had no trouble overhearing. Not that her father ever minded people overhearing him, especially when he was talking about something controversial. "The roof's falling in. Someone is going to be seriously hurt."

What was he talking about? She'd talked to Luther not an hour before. Cold, clammy dread shivered up Jaime's spine as she twisted around in her seat.

Mason wore his usual uniform of navy pants and light blue, short-sleeved dress shirt with the Gulliver's Island Police Department logo over the breast. "Department" was a bit of a stretch, she knew. Other than Mason there were two full-time employees and one was the island dispatcher. It was all the small community needed, except during the summer months.

He continued. "That old school has got to go, there's no ifs, ands, or buts."

Jaime's jaw dropped. When the Gulliver family had bought the island two hundred years before, they'd planted their vineyard and built the school, which was what had grown the tiny village of Gulliver Township. The school's brass bell hadn't rung in decades, but the place was still important to the island.

It was important to *her*, and not just as a distraction over the whole ten-year nonsense.

Jaime wiped her mouth and pushed up and out of her booth to step closer to their table. Her father spoke to Tom Gulliver, her boss at the winery, and a few other township trustees.

"Excuse me," she said. "The construction crew is making good progress. I don't think we need to call it quits so soon." The lie tasted bad in her mouth.

"The crew isn't coming back. Luther made it official when he stopped by the township office a half hour ago." Mason sighed. His patronizing tone set the hairs on the back of Jaime's neck on edge.

"What do you mean they aren't coming back? I was with Luther not more than an hour ago. He left, but only for the weekend." Jaime couldn't wrap her head around what her father was saying. This was bad. Really, really bad.

"The renovation wasn't thought out clearly enough."

"Answer my question. How do you know the crew is walking out of the job?"

Mason sucked in a slow breath and Jaime fisted her hands at her sides. "I mean he stopped by the township office with the *unsigned* contract and said he was through being monitored by a party planner and walked out."

Party planner? Monitored? She'd been doing her job. Mason continued before Jaime could defend herself. "And, Jaime, sweetheart, I'm not sure you have all the facts about Gulliver School."

"I know it's a historic landmark. I know it educated several generations of Gulliver residents and mainland kids." She straightened her shoulders. "I know during World War II the Red Cross used it as a meeting place of sorts for the women left behind." Just because something didn't work the way some thought it should didn't mean that thing should be destroyed. "The building has a lot of issues, but it isn't as bad as we initially thought—"

"Did you know little Andy Grapple broke one of the windows over the weekend, crawled inside and then fell from the second-floor landing?" Tom Gulliver's voice was deep and passionate.

Tom and her father had been buddies as long as Jaime could remember. Other than her father Tom was the only person on the island who knew exactly what had happened ten years before. All those years ago her father helped her hide her scars, and thanks to Tom she had a good job, but this was not the same. "No, I—"

"Did you know some of the high school kids have used that place as a parking spot?" her father chimed in. Of course she knew that. *Everyone* knew that.

"Or that the roof is collapsing?" Rick Meter, another trustee, joined the conversation.

Yes, she knew more about the old school than anyone else on the island at this point. She hadn't known about Andy's fall, though, which was odd, but she knew renovation could save the old brick building. Throwing it away like a broken toy was just…wrong. "Roofs can be fixed, windows replaced."

"We can't station a guard outside 24/7 to keep kids out of it."

"You could install an alarm system," a new voice joined the conversation. The hairs on Jaime's neck stood up again. The man in the corner. This time it wasn't annoyance at being talked down to that caused the reaction. It was the voice itself. A voice she never thought she'd hear, at least not while she was on Gulliver.

The broad shoulders.

The not too long but not too short black hair.

Sure, his face was turned away, but she should have known or at least suspected. Ten years.

She turned slowly and felt the blood drain from her cheeks. The man from the corner booth wasn't so much stranger as long-lost resident.

Emmett Deal stood there, listening to her argument with the trustees. Sunlight glinted off the pristine windshield of an unfamiliar work truck. Stenciled on the side were the words *Deal Construction*. Here was Emmett and here was his truck. She blinked and he was still standing at a table near the front door. She wasn't imagining him.

His eyes were bluer than she remembered. More of a cerulean than the baby blues that invaded her dreams when she was overly tired. He was taller, too. Not by much, maybe an inch. His shoulders more broad and his hips— Jaime gave herself a mental shake and brought her gaze back to Emmett's beautiful face. Chiseled jaw...hint of stubble.

Before he'd left Emmett had hated that he couldn't grow a proper mustache. It didn't look as though that was a problem any longer. Black, black hair flirted with the collar of his tight T.

He seemed to look straight past her, though. Jaime swallowed and tried to ignore her rapidly beating heart.

Okay, so looking at his face wasn't the right thing to do, either. She turned back to the men at the table.

"An alarm." She swallowed, hating that her voice slid up an octave. "An alarm system is a good start, and better than razing a building that is important to Gulliver," she said, this time keeping her voice steady. "We can hire another reno crew." Somewhere in the state of Ohio there had to be a construction crew available. There had to be. "With so much activity, the kids will stay away."

"Even during overnights and weekends?" Her father shook his head and folded his beefy arms over his chest. He sat back in his chair. "We don't have the staff to run over to the school every time a squirrel sets off the system. We should reallocate the budget into teardown and creating a city park on the land."

Jaime cleared her throat but her mind was blank. "A memorial park isn't better than a building that has stood watch over this town, this island, for two hundred years."

Emmett refilled his to-go coffee cup at the counter. "A good system will know the difference between a squirrel and a person. Parks are great things but there is plenty of undeveloped land on the island that could be used for a new park. Not that it's any of my business." He paid Anna and faced the table while he sipped his drink.

Jaime wasn't sure if she should hug Emmett for taking her side or demand that he let her handle this on her own.

"No, it's not." Her father's words were curt. "This is a township decision."

Demand he leave. Definitely, definitely demand he leave. Mason was about to go ballistic about outsiders versus islanders. "Thank you—"

Emmett cut her off. "I may not live on Gulliver any longer, but my father does. He came close to having the school declared a historic landmark a few years back." He sipped his coffee, looking at the men at the table and studiously avoiding the section of the diner where Jaime now stood. That annoyed the bejesus out of her.

"As I said, this is a township decision. Before we spend more money on another crew that will leave us high and dry, I think we should seriously consider demolition. And as you said yourself, you're not part of the township. Haven't been for ten years."

"Seems like it wouldn't take much work to fill in the gaps in that old application. Renovating is never cheap but a lot of times it is cheaper than tearing down."

"Maybe you should stick to what you know." Mason's voice was low in the quiet diner.

"As it happens, I know old buildings. I could take a look at it."

"And then leave when things get tougher than you imagined?"

Color flooded Jaime's cheeks. This wasn't about the school building; not any longer. Her father was being his usual bullheaded self. Blaming Emmett for something that wasn't his fault.

Before her father could say something he didn't mean Jaime pushed back into the conversation. "Then the township should decide, not just the board of trustees. During the island's bicentennial last summer every

Gulliver business benefited from the increased tourist traffic. If the school is renovated, we would have that kind of draw all the time. A few artists stop every summer to paint the old building. Renovation will give them more of a reason to come back than a park."

From the hand in his pocket to the hunched shoulders, Emmett looked anything but comfortable. As if this conversation was not going the way he'd thought.

Well, then, he should have butted out from the beginning.

"Are you willing to take a look? So we know exactly what to talk to demolition *or* renovation experts about." Tom Gulliver practically preened as he said the words.

"I'll be on the island for a few weeks. Whatever you decide, I can offer my opinion."

The bell over the door tinkled as Emmett pushed through it. He got into his truck without looking back and drove away.

Jaime realized she was staring—again—and looked back at her father.

"I still say we should vote on demolition at the meeting tonight," he said from his side of the table.

"Dad—"

"The Deal boy might have the right idea. Could be cheaper to restore the building, I've said that from the beginning. It's part of island history." Rick Meter picked his teeth with a toothpick and Jaime shivered. Of all the times for her to agree with Rick Meter. "We hired Luther's crew after a light appraisal from Troy Turner at the real-estate office. Emmett will know better what exactly the building needs and we can go from there."

Jaime clenched her hands. *Emmett will know better, indeed.* He knew all about running away, but staying? Fixing what was broken?

"Restoring the building will bring more tourists to Gulliver, and not just during the summer months. Tourists already visit the islands to see Perry's Monument—" she mentioned the memorial at Put-in-Bay "—and the Marblehead Lighthouse. Gulliver School could become one of those draws."

"Getting a true estimate before we start the hiring process, for demo or reno, is smart." Rick leaned back in his seat and plucked another toothpick from the table dispenser. He stuck it between his teeth and then put his hands behind his head. "Even if we voted tonight we wouldn't have the permits or contracts for demolition before the summer is over. We've already got permits for renovation."

Tom nodded. "Mason?"

"We should just vote. That building is a menace." Her father tapped his fingers against his biceps as if his opinion settled everything. Probably he thought it did.

Jaime held her breath.

Finally, Tom said, "Okay, we'll get that estimate. I'll call over to the Deal house this afternoon."

"I'll do it. You asked me to head the project, which includes estimates and new hires." Jaime kept her voice steady and looked from Rick to Tom and then to her father.

Mason's expression remained impassive but his eyes studied her as if she had two heads. Maybe she did. She hadn't left her father's house for weeks after the senior trip. Then Emmett had stood her up on prom night. She hadn't mentioned his name in years. Now she was suggesting the town hire him for a job that would keep him around for an extended amount of time.

Well, she wasn't the same girl she'd been when he'd left.

Emmett being back didn't change that.

CHAPTER TWO

EMMETT APPROACHED THE front door of the dilapidated Victorian home with dread. When he'd left Gulliver's Island ten years before the gingerbread trim along the roof was an inviting green, the porch painted a delicate peach and the second floor a deep navy.

The painted lady he remembered was chipped and stained.

There was no trace of the peach color on the porch, although sometime in the past few years the porch steps had been painted what appeared to be a bull's-eye red color. A few strips of navy remained along the windows on the second floor. The gingerbread trim looked like the rotting wood it was.

From a professional standpoint the place was a mess, but he knew he could bring her back to life.

From a personal standpoint, he didn't understand how things had gotten this far.

How had his stickler father allowed this to happen to their home?

The doctor's voice echoed in his mind, reminding Emmett of his father's diagnosis. He clenched his hands. He'd failed his dad in not coming back for all this time. Maybe if he had…

Staying off the island had made it easier to move forward. Easier to forget the careless boy he'd been and to become someone capable, dependable.

The boy who'd been careless enough to ruin the life of his best friend was gone and in his place was a man people came to, to solve their problems.

Jaime Brown's big brown eyes seemed to dance in front of him. He'd left to make things simpler for her, but seeing her again... She was no longer the broken girl who'd come back from Pittsburgh, but she wasn't the girl he remembered from before the attack, either.

The front door creaked open and Gibson Deal stuck his head around the corner, a shock of white hair falling forward to hide eyes that were once a clear, bright blue and were now faded like Emmett's Levi's.

"I'm not buyin' nothin'," Gibson said in a voice that still held the iron Emmett remembered from his youth. To listen to the old man, nothing had changed. It was probably one of the reasons no one on the island had figured out Gibson was fading. He could still talk a blue streak; had opinions on everything. Hell, during his visit to Cincinnati last fall Emmett had thought his father was fine. Last week the doctor had assured him that during that visit his father had already been losing his mind.

Emmett was doing more than listening for the first time in years. He was observing and what he saw left no doubt in his mind that the doctors in Toledo were right. His father was fading.

Gibson's hand tremored against the door and there was a confused look in his gaze.

"It's me, Dad. Emmett."

The door creaked open a few more inches. Gibson pushed the hair from his face, squinted faded blue eyes and pressed his lips together while he inspected Emmett as if he'd never seen him before.

"Well, what the hay are you doing on the porch? Come on in, boy. I've been expecting you." As if nothing was wrong. As if Emmett landed on this doorstep every other weekend. "You said you'd bring paint. Did you bring paint? Mary Margaret loves to paint."

Emmett motioned to his truck loaded with enough paint, wood and various other supplies to fix up every house on the island, which was good since he'd volunteered to—at least— take a look at Gulliver School, too. Maybe his father wasn't the only one losing his mind.

Thinking about the school brought back the image of Jaime.

Wearing white pants and a silky blue top. In eighty-five-degree weather. When he'd known her she'd worn sundresses on any day the temperature breached seventy.

He could still see her standing on her front porch in a white sundress with pretty blue flowers long into October that last year he'd been on the island. It had been unseasonably warm that fall and when anyone had reminded her of the changing seasons she would smile and tell them she wasn't ready for turtlenecks and snow boots just yet.

The calendar would change over to June in a few days and already it felt like August on the island.

She'd also cut her hair and the shoulder-length blond curls suited her face. She was thinner than he remembered, but those brown eyes were still deep enough to drown in. Not that he had any intention of drowning.

The Jaime he remembered… The Jaime he remembered had grown up, Emmett told himself. Just as he had.

"I've brought everything we'll need with

me." He wasn't sure what he would need when he'd left Cincinnati, only that the sooner he had the place fixed up the sooner it would sell. The sooner he could get Gibson into the assisted-living facility in Cincinnati where he could begin treatment. Not that treatment would change anything.

He'd done enough late-night internet surfing to know there was no coming back from dementia. There would be good days and bad, and eventually he would lose his father altogether, even though the man might still be alive.

Emmett's heart beat rapidly at the thought. Gibson was his only family and he didn't want to lose the old man.

He shouldn't have made such a big deal about coming back to Gulliver. Should have made more of an effort to put the past to rest. He'd lost ten years he could have had with Gibson and for what? Because he'd made a few mistakes as a teenager? Didn't everyone?

"You thirsty? Want a sandwich before we get started?"

Emmett couldn't stomach what might be on the inside of the refrigerator. "I thought we'd just make an inventory list today." The farther into the house they walked, the more Emmett's hopes sank. When he was a kid, the hardwood floors would have gleamed, the end tables sparkled. A few magazines might have been stacked on one end of the coffee table and there would have been a basket for the TV and radio remotes beside his father's favorite green recliner. His mom would have been baking something and, more often than not, Jaime would wander in through the back door.

Emmett refocused on his father.

What he saw now were stacks and stacks of newspapers. A few empty food containers. The TV was on but muted. Two lampshades sat askew because of the jackets hanging from them. Envelopes—some opened and some still sealed—littered the dining-room table and a thin film of dust covered everything.

Emmett swallowed. How much worse would it be if his father hadn't taken the ferry to the mainland last month? He'd boarded a bus for Dayton at the ferry stop and become so disoriented that a restaurant manager had called the police. The police had called Emmett and now he could see for himself that things were very wrong. He dragged his finger through the dust covering his mom's favorite side table and then wiped his caked finger on his jeans.

"Dad, I thought you hired that local company to clean once a week after Mom died." He tripped over something and picked it up, holding the cracked leather shoes by their strings. What were his old football cleats doing in the hallway?

Gibson waved his hand as they continued through to the kitchen. He grabbed a bottle of water and passed it to Emmett. "Those girls didn't know a broom from a dust rag. I let them go a while back."

His mother had passed away the summer after he'd left the island. God, how had he missed all of this in their weekly phone calls?

Once more Emmett racked his brain, trying to remember any incident that could have alerted him during Gibson's last visit. He'd been a little more crotchety and particular than normal, but when had Gibson not been particular? From the pressed pants and natty ties he'd worn every day to school to the way Emmett's baseball uniforms should be washed after the games, Gibson had ideas. Ways of doing things. Emmett and his mother had become so used to his opinions that they'd forgotten any other way of doing things. So it was normal to fall into that routine when his father had visited for a couple of weeks in October.

When he'd left Emmett had found a stack

of newspapers under the bed but hadn't thought anything of it.

Now he wished he had.

"I was thinking we'd start with the porch. You know how your mother likes a clean and pretty porch. Peach. That was her favorite color." Gibson finished his water and wiped his mouth on his sleeve. "The upper level should be navy and I think green would be a nice color around the eaves."

"Dad—"

"And in here, I know your mother likes her wallpaper, but I think paint is more practical. And if we used some of that blue, it would be a nice accent for her paintings and things."

"Dad." Emmett tried again, but Gibson kept talking.

"Now, we turned your bedroom into a sewing room for your mother a few years ago so you'll be staying in the guest room. If we could just update the closets and bring in a little more storage space for your mom's bits and bobs, we'll be in good shape, don't you think?" He looked around the dingy kitchen with pride, obviously not seeing the dirty stove or ancient refrigerator. "We'll bring this place back to life yet."

Emmett tossed their water bottles into the empty trash can and then grabbed several old containers from the cabinets to throw away. He considered running scalding-hot water into the sink to wash the piles of plates and cutlery but decided against it and tossed it all into the trash. No amount of dish soap or hot water could bring those things back to life.

"Dad, we're fixing this place up to sell it, remember? You're coming to live in Cincinnati, near me." He was careful not to say "with me." The doctors had been clear. Though his father was in the early stages, he needed more care than Emmett could give on his own. And patients like Gibson would grab on to any chance to stay in their homes. Emmett had failed his father so far; he wasn't going to fail at this. Gibson would come to Cincinnati and get the care he needed.

"Your mother loves the island, you know she won't move."

Emmett took a breath and closed his eyes. His mother was buried in Toledo in one of the plots she and Gibson had picked out years before. "Dad, Mom isn't here anymore. She's gone."

Gibson gestured dismissively and began adding more things to the trash. "She's just gone to get groceries. She'll be back in a while. She was going to bake shortbread cookies for you but forgot we were out of vanilla." He cleared one corner of the kitchen table and started on another, tossing things willy-nilly into the big trash can along with Emmett.

Emmett reached for his father's hands; stilled them. "Dad, let me do this, okay? I'll make sure everything that is thrown out needs to be trashed. Why don't you rest?"

"I don't need to rest. I'm healthy as a horse." He pounded once on his chest as if that would sway Emmett. Maybe he really thought it would.

Maybe he didn't remember why Emmett was here in the first place.

"Dad, we're selling the house, remember? We talked to the doctor about it last week. You're moving into that nice apartment that's just down the road from my house."

Gibson was quiet for a long moment. "You're here to renovate the house. Our house."

"Yeah, I am, Dad. And then we have to sell it. You can't stay up here on your own and my work is in Cincinnati so you're coming to live with me." Emmett winced. "Near me, at that nice apartment."

"I don't think your mom will like living in an apartment. She likes to have room to move."

"Do you remember the bird room? With

all the parrots and cockatiels?" Emmett led Gibson to the table, cleared another space and they sat. "And there was that nice walking path around the pond, remember? We saw that big, Great Dane when we walked around it last time."

"His name was Percy. And the parrot wouldn't repeat anything we said."

Emmett smiled. "That's right. The nurse said he was shy, remember? And you said once you got acquainted, everything would be all right."

"But your mom didn't see the place. I'm not sure she'll like it. Maybe we should just do the painting and things here." Gibson clasped his hands, twisting them around. "We could take her down in a few weeks, when she's ready."

"Dad, Mom isn't here. She died several years ago."

Gibson's brow furrowed. "Mary Margaret is at the store, getting vanilla for snickerdoodles. Emmett's coming home."

It had been shortbreads a few minutes before but Emmett didn't correct his father. He looked away and squeezed the bridge of his nose. Oh, God, it was happening.

"Dad, do you remember visiting Cincinnati?"

Gibson pushed away from the table and stalked to the kitchen sink. "'Course I remember Cincinnati. Terrible football team, pretty good at baseball, though, depending on the year. My son, Emmett, lives there. Mary Margaret and I go down every few weeks because he's too busy to come up here. You went to school with him, didn't you?"

Emmett rose from the table and began stacking old magazines and junk mail into piles. When the pile looked ready to topple, he pushed it into the trash can and started another. "I'm Emmett, Dad. I'm here to help you get the house ready to sell."

But Gibson kept talking, as though Emmett hadn't said a word. "You know, it's summer and Emmett doesn't like coming back here. But I'm hoping he makes it this year. Big party planned for July. Reunion, you know."

Emmett thought about the invitation he'd left on his office desk before coming home. He planned to be off Gulliver by the time the reunion came along. Off the island and back in Cincinnati where the only thing people knew about him was that he was good at restoring old houses.

"Dad, do you still read these tabloids?" He picked a few issues from the floor, dated last summer.

"I never read that trash. Mary Margaret, she likes those celebrity stories. Likes to stay on top of Hollywood," he said, his voice lilting into a laugh. "Hey, do you think that's what's holding her up? You think she's reading the magazine in the store because she's tired of me ribbing her about it? We'll have to tell Emmett that when he gets here."

Emmett gave up. He couldn't say those words—*Mom is dead*—one more time. He couldn't. Mary Margaret Deal was very much alive in this house. Emmett shook his head. Even if he could say it, Gibson very obviously couldn't believe his wife was gone. Maybe that was why his father was having such a hard time letting go, because he could still feel her here.

No, Gibson's inability to let go had nothing to do with the magazines stacked around the house or the sewing room that probably still had whatever project on the sewing table Mom had been working on before she died years before. He couldn't let go because that was part of who he was. Determined. Particular. Obstinately convinced he was right until the last leg of whatever crusade he was on crumbled.

He'd been the last man standing in the quest to save the old school all those years ago. The first to defend Emmett when the rest of the town went on the attack.

The doctor said Gibson was living in a world that was more comfortable for him; Mary Margaret always made things comfortable. Maybe it was okay for Emmett to just let this one illusion stand.

"Could be, she always liked the pictures best," he said as he pulled one full trash bag from the can and replaced it with another. He started filling that one up, too. "Did you know they're talking about rehabbing the old school? Well, maybe. They were actually talking about tearing it down, but I volunteered to have a look."

He kept talking about the school, about the Reds and Indians. About anything he could think of as Gibson stared out the window. Emmett cleared the kitchen table of junk and filled another bag with trash, hating the sound of his voice but more afraid of the silence if he stopped talking. Mentally he tacked another week on to his plans to stay on the island. It would take at least that long to get the junk cleared out so the real work could begin. He'd need more supplies, which meant another ferry ride to the mainland. Might as well unpack the truck and reload it for the landfill. Once most of the junk was cleared away he would call the cleaning crew to start working on the inside of the house.

Emmett tied up a third bag of trash and started on a fourth, this time pulling crusty pots from the stovetop and putting them into the bag. He would do all of this and he wouldn't complain, not once.

"Hey." Gibson turned away from the window. "Emmett, I didn't hear you come in, boy. You're early."

"It's almost noon."

Gibson grabbed another bottle of water from the fridge. "I didn't figure you'd get here much before five, what with traffic and coming up from Cincy. I didn't get to the store before you got here, so we'll have to eat at Gulliver's Diner tonight. They still do that prime rib you like."

Why was it suddenly easier to breathe? His father was back. "Sure, Dad, that sounds great. And we'll stop by the grocery to get a few essentials after."

"It's good to have you home, boy." Gibson looked around with sadness in his eyes. Where there was confusion before, now Emmett was certain Gibson saw what he did: a cluttered, messy house in need of repair. No ghosts. No memories that seem more real than the present. "I don't want to leave this place."

"I know, Dad."

"Mary Margaret and I had a lot of good memories here."

"I remember." Emmett swallowed. This was the man he remembered. A little thinner and more vulnerable than he had ever seen him, but this was the Gibson he remembered.

This was his dad.

"I don't, sometimes. Sometimes, all I know are the memories." Gibson squeezed his hands together, looking around the room as if he might find the one thing that would keep him here.

"That's why you're coming to Cincinnati, so the doctors can help you."

Gibson sighed. "You shouldn't have to deal with this, boy. It isn't fair."

Emmett agreed. Losing his mother had been hard. Watching his father fade away… he didn't know how he could deal with that, too. "Who said life was fair, right?"

"Emmett." Gibson shook his head. "Life is what you make of it."

Up until a month before Emmett had thought he'd been making a pretty good life. Since they'd met with his father's doctors, he wasn't so sure the choices he'd made were anything but selfish.

He didn't know if the trustees would call about the school, but if they did he would answer. Why he'd ever offered to do an estimate on the building he couldn't explain. Just that there had been a look in Jaime's eyes, a determination to the set of her shoulders and her fisted hands, that he'd had to encourage. He owed her at least that much.

CHAPTER THREE

THE NEXT MORNING Jaime paced her office and one question kept repeating over and over.

What was Emmett Deal doing back on Gulliver? While she waited for a clerk in the Historic Registrar's Office in Columbus to pick up the phone, she pulled at the collar of her fitted navy T and this time her nail bumped along the scar that ran from her collarbone to the top of her breast. She shivered and blew out a breath before busying her hands with the pens and markers in the tree-trunk coffee mug on her desk.

It didn't matter why he was back. It didn't matter that he had the absolute worst timing of any human who'd walked the face of the earth. What mattered was getting through the next six weeks and getting her life back to normal. Quiet and so boring that she faded into the background and people forgot about Pittsburgh. No more reading through the accomplishments of her former classmates and realizing she didn't like the life she'd been perfectly happy with just a month before. No more wishing she'd made different choices all those years ago. Wondering if was too late to make those changes now.

Jaime ran her index finger under the crew neck of her T, trying to scratch the itch that normally didn't make itself known until the first tourist-filled ferry docked at the pier. Her life might not be as big as some of those on the reunion questionnaires but it was hers, built from the ashes of a time when she'd been afraid to leave her own house. She had a challenging job at Gulliver Wines. Lived in a perfect little bungalow with water views. Had friends she could count on. She wasn't jealous. She wasn't sure what she was but it wasn't jealous.

Calling the registrar's office was step one. Going to the Deal house was step two and getting the renovation back on track step three.

The registrar's secretary came back on the line and asked Jaime to leave a message. Screw it; she'd deal with the state paperwork later. After leaving the message she hung up the phone and willed her mind to focus. She composed a quick email to the registrar to underline the importance of the school, and to reiterate her request that he call. Then she made a list of local contractors she'd dealt with for the winery; once this project got its second start it was important for it to go smoothly. No more Luthers.

Maureen arrived with steaming containers of fresh fish and chips from a dockside restaurant a few minutes later and Jaime's stomach growled as if on cue.

"I'm so glad you're flexible. When the school called this morning I couldn't tell them no." Maureen rattled the containers before setting them on a side table and tossing her purse into an empty chair. "God, I love your office."

Jaime looked around at the mostly white space. She'd framed a few pictures of the Marblehead Lighthouse a few years before, and her computer was new, but other than that it was just an office.

"It's quiet. No seven-year-olds asking for another chapter of *Junie B. Jones* or another round of Heads Up, Seven Up."

Jaime pushed the take-out container filled with deep-fried fish away and busied herself with the reunion file. "What are we going to do about this?"

"As de facto cochair of the reunion committee with you, I think we're going to order cake and punch and call it good?" Maureen answered hopefully.

"Fine." Jaime sighed and twirled her pencil in her hand. "We'll start the dinner shifts at four on Friday and be fine. Winery tours on Saturday before the big party?"

"And that brings us to the school and the big party…but first we need a new estimate, right?"

Jaime narrowed her eyes at Maureen's innocent expression. "New estimate?" Lord, why was she always surprised at how quickly the grapevine worked on Gulliver. Of course Maureen knew not only about the possible demo but also the new estimate.

And Emmett.

Maureen blinked. Jaime tapped her foot. Maureen rolled her eyes. "Fine, Rick called Clancy and you know my husband is a dear, sweet man who can't keep anything to himself. Emmett's back. The school is on the chopping block. You're in the middle. You could have told me all this yourself, you know, instead of pacing around your office and fiddling with your shirt."

Jaime dropped her hands to her sides. "It's just an estimate, and then we get the project back on track and save the reunion."

"Do you think Emmett was serious?"

"About saving the building? You know as well as I do that he loves old buildings. I'd say he was serious."

"And how are you?"

"Why would I be anything but fine?" Jaime doodled on the corner of her desk blotter. "I'm not pining for the one who got away."

"I only ask because there haven't been very many since The One."

Jaime made a face. "That's only because most of the available men on the island are my dad's age. Not interested."

"One semiserious relationship that ended more than three years ago."

"As I said most of the available men—"

"Clancy works with a couple of guys on the mainland—"

"Maybe after the reunion." But preferably never. Jaime didn't want to be fixed up. She didn't want to be alone, either, but maybe that was for the best.

"Jaime, you can't want to be single for the rest of your life. You don't date locals. You don't go to the mainland to meet new people."

"I'm busy." Her gaze snagged on the folder filled with the highlights of her former friends' lives. She didn't want to read about the big lives of her classmates. Didn't want to argue with her father about the old school.

Didn't want to be alone but didn't want the whole This Is Why I'm Disfigured conversation, either.

"You make time for the things that are important."

"Right now the school is important…the reunion."

"Maybe you and Emmett—"

She shook her head. "Not happening and not because he disappeared on prom night. He's back but he won't stay. I won't leave."

"How do you know he isn't back for good?"

Jaime snorted. "Emmett Deal has a successful business, a television show and zero ties to Gulliver."

"His dad is here."

"He didn't come back for his mother's memorial service, Mo."

"He attended the funeral services on the mainland. Besides, the 'service' here was more of an impromptu Remember When gathering."

"Don't defend him."

"I'm not defending. I'm saying he was with Gibson at the actual funeral, and you know Gib goes down to Cincinnati a couple of times each year."

"Whose side are you on?"

"Yours. You know that, I just… You keep

telling me it's been ten years. Maybe he's ready to come home?"

Jaime swallowed. Thinking of Emmett as the aloof person he'd become after Pittsburgh was so much simpler than thinking of him as someone who missed home. "I don't think Gibson being on the island is the huge draw you think it is," she said, but her voice sounded breathy to her own ears.

Maureen plucked the phone from Jaime's desk. "Then call him. We can't do much more planning until we know the school will actually be available by reunion weekend."

Jaime watched the handset as if it might reach over and bite her. Then reluctantly took it from Maureen's hand and put it back.

"I might have better luck if I just show up."

Ten minutes later Jaime turned her golf cart off the main island road onto the long drive to Emmett's family home. She couldn't remember the last time she had been here. Definitely before his mother had passed away.

The house came into view and she stopped abruptly. The pretty old Victorian looked… worse than the school. The front porch sagged, most of the paint had worn away and the lawn was not mowed. Gibson Deal had always been particular about the house; the sight of its disrepair didn't make any sense.

But Emmett's coming back suddenly did.

EMMETT WAS JUST getting ready to go to the dump when he spotted Jaime sitting in a red golf cart in the driveway. "Hi," he said and tossed the keys onto the front seat of his truck. He walked to the golf cart. "The trustees didn't call. I figured they won the argument."

"Not yet." She mumbled something else that sounded suspiciously like *not ever* and then smiled brightly at him. "I'm here to take you up on the offer of an estimate. We've already had one, but after Luther Thomas walked out on the job the trustees want to make sure there are no more surprises."

"And if I have plans?" He raised an eyebrow at her.

"You don't." She waited a long moment and finally said, "Are you coming or do I also have to look for another estimate?"

"I haven't been asked onto the project yet."

"I just did." She blew out a breath that made the curls at her forehead dance. Emmett bit back a smile. She was still so easy to rile up.

"No, you said you were here to take me up

on my offer. But you didn't actually ask me to give an estimate, and as part of my offer I did say the trustees should call if they wanted my help."

"I'm as close as you're getting to a trustee today so either get in or get out of my way."

Emmett clicked his tongue against his teeth. Maybe he'd misjudged Jaime yesterday. She'd looked lost and forlorn in those baggy clothes and, despite the determination in her gaze, it was obvious she'd been about to cave to the trustees' demands. This Jaime was different. She wore khaki pants and a fitted top and her manicured nails were tap-tap-tapping against the golf cart's steering wheel. This Jaime was in charge. It was nice to see.

"I'm not in your way," he said, making a flourish with his hands as he moved farther into the yard and away from what was left of the circular drive that led back to the lane.

"You know what I mean. Just get in the cart. Please?" she added almost as an afterthought.

He hadn't actually called the trash barge. He could go to the school and then deal with the load of trash. "Fine, just let me get a couple of things," he said.

A few minutes later he was in his dad's golf cart with a pencil, level and a few other tools in a belt on the front seat and following Jaime to the school. Most islanders chose bicycles or golf carts to get around. The wind on his face felt good. He hadn't been in a golf cart since he'd left.

He sighed as they turned into the school's drive. The roof bowed in the middle, which didn't bode well. One of the side windows was broken. The front door hung slightly askew. If the inside was as bad as the outside this was more than a surface remodel job. The city would need tens of thousands of dollars to fix it up. That didn't give the other crew reason to walk out, but some guys took on jobs before knowing the full details.

Jaime led the way inside and his hand clenched across his clipboard as he watched her hips sway side to side. It was silly, really. He'd known he would see her sooner or later when he came back, and had tried to prepare himself for that by looking her up on the internet. He'd found a few pictures in the Gulliver's Island weekly newsletter, and saw her profile on one of those professional social networks, but there were no personal social media pages. She pushed a flyaway strand of hair behind her ear. Nothing he'd found had prepared him for how much she had changed.

Or how much she had stayed the same.

Those brown eyes were still slightly too big for her face. Her bottom lip slightly too thin and her chin too determined. He hadn't seen her smile yet, but he knew that would bring out a single dimple in her left cheek. And, if she were really amused, small flecks of gold would twinkle in her eyes.

Not that any of that mattered even a little bit. He was here for a few weeks to get his father ready for a move. That was it.

"Well," she said as she pushed open the front door. "What do you think?"

He thought she looked good from the tips of her toes to the blond crown of her head. And that was so not what he should think. He wasn't good for Jaime. That's why he'd left Gulliver in the first place. It was why he hadn't come back and why he needed to get off the island just as quickly as possible.

Why he should have kept his big mouth shut yesterday in the diner.

Why he should definitely, totally, not check out how her pants outlined the gentle curve of her hip. She moved away from him and for a split second he forgot not to look. His hand slipped off his clipboard and the clip snapped down on his finger. Emmett cursed violently.

"I think this place needs a lot of help," he said, shaking his hand to dull the pain.

She clasped her hands in front of her. "Are you all right?"

"Old clipboard. Should have thrown it away years ago," he lied. "Where should we start?"

Jaime led the way through the main room, pointing out where the other crew had started. As she talked about an open-floor-plan main room with display cases along one wall and high tables scattered throughout, the room seemed to take on new life. The broken-down walls disappeared and Emmett could almost see sunlight pouring through a newly hung stained-glass window onto to honey-colored wood floors. The room could serve multiple purposes from tourist attraction to rental hall.

"How did you get the trustees to sign off on a Cleveland crew?"

"They were available. And I was here to be the local lookout, to make sure they didn't abscond with any nails or screws that were once sold at Island Hardware."

Emmett chuckled. "No wonder the crew walked out."

"I didn't actually frisk them as they left."

Emmett squatted to look at the warped floor. "Is that why you're here now? To make sure I don't steal a broken windowpane?"

"They wanted a local." Her mouth twisted in apology.

"Local?"

"Someone who lives on the island. Has island interests at heart. You know the drill."

Yeah, he knew the drill. He hated the drill of treating those who lived off Gulliver differently than those who resided on the island. People moved in and out of his neighborhood in Cincinnati all the time. His business, in fact, was based on people buying, selling and moving on to the next project. Still, it rankled that they didn't think of him as local. His father still lived here, for God's sake; had been the superintendent of schools until he'd retired a few years before.

And, again, none of this matters, he reminded himself as he made a notation on his paper. What the islanders thought of him was no longer his concern. He'd left; made something of himself. What a handful of strangers thought of the boy he'd been was so far off his radar it was barely a blip.

"The floors seem to be in good shape, other than the slight warp here in the old principal's office," Jaime began. He shot her a curious look. "I've been here for the past week, remember? We're thinking of using this place for the reunion this summer."

"Oh."

"Our ten-year reunion," she said, as if he was dense.

"I know how long it's been since high school."

"I wasn't sure. Most of the class has RSVP'd."

He'd tossed the unopened invitation onto his desktop as soon as it arrived, knowing from the off-white envelope with streamers embossed on the front what it was. "I'm not sure I'll be here that long." Didn't want to be here that long was more to the point.

"I figured," she said and sounded almost happy about it. That rankled even more. "With your big life in Cincinnati. Must be hard to get away at all."

"It is. And I don't have a 'big life' down south. It's just a life." Emmett picked at a bit of loose wood around one of the window-panes and it flaked off easily. Rotten. Great. He made another notation on his clipboard and moved to the next window. "I'm here to renovate my dad's house. He's selling and moving to a place in Cincinnati."

"Gib's moving? Why? He loves the island."

Emmett wasn't sure how to answer that. His father hadn't said he couldn't tell anyone about his illness. But then, he'd also avoided leaving the house today when, in the past, he'd have been all over a trip to the mainland. Last night, he'd been upset that he lost himself for a while, and Emmett had to believe that was part of the reason. He didn't want to lose himself in front of his friends. "He wants easier winters. Besides, the old place is too big for one person."

"Oh. It looked, uh—"

"Like we're thinking about torching it for the insurance money?"

"It's not that bad."

"He's getting older. It's harder to keep everything up."

Jaime followed him as he tested the walls and floor. They started up the back stairs and he pointed to a loose board before Jaime tripped over it. She wobbled and he took her hand, the contact heating his skin.

"Emmett—"

"Don't." There was a look in her eyes that he remembered. A look that said she was going to say something he didn't want to hear. Something he couldn't hear. And it had to be about one of two things: prom night or Pittsburgh.

In either case, Emmett didn't want to hear it. He didn't want her to tell him she was okay or that those events didn't matter. They did. For better or worse leaving Jaime in Pittsburgh and then again on the island, changed his life.

They reached the summit and he released her hand. Emmett looked around. Not bad. The old wood floors were scarred but solid, and though the ceiling had a lot of water damage, neither the ceiling nor the floors below the water spots were warped. He'd need a ladder and an inspection of the outside roof to be positive.

"I just wanted to say—"

Emmett cut her off. "This isn't as bad as I thought." He pretended to push against the wall nearest him. Then continued down the hall, away from Jaime and the memories he wished he could forget.

She followed. "Can it be fixed?"

"Anything can be fixed with the right budget." He knelt to pick at a corner floorboard that showed a slight upturn. He pulled it away from the wall. No surface mold—that was a good sign. Jaime stepped to the wall. Her legs were as slender as ever. Not such a good thing, he decided as his heart pounded in his chest.

"We don't have a huge budget."

"There are other ways. Historical markers. Grants."

"We're talking about six weeks."

"Obviously the entire building won't be restored within six weeks, but you could get the main floor ready, repair the roof. The rest could be completed over time." He stood and checked a few more things off the list on his clipboard.

"Emmett, why are you here?" She put her hands on his shoulders and the contact seemed to burn along his nerves. That was silly. He and Jaime had paired off all those years ago but he'd never burned when she'd touched him. She turned him to face her. "Why now?"

"I told you, to fix up Dad's house and move him to Cincinnati." His voice sounded rough even to his ears. Emmett swallowed.

"I'm sure you could hire a crew to paint the old house."

True, but he'd lost enough time with his father. Only, he couldn't tell Jaime that until he knew his father was okay with news of his condition being public knowledge.

"It's time." That was the best answer he could come up with, and he could tell from the look on her face that it wasn't enough for Jaime.

CHAPTER FOUR

JAIME WANTED TO press him. There had to be more to his showing up out of the blue than a simple move to Cincinnati.

But this Emmett was different from the boy she remembered, and not just in the way he looked. There was a quietness about him that had changed from the exuberant, prankster guy she'd loved all those years ago. And, obviously since her hand still burned from his light touch on the stairway, she was even more attracted to New Emmett than she had been to Old Emmett. She'd kissed him a million times. Held his hand. Made out in the back of Gibson's old Pontiac hundreds of times and each time it had been simple to stop. Take a moment and keep things under control.

She pulled her hands to her sides and then shoved them into the pockets of her khakis. Not once in all the time they'd dated before had she felt such a strong jolt of attraction for him.

"I saw your television show once." Or

maybe a thousand times, she'd stopped counting after having a particularly vivid dream involving Emmett wearing nothing except his construction belt, a giant bed and her without the scars on her torso.

"I heard you're working at the vineyard. What happened to becoming a female Indiana Jones?"

"I didn't go."

"Because of Pittsburgh." His voice was flat. Emmett and Gibson had been the most vocal of the people encouraging her to pursue archaeology. Well, at least he could name the city. Most people trailed off before saying the name, looking away from—or worse, looking through her.

She offered him a lopsided smile. "Actually no, although a lot of people think that. Having an interest in old things doesn't mean I'd make a good dirt digger."

"Most people would jump at the chance to be a famous archaeologist."

"I'm not most people." And she didn't want to talk about herself. She'd decided a long time ago what she wanted, and what she wanted was to live on the island.

She started down the stairs and Emmett followed.

"No, you're not."

"Is that a compliment or an insult?"

He studied her for a long moment and Jaime thought he would say "insult." Instead he said, "Compliment. And here's another. You're just as pretty as you were in high school."

Heat rose in her cheeks, but Jaime was determined to keep this meeting at a professional level. She didn't need empty compliments from Emmett; she needed his help to save the school. "So, your final verdict is that this place can be saved?"

Emmett stopped at the landing and looked around, as if he saw more than the roof and floorboards.

Sometimes when Jaime looked into a glass of wine she thought she could taste hints of the individual grapes. What did he see when he looked at old buildings like this?

"I'd say it can be saved."

"In time for the reunion? Because the picnic shelters are all reserved and we're not stringing up lights along the beach and I refuse to decorate the high school gym one more time."

"There's always the winery," he said, and there was a twinkle in his blue eyes, as if he already knew Tom had nixed that idea.

"You and Jason and Homecoming Week."

"He's still pissy about rerouting a few casks?"

"'Pissy' almost covers it." Jaime smiled as she put her hand on the railing but it wobbled. She pulled back.

"This big issue I see is the roof." Emmett twisted his mouth to the side. "Yeah, I'd say you could have the main floor cleaned up and party-ready in time for the reunion, assuming I don't find more issues in the basement than I've seen up here."

"More issues?"

"Cracked foundation. Water. That kind of thing."

Back to the project, Jaime.

"If you'll give me your evaluation, I'll take it to the trustees this afternoon." She started back down the stairs but tripped over one of the bad steps and fell against the rickety railing. It held, but just barely.

Emmett's hands were firm as he steadied her. The ten feet between her position on the step and the ground floor seemed to yo-yo in front of her, making her stomach feel weak. She closed her eyes and steadied her breathing.

"You're okay." His voice was soft against her hair, his strong hands reassuring against her upper arms.

"Forgot about that step," she said, her voice

a hair higher than normal. Jaime cleared her throat. "Thanks, but I'm okay." She looked into his blue eyes, mere inches from hers, and felt lost. Pulled back to a time when it was normal to leave her hand in his. Breathing ragged, she tried to get a grip because although this was Emmett, he wasn't the boy she'd known. Maybe the boy she remembered had never existed.

"Do you remember when we broke in here New Year's Eve? Maureen and Clancy, Jason and Rebecca. Clancy brought leftovers from the diner. Maureen snatched a bottle of schnapps from her dad's liquor cabinet."

His voice tickled over her nerve endings and Jaime couldn't stop the smile that crossed her face.

They'd laughed and told stories and danced to the tinny music from Emmett's iPod speaker. Fallen asleep sometime after midnight, huddled together in sleeping bags until the slamming of a car door had woken them. One of her father's patrol officers nearly had caught them, but Emmett had distracted him while the rest of them had fled out the back door.

"You were assigned twenty hours of public service picking up litter at the beach."

"God, it was cold that winter. I nearly got

frostbite keeping the beach clear." He pushed a strand of hair behind her ear. "We had some good times." Was that a hint of sadness or just nostalgia?

And if it was sadness, why? Sad because of the way he'd left? Sad because of what had happened that night? Sad that he'd left and the talk had started with the not-so covert looks?

She straightened her shoulders and pretended nothing had happened at all.

"What made you choose Cincinnati?" She would not ask why he left. She didn't need to know. Wanted to know, yes, but that was different. So focus on the present, not the past.

Emmett's mouth twisted to the side and he fixed his gaze somewhere over her shoulder. "I needed to get away. Cincinnati was away, but it was familiar."

"Away from what?" From her?

"Just…away." His expression closed off and, just like that, the glimpse of the Emmett she'd known was gone.

He stepped around her, but kept his grip strong against her hand, helping her down the stairwell. Jaime tried hard to stay focused on the renovations and not the feel of his callused hand against her smooth palm. It wasn't so bad this time. The burn was just a mild heating. See, she was already getting used to Emmett being back on the island.

This wouldn't be hard. Not at all.

That moment was just a moment. A split second in time that didn't mean anything. Not really. Her life was here, on Gulliver. His wasn't. The words he hadn't said, "away from you," echoed in her mind.

It didn't hurt that she was the reason he'd left, she told herself, but still she rubbed the heel of her hand against her chest. Felt the scar through the thin fabric of her high-necked dress. She put a smile into her voice. "And now you're back because…?"

"Sell Dad's place. Get him moved to Cincinnati." They reached the bottom step and he released her hand as if it burned him. He also wouldn't look directly at her and that annoyed Jaime. She was the one who'd had to face the worried looks, to pretend she hadn't heard the abruptly stopped conversations.

"Gibson will be happier here. If he wanted to move, he'd have done it after he retired from the school. Or after your mother died. He has friends here. You know how islanders take care of their own."

His full lips formed a hard line for a moment before he said, "It's for the best that he comes to Cincinnati."

"So, you wanted off the island and you left. Now you're dragging your father off the island, too? What good will that do?"

Emmett shook his head, but he didn't answer. A moment later he handed her the paper with his notes and estimated costs for the main floor renovation.

"It was good to see you, Jaime." Finally, he looked at her, but it was as if he were a stranger. His blue eyes were flat, remote. Businesslike.

"It was good to see you, too." She lied. It hadn't been good to see him. All sorts of questions tumbled around in her mind, demanding answers he couldn't or wouldn't share. Why he left...why he was back...and what those answers meant for her. She liked her life, damn it, she didn't need to be on the arm of Emmett Deal to be complete. Emmett coming back shouldn't impact her at all. So why let it?

"Maybe we'll have lunch before you leave." She didn't want to, but it was the polite thing to say. After all, he'd taken time away from his house project to give her an estimate on the school, and it was impossible to avoid anyone on Gulliver for long. Besides, avoiding Emmett would encourage the gossips more than being seen with him.

He nodded and stuck his pencil under the clip on his board. "Maybe."

He put his hand at the small of her back as they started for the front door and a little jolt of electricity sped along her spine.

She wished she could blame the singe on faulty wiring.

EMMETT CLOSED THE front door of his childhood home and leaned against it for a second, trying to pretend none of that had just happened. He hadn't taken Jaime's hand. Hadn't nearly told her he'd left her alone all those years ago because he'd blamed himself for Pittsburgh. Hadn't thought, at least three different times, that he'd like to know if she tasted different now than she had back then.

The feel of her smooth palm against his and the softness of her arms refused to let him pretend.

He couldn't get involved with Jaime. Not now and not ever. His actions all those years ago had imploded her life. She could say all she wanted that she'd never wanted to be an archaeologist, and maybe she hadn't. What she had wanted was to leave Gulliver. To travel and see the world. She'd known the ferry schedule by heart; collected hotel pamphlets on vacations. He'd given her a world atlas for Valentine's Day, for goodness' sake, and she'd glowed as if he'd given her diamonds. Jaime had wanted to experience world cultures and Emmett had taken that from her with one careless action.

He blew out a breath and pushed off the door. He couldn't change what he'd done or how that had affected her. How all the looks and hastily stopped conversations had changed her. He'd seen it happening and hadn't been able to stop it. Then he'd actually overheard one of those hushed conversations and realized everyone had been talking about him. What a bad influence he was on her... how it was his fault. He'd already blamed himself but knowing that his presence on the island had kept people talking and was beating her down had been more than he could take. He'd left, hoping that with him gone the talk would die down and Jaime could get her life back on track.

And obviously failed her all over again.

She didn't seem to need him now, at least not today. Yesterday...? Maybe he had wanted her to be vulnerable. In need.

Wasn't that what Kasey had insisted when she'd walked out just before Christmas? That he only wanted to fix things for her; that he didn't want to really know her. Wasn't knowing a person about helping them? He didn't like the word *fix*. He fixed houses. He had no illusions about his ability to fix people. But helping? He could help.

He'd met Kasey on a job; a rehab in a bad neighborhood just outside downtown Cincinnati. They'd had dinner and then drinks and, before he knew it, he was rewiring her house. When she'd told him about her awful boss, Emmett had offered her a job doing some accounting for his construction company. They'd been comfortable.

He'd chalked up her complaints as excuses to quit the job and their relationship, but now…

Did he have some kind of latent hero complex about women?

Emmett shook off the question. He loved women; he didn't feel superior to them. Helping people out was part of his DNA. Bottom line: he was hardwired to solve problems. Jaime had a problem, he offered his advice. Actually getting the old school renovated was completely in her court. Nothing he could or would do about it.

The image she'd painted when they'd toured the school shimmered back into his mind. It would be pretty, though. A draw to tourists; a place to instill pride in the locals. Maybe there was one more thing he could do.

JAIME TAPPED HER foot against the carpeted floor outside Tom's office at the winery and watched the clock tick toward three. The registrar's office had emailed after lunch with instructions to finish the paperwork; they seemed excited for the project. After Google-searching construction firms and calling everyone listed on the search results, though, she was no closer to finding a crew that could start work next week. Much less one that would finish the job in time for the reunion.

The clock ticked past the big three on the dial and her mind wandered. Since leaving the school, for every five minutes she'd spent working on the renovations, she'd spent twenty more thinking about Emmett.

How the sun shone against his jet-black hair. How her hand felt in his. Mostly about that moment on the stairs, the moment she thought he might kiss her. How ridiculous was that?

She hadn't spent the past ten years pining for Emmett Deal. He'd left. She'd moved on.

Emmett being back didn't mean anything in her life had to change. In fact, since he'd made it clear this was a short—and very final—visit, nothing in her life would change. She tapped the folder on her lap. These projects would keep her busy. She liked busy. Busy meant days with no time to wonder and nights when she was too tired to dream. Everyone knew she liked busy.

Tom opened the office door, thanking someone on the other side for stopping by. Emmett's voice inside the office kicked her heartbeat into overdrive. That was as ridiculous as wondering about Emmett's life in Cincinnati.

"No problem, it's a solid project and several of my guys were interested." Emmett stopped when he saw Jaime sitting in the hall. Her heart pounded harder and her mouth felt dry. What was happening to her? First, she drooled over the man in the diner, now she couldn't be in the same room with him without losing control of her body.

"Tom mentioned you had trouble finding a crew the first time around."

Jaime quickly stood, holding the folder to her chest. "H-he did?" And now she was stuttering. Perfect.

"Emmett called about the estimate and one thing led to another. Are those the papers?"

"Yes, Laura mentioned you wanted to take a look," she said, pointing toward the empty secretary's desk at the opposite wall. She should have known something was going on when Laura wasn't at her desk.

In the twenty-four hours since Emmett had landed on the island Ronda at the post office had waved her inside to pick up a package that had mysteriously disappeared and, of course, to ask if Emmett was really back on the island. Since Ronda was the second person any of the island gossips would call, the innocent-sounding question was a ploy to find out *why* he was back, and not *if.* Anna had avoided eye contact this morning over coffee. Anna never avoided eye contact; the waitress was usually direct to the point of pain. Now Laura had called Jaime about the estimate, disappeared and Emmett came strolling out of her boss's office.

"And the final decision?" Jaime had a feeling she already knew and she didn't like it. Not even a little bit.

"I called in a couple of favors and found a crew willing to come up here for the summer."

"You did?" She focused on Emmett. Okay, a crew was good, especially since she'd had no luck this afternoon.

Tom saluted them with the folder and shut

the office door, mumbling something about meeting with the trustees over drinks.

"Wasn't too hard. I already knew they were available."

The sinking feeling in Jaime's stomach grew to a gaping hole.

"Your crew?"

"One of them."

"One of them," Jaime repeated.

"Yeah, I have a crew that focuses on older homes in Cincinnati and another that goes where the projects are—"

"That would be the television crew."

"Right, but they're on summer hiatus and thought this sounded like fun."

Jaime felt as though the project was slipping away from her, which was silly. She was never on the actual project team. Her job was to write checks and meet scheduled deadlines. Not knock down walls and install windows. "I thought you said you were here to fix up your dad's house, not renovate the old school."

"I am. Was." Emmett squinted. "Am. Mostly, I'll consult. Like you."

"I'm not a consultant."

"And you don't think this is a good idea."

Jaime led Emmett to her office and motioned him to one of the chairs. He crossed one jeans-clad leg over the other and she swore his abs rippled under the tight shirt he wore as he sat.

From her seat Jaime folded her hands together and leaned her elbows on the cherrywood desk. She wanted to move, but she settled for tapping her toes against the cool leather soles of her sandals.

"I think you're trying a little too hard."

Something flashed in his eyes. Anger, maybe? Whatever it was Jaime refused to apologize just as she refused to pace.

"I think you're dreaming if you think you'll find a quality crew by cold-calling out of the phone book. Hoping one of them will drop their deck-building, roof-replacing, pool-installing summer isn't going to give you a renovated school for the reunion."

"You'll complete the main floor by July first?" Jaime took a breath, hating that her words were nearly an echo of her father's from the day before. "We've already had one false start, so if you aren't going to see this through you can leave now."

He stood and held out his hand. "I always see my projects through."

Jaime hesitated but then stood and took his hand. The contact zinged along her nerves, but she didn't pull back. "Then I'll see you Monday morning."

Emmett closed the door softly on his way out. Jaime rubbed her palm down the leg of her trousers.

And began to pace.

Finish what he started.

When the project was finished Emmett would leave. She would stay here, on Gulliver.

Alone.

Jaime watched the closed door for a long moment. She didn't want to be alone.

Where did that leave her?

CHAPTER FIVE

EMMETT REPLACED THE keys to the old golf cart on the peg near the front door. *Stupid, stupid, stupid.* He'd gone to Tom Gulliver's with the intention of giving him a few names and reassuring the man the project would be a good investment for the island. How he'd wound up volunteering his crew he had no idea.

He couldn't back out, though. Not now. Not after Jaime's veiled certainty he would walk out on the project. Thankfully his guys lived for projects like the old school, and an extra payday was always nice.

Emmett frowned and looked around carefully. The house was too quiet.

"Dad?" he called into the crowded space. No reply. No shuffling of feet. He glanced out the front windows, but there was nothing in the front yard besides his golf cart and the overgrown and untrimmed trees that hid the house from the street.

Continuing through the living room and kitchen, Emmett looked for his father. A steamer released little puffs of moisture into the dining room, but none of the wallpaper was off the walls. Emmett checked the upstairs bedrooms. Empty. The back porch. Nothing. His breathing quickened and he hurried into the backyard.

Gibson's old Jeep sat under the carport with Emmett's truck behind it. At least he wasn't in a motorized vehicle.

"Dad?" he called again, louder this time, and his voice echoed back to him from the thicket of trees at the rear of the property. Their home was one of the few on the north side of the island; most of the development was on the south side because that harbor was less rocky. The first Gulliver built his general store there and the town had grown up around it. Another reason Emmett needed to get him off the island and into a care facility.

There was an old deer trail that led into the woods and eventually to the rocky north shore of the island. Gibson used to walk the trail a couple of times a day with his camera. If he'd gone alone, if his memory failed, there was no telling what might happen.

Briefly, Emmett considered calling the township police, but to say what? No one on the island knew about Gibson's condition yet. Sunlight slanted across the green leaves of oak and maple trees and he started for the short trail. He'd find Gibson and bring him home. Protect the older man's secret.

Emmett hadn't been on the trail in years and it looked as if no one else had, either. There were clumps of composting leaves left from the winter months, families of chipmunks and squirrels rustling in the underbrush. In a few places it seemed the trees were closer together than he remembered. Probably he had been smaller back then. There was no sign of Gibson in the woods. No stray buttons or pieces of fabric caught on a branch. That was silly. The man wasn't running for his life. He was out for a stroll. At least Emmett hoped that was it.

Finally the trees opened onto the rocky beach. Emmett inhaled a long breath and for a short moment closed his eyes. The water smelled fresh, no hint of washed-up or decaying fish bodies. Here the tree line seemed closer to the water, but he supposed that was natural. No one came to this side of the island. Years before the quarry companies had owned it. When they'd left, the beach had fallen into township hands. But locals and tourists had wanted sand. Removing the big slabs of rock would have eroded most of the island to nothing so they left it alone.

A blue windbreaker fluttered against the rocks on the far side of the beach and Emmett started in that direction.

He finally spotted Gibson kneeling over a tide pool, running his hands through the cold water.

"Dad?" Emmett spoke quietly, not wanting to startle the older man.

"Emmett. How'd you find me out here?" Gibson continued running his hands around the pool, a content expression on his face as if he'd never felt the sides of rocks smoothed by centuries of running water.

"Followed the trail, like I did when I was a kid and Mom would send me out to bring you in for dinner."

"Mary Margaret was always a stickler for five-thirty dinners, wasn't she?" Finally he wiped his damp hands on his khaki pants and stood. "Is it time for dinner?"

Emmett's belly clenched. The rabbit hole was opening again. "No, maybe lunch. Dinner's a while off. What made you come down here?"

Gibson shook his head. "Nothing, really. I thought maybe I'd find a piece of sheared rock to take with me to Cincinnati. And it's been a while since I walked down here." He patted his pocket. "Your mom convinced me to downsize to a pocket camera a few years ago, so I took some pictures, too."

Emmett took his father's elbow and tried to help him back to the grassy area but Gibson shook him off. Emmett blew out a relieved breath. His father hated accepting help. It wasn't the rabbit hole opening with that question about dinner, just the simplicity of losing track of time. He could relate to that. Somehow being in the old school had made him feel as if he'd been back in high school with Jaime, not facing an uncertain future with his father.

"I'm not an invalid yet," Gibson said and turned on his heel. "If your being here means I can't take a walk without checking in, you can just haul yourself back down south and I'll hire a crew to clean up the house. Toledo or Cleveland has assisted-living apartments I could move into, too, you know."

Emmett knew that. Of course he did. But Toledo and Cleveland were too far from Cincinnati for him to get to his father if he was needed. He wasn't budging on this. He'd missed too much of his mother's last years. Too many of his father's. He might only have a few months left and he damn well wasn't going to lose them, too.

"Toledo and Cleveland don't have Skyline

Chili." He used Gibson's favorite Cincinnati treat as enticement.

"They do in the freezer section."

Emmett chuckled. "You tried that before I left home, remember? One bite and you tossed it in the trash."

"Maybe my tastes have changed."

"We have Graeter's," Emmett said, mentioning an ice cream chain where his father always managed to eat on visits to Emmett's home. "And you know the hot dogs are better at the Reds games than at the Mud Hens or Indians."

"True." They began walking back to the trail leading home. "But according to one celebrity Toledo is the Paris of Ohio," his father said.

"A river running through town doesn't make Toledo Parisian." Not that Emmett had been to Paris.

"Well, that actress is hot."

"I don't—Dad—which actress?" Emmett stumbled over his words. "Nevermind. When I was a kid you said hotness was more a state of mind than body."

"You paid attention. You know, the one. Blond hair, pretty eyes. In all those black-and-white movies." No, Emmett didn't know. Gibson could be describing one of about twenty starlets, but before he could ask anything more Gibson patted his shoulder as if Emmett had just won the national spelling bee. "Beauty is still only skin deep, it's the mind that keeps us coming back."

Emmett wasn't sure what to make of his father. He'd never seen Gibson so much as notice a pretty girl, and now the old man was crushing on an elderly actress. The doctors didn't tell him dementia would turn his father into a teenager again.

"Those actresses would be about a hundred and fifty years old."

"So am I."

"You're seventy-two."

"I always did like cougars." Gibson looked at him, an innocent expression on his face. "What? You thought after seventy a man's needs became irrelevant?"

He'd hoped not, but wondering what his own sex life would be like post-retirement and knowing what his dad thought about… those were two very different things. "I really don't want to talk about this."

Gibson shrugged. "A man has needs. We had this talk when you were about twelve."

They'd talked about girls and kissing and where babies came from in a very abstract way. Emmett was so not having the sex talk with his dad. Especially not when the talk was *about* his dad.

"Dad."

"Do you know your mom never let me watch game shows? Those great old dames used to guest star and she knew I had little crushes on a few of them."

"Mom was afraid you'd run off to Hollywood to have an illicit affair with a star because she was on a game show?" His mother jealous of a woman Gibson would never meet because he'd never wanted to leave the island? Didn't sound like the Mary Margaret that Emmett remembered. His mother was feisty. Single-minded, completely head over heels about Gibson, and confident he was crazy for her.

The tree line thinned as they neared the house. "Nah, Mary Margaret knew she was the only girl for me." He was quiet for a moment and Emmett watched him carefully. A twinkle came into his eye. "It was because of the letter."

"Letter?"

"I wanted to be a contestant so I wrote to the show."

They stepped up onto the back porch. Emmett opened the drink refrigerator on the porch, pulling out two cold bottles of water. They sat on the old porch swing.

"Sure. I'd have taken any of the shows, but *Password* was my favorite. It would have been fun. I was always good with clues." He chuckled. "Funny, my mind used to be sharp. I could remember anything." He didn't say anything for a moment. "Now, some days I wonder if I'll remember who I am."

"We're getting you help, Dad. They have treatments."

"They'll work for a while, I know." His dad's voice was stoic. Resigned, maybe. "I remember today, and I'm not going to ruin that. Where was I? Right, the letter. So I wrote the show and made it through the first phase, and that meant a trip to LA for a screen test."

"You guys never left Ohio."

"Sure we did."

"Not once. We might have crossed the lake to Detroit a time or two, but I can't remember ever leaving the state when I was a kid."

"Huh. There was the trip to Gatlinburg. No, that was before you were born. St. Louis. No, that was our honeymoon. We never did get that cruise we talked about. Maybe we didn't travel much when you were younger. I'm sorry, son."

Emmett swallowed some of his water. "It

isn't a big deal. I always thought the two of you, or at least one of you, was kind of afraid to travel."

"Huh." His father was quiet for a moment. "I never did tell her."

"Tell her what?" Emmett's mind reeled. His father had a whole life he knew nothing about. He'd wanted to be on game shows? And his mom had been jealous of Gibson's crush on an actress?

"The screen test. I got it, but never taped the show because she got so mad on that trip. After the audition we went to the Santa Monica Pier and Betty was there. Your mom was busy buying souvenirs and I was watching Betty. Betty flirted with me I flirted with Betty, and Mary Margaret didn't like that at all."

Which Betty? Grable? Davis? White? Emmett was torn between trying to figure out his dad's celebrity crush or chalking it all up to rambling. None of this sounded like the parents he knew. The devoted, loving people he'd grown up with. He checked Gibson's eyes but they seemed clear and his hands weren't doing that clench-and-unclench thing they did when he was upset or having one of his spells. "The thing I never told your mom is the Betty who flirted with me was a female impersonator. Just some street performer looking for a tip."

Emmett choked on his water. "You flirted with a drag queen on the Santa Monica Pier?" His buttoned-up, tweed-wearing dad?

"When was I going to meet the real woman? I was a schoolteacher from a tiny island on Lake Erie that no one outside the state has ever heard of. And I was in LA, auditioning to be a contestant on my favorite show. It isn't as if the impersonator was a hooker or anything. She didn't talk to me for the rest of the night."

"The hooker?" Emmett couldn't keep it all straight. He checked Gibson's eyes again but his gaze was unclouded.

"No, your mom."

"Mom always had something to say."

"Not that night. She wouldn't say anything. By the next morning I knew better than to bring it up, even to explain, so I dropped the subject and we came home."

"And you didn't do the show."

Gibson shook his head and then finished his water. "I think I'll take a nap. Wake me in an hour and we'll start on the porch."

The screen door slapped shut behind him, leaving Emmett alone on the back porch wondering about the life his parents had had before he was born.

He wished he'd seen it.

They'd had him late in life. Gibson had been in his forties by the time Emmett was born. Although they'd never seemed old to him, they'd also never seemed young. They were his parents. Boring. Loving and attentive. But boring.

This peek into their life before him was odd. Made him wish he'd made more of an effort to get to know them as adults.

He pushed off the swing.

He was here now. It was too late to get to know his mom, but he still had time with Gibson. A very short window of time—and he wasn't going to waste it.

Maybe, just maybe, he'd be able to right things for Jaime, too.

CHAPTER SIX

"YOU HUNGRY?"

Emmett pulled another wide strip of wallpaper from the dining-room wall before stuffing the steamed paper into the big, barrel trash can he'd brought in from the back porch. Gibson stood in the doorway, hair wild around his face and a baseball cap on his head. Emmett couldn't place the mascot on the brim.

"Sure." He wiped his hands on a damp towel and then put it back on the cleaned corner of his mother's mahogany dining table.

Saturday afternoon and Gibson had lasted a half hour before going to his room to rest. In the time since, Emmett had torn most of the wallpaper from the dining-room walls and worked up a sweat. Thought a lot about Jaime. She wasn't the girl he remembered, and it bothered him. His leaving the island was supposed to help her regain her confidence. Find her footing. Insert clichéd statement here, Emmett thought wryly.

Sure, she talked a good game about the school project, but he couldn't get that look he'd seen out of his mind. In the diner that first day she'd been almost haunted, and he didn't think it was 100 percent about him.

"How about the diner? It's meat loaf night."

"I'll call in the order."

"We should go there, eat it while it's nice and hot on real plates with real silverware," his father said. Emmett couldn't say no to that.

Once they were in the golf cart Gibson didn't seem to want to talk and Emmett's thoughts circled back to where they'd been all day: Jaime.

Seeing her made him realize two things. One, for better or worse, Jaime was the reason he hadn't had a serious relationship since he'd moved off the island. Kasey was the most serious, but he could admit to himself that he'd never really let her in. Maybe that was what she'd meant by him needing to fix her. Once her life was in order, he couldn't figure out what he had to offer her. There had been other women, but they'd been easily put out of his life when the time came, and it always did. They were too talkative or too secretive. Too tall. Too short. Had weird laughs. One he'd cut out of his life because she tried to friend him on Facebook. Heinous crime, that. Now he realized it wasn't the perfectly normal things he found odd it was that none of them were as perfect as his memories of Jaime Brown.

Two, he needed to get laid. That was the only explanation for the tingles along his nerve endings when she was around. Jaime had been a pretty girl and had grown into a gorgeous woman, but the residual burning he could feel where his hand touched hers, the weird feeling in his gut when he remembered how her eyes dilated during that moment on the stairs, could only be physical.

Needing physical contact didn't mean he wanted Jaime, though. He couldn't desire her in the long term when he couldn't kiss her in the short term. Couldn't bring up those old feelings. She was Gulliver's Island. He was Cincinnati or whatever other city where no one knew him. Where he could be Emmett the Construction Worker and not Emmett the Prankster.

"We eating at the diner or the fish shack?"

Emmett blinked and the main street came into focus. He parked the golf cart under a sprawling oak. "Diner," he decided.

Anna told them to sit wherever, and there were plenty of places. At a quarter to five on the Saturday before Memorial Day they were Anna's only customers. They chose a side booth and picked up menus from the table.

"What can I get you?" Anna asked after she delivered two glasses of water.

Damned if he knew what he wanted. Emmett shook himself and looked at the menu in his hands. Anna wasn't asking about Jaime, and she was entirely too perceptive for him to be focused on anything other than the food.

"We came for meat loaf," Gibson said. "But I changed my mind. I'll have the prime rib and a loaded baked potato, and don't skimp on the sour cream."

"Glass of milk with the meal, like usual?" She didn't bother to write down Gibson's order. After twenty years of waiting tables at the diner she probably knew the preferences of every island resident. Gibson nodded his assent and she turned her attention to Emmett.

"Same, although I don't need enough sour cream to clog all my arteries, just the one will do it. And a beer, whatever you have, instead of milk."

She smiled at him, the first real smile he'd seen from any of the island residents. "We've missed you around here. You staying for a while?"

"Through the reunion, anyway," he said, unsure how much she already knew. Anna wasn't the gossip that most islanders were, but she knew a good story when she heard one. When she left Emmett turned to his father. "Do you eat here a lot?"

"Couple of times a week. They started doing a delivery service a few years back so mostly I order in. Why didn't you tell Anna we're leaving before the summer's out?"

"Come on, Dad—"

"Not like it's a secret."

"It was a nosy question."

"It was just a question. From a woman who babysat you until you were school age."

"A woman I haven't seen in years."

Gibson unwrapped his silverware from the paper napkin and set it just so on the chipped tabletop. "It was still rude."

Emmett twisted his mouth to the side, not wanting to agree with his dad. "What was I supposed to say?"

"You were supposed to answer the question."

"But how?" Emmett clenched his jaw for a second and then made an effort to relax. "We haven't talked about what to tell your friends. So when I tell them I'm here long enough to fix up the house and list it, then what? Do I tell them you're moving to a nice retirement community? Or do I call it assisted living? And while we're talking about it, when they ask why you want to move what do you say?" Although they were alone in the restaurant, Emmett kept his voice low.

Gibson fiddled with his fork and knife. "You call it whatever you want."

"What do you want, Dad?"

Gibson sighed. "Doesn't really matter what I want, not now." He circled his hand near his head. "This can't be a secret for long, anyway. People might as well know I'm headed to the crazy house."

"You don't have to call yourself crazy."

"We're all a little crazy, Emmett, that's no secret."

"Dad…" This was so not the time for Gibson to go all school psychologist on him.

"What? It's like that old comedy bit. 'You didn't know you were terminal?'" He threw his voice, pretending he was on a stage for a second. He sipped his water and when he spoke again, it was with the voice Emmett remembered reading to him from the *Iliad* or *Tristan and Isolde*. "We're all terminal, Emmett, and we're all a little crazy. My crazy just happens to be linked to losing memories and who I've always been." His father reached across the table and touched his hand. Unlike when he was a kid, his father's voice wasn't calming and didn't leave him feeling peaceful. "You can tell anyone who asks whatever you want. I don't have any secrets."

They talked about nothing for a while. Emmett watched one of the ferries motor toward the dock from Put-in-Bay. God, he wished he was on it. Wished he was anywhere but in this purple booth avoiding talking to his father about dying.

"We should replace the pull-down steps to the storage area over the garage," he said, trying to keep the conversation going.

"The floorboards in the cupboard of the bay window need to be finished."

"I thought you did that years ago."

"I pulled up the old, never did get new ones in there."

A few hungry, island residents came in. Ronda from the post office waved to him, and took a table near the window. An elderly couple sat at the bar. It was so familiar to listen to the bell ring as the door opened, Emmett could almost forget he didn't belong on Gulliver.

The ferry slid to a stop at the dock. It looked to be the size of his water glass. A few more weeks and he could load up the truck and take the ferry back to his life. Until then, he would deal with the present because there was nothing he could do about the past.

Anna brought their meals and the scent of perfectly prepared meat and potatoes made the peanut butter sandwich he'd eaten over the kitchen sink at lunch seem like an ancient memory. He inhaled, savoring the smell of steak and melted butter, grilled onions and baked potato. The steak in front of him sizzled against the cast iron of the skillet.

He forked up a bite and then froze. Jaime walked through the door, waving to Anna at the counter. She put her bag down at a small table on the other side of the restaurant and then saw him. She froze for a second and then strode to the table.

She pasted a smile on her face for him, but when she spoke to his father he heard genuine caring in her voice. "Gibson, I haven't seen you here in ages."

Gibson swallowed the potato in his mouth and tipped his imaginary hat at Jaime. "Been too busy to come in. Mostly Anna has my order delivered."

"Well, you should make it a point to come in more often. We can always use a Gibson story." She studiously avoided looking toward

Emmett, which only made him want to get her attention.

That was stupid. He didn't need her attention. He didn't need her anything.

"Why don't you join us? You can tell me more about this school renovation and I might just share a story or two with you."

Jaime shook her head. "I'm going to eat and run. Big day tomorrow."

"You could eat and talk, then run. Wouldn't take too much more of your time." Gibson shot her a smile and Jaime chuckled.

"There isn't much to tell." Finally she looked at Emmett, a plea in her big, brown eyes.

Before he could back her up, which was the smart thing to do after what had happened at the school, the prankster part of Emmett decided to join his father's challenge.

"He's got a great one about the old school, the Gulliver family and Prohibition."

Damn it, why did he say that? Jaime loved history. She lived for historic scandals and adventures. Maybe Gibson wasn't the only Deal with a mental health issue because Emmett seemed to have developed a split personality since he'd landed on Gulliver Dock yesterday. He wanted off the island and away from the people one minute and wondered what it would be like to be back in the middle of everything in the next.

Losing it, buddy, you are losing it.

"It might be your last chance to hear it. I'm moving to Cincinnati in a few weeks," Gibson said. "And it's a doozy of a story."

Jaime seemed conflicted. She chewed on her lower lip for a moment. Then her hands unclenched from her sides and Emmett knew she'd decided. He grabbed an extra set of utensils from a neighboring table, and set them next to his father.

"Okay, but I really do have to eat and run." She picked up her purse from the other table and returned just as Gibson moved the new set of silverware to Emmett's side of the table.

"I'm not going to hear a thing you say if you're on my left." He shrugged and shot Emmett a triumphant look.

It wasn't a challenge to Jaime, Emmett realized. His father had been challenging him. To have dinner with Jaime.

"You don't—"

A sharp kick to Emmett's shin stopped him from telling Jaime that Gibson's hearing was fine. He stood so Jaime could slide into the booth. She sat as close to the wall as possible. So this was as uncomfortable for her as it was for him. That was something. Not wanting to crowd her, Emmett sat at the edge of the booth seat.

"I don't tell a lot of people. But when you hit retirement age things in your body just seem to start breaking down."

"I don't believe that for a second." Jaime paused when Anna brought a salad to the table. "Could I get a shredded chicken sandwich, too? I forgot about lunch today."

"Back in a sec," Anna assured her and left the table.

"I see you and my dad are keeping the diner's cash flow going."

Jaime shrugged and ate some of her salad. "Cooking for one is boring. It's easier to grab meals here or order something from the kitchen if I'm working late at the winery."

The way she ate her salad fascinated Emmett. First, she dipped her fork into the pot of dressing Anna had left at the table and then she stabbed a leaf of lettuce or tomato, lifting it to her full lips.

Gibson cleared his throat and Emmett realized he'd been staring. He forked up some steak and shoved the food into his mouth. Gibson's brow creased as he nodded his head toward Jaime when she wasn't looking at him. Emmett pressed his lips together. He was not falling into that trap. Whatever his father was up to, Emmett was not interested in telling Jaime anything. He shook his head.

Gibson widened his gaze and nodded once more. Emmett pretended to be entranced by the view and forked up another bite of his dinner. Gibson had invited her to join them; he could darn well entertain her, too. Actually, that wasn't a half bad idea.

"You should tell her about the basement, Dad."

"Basement? At the old school?"

"They used it as storage." Gibson shook his head and cut another chunk of steak from the prime rib.

"Oh." Jaime's voice was disappointed. Emmett couldn't blame her. Gibson's stories were legendary when he was growing up. His dad knew as much about the island as the Gulliver family. "I thought maybe you knew something that would help with the landmark committee. I've been researching what they need for the application. The age of the building helps, but historic details would be even better."

Gibson waited a long moment and Emmett was about to step in to tell the tale when he began talking about the deal the school district had with the Gulliver family all those years ago. Jaime was fascinated by the telling, and Emmett was fascinated by her.

He watched her posture change from polite interest to full-on engagement. Jaime leaned forward as if Gibson's voice pulled at her. For a moment she held her breath and just as suddenly began breathing normally once more. She forgot to eat, but held on to her fork. Eyes shining, expression rapt, she took in the details Gibson had learned from the diary he'd found.

"How long did they use the school?"

"Through Prohibition and into the war years, that's how the diaries read." Gibson scratched his head. Sipped his water. "Do you think they lost our order?"

His father's words snapped Emmett out of the near-trance he'd been in and firmly into the present.

"Did you guys order the pie? Maureen and Clancy stopped in at lunch for a slice of the apple caramel and she's been texting me drool emoticons ever since." When Anna brought her sandwich to the table, Jaime asked for a slice of pie to go.

Gibson asked for a slice, too, and before Emmett could ask for the check, Anna disappeared into the kitchen. He studied his father. The vacant look wasn't there, but he'd started to flick his thumb against the pads of his fingers. The way he'd flicked the other day when he completely forgot who Emmett was.

He needed to get his father out of here. Home. That was all Emmett could think about. Getting his dad home before something bad happened.

"You said you were going to eat, talk and run, but we should probably get out of here."

"I want my pie." Gibson looked around, his expression confused. "Why don't I have pie?"

"Anna's bringing it, Dad." He turned to Jaime and asked about the renovation project, hoping she wouldn't notice what was going on with his father. She looked up and her eyes moved from him to Gibson and back again. Gibson's thumb flicked faster against his fingers.

"Why don't I...?" Gibson's voice trailed off and the look on his face went from worried to vacant. Emmett saw it happening but was powerless to stop it. Gibson's fork clattered to the tabletop.

Emmett stood quickly. He pulled a few bills from his wallet and then shoved it back into his pocket. "Would you apologize to Anna for us? I just remembered we have an appointment." He took Gibson's arm. "We have that appointment, remember?" he said, hoping his dad would just go along with it.

Gibson didn't say anything, but he didn't resist when Emmett walked him to the door.

He didn't look back. Not when they got to the door and not when he put the key into the golf cart's ignition. Emmett fastened the passenger's-side seat belt around his dad, and pressed the accelerator as hard as he could. The golf cart surged forward and then settled in to its ten-mile-per-hour pace. Emmett couldn't help himself. He looked back.

Jaime stood on the walk outside the restaurant, looking after them, frowning.

So much for dealing with the present.

WELL, THAT WENT WELL.

Jaime returned to the table, listening to the tinkle of the bell over the door as it shut behind her. She should have stayed at her own table. Maybe she should have gotten her meal to go. She sat at the booth and picked at the remains of her salad. Definitely shouldn't have sat beside Emmett, not even squeezed into the far corner of the booth even with at least twenty-four inches of space between them.

Listening to one of Gibson's stories was

too big a draw. The man knew more about Gulliver than anyone else on the island.

Anna came by the table, taking away the half-eaten plates of food Emmett and his father had hastily left behind. She left mumbling about doggie bags and starving children in Africa. It almost made Jaime smile. She collected her check and started toward the counter, thanking her lucky stars she'd ordered the pie to go so she wouldn't have to sit at that table any longer. Anna met her at the counter with two bags.

"Since both orders are already boxed, you might as well take them all," she said as she rang in Jaime's bill. "They'll just get tossed in the trash otherwise. You know how Hank is about day-old pie."

"Crime against sugar."

Anna rolled her eyes. "That man... So, you ate with Gib and Emmett." The statement sounded like a question, but Jaime didn't take the bait.

"Gibson told me a story about an old storage space in the basement."

Anna counted back Jaime's change. "Is Emmett staying long?"

"Couldn't say." Jaime bit back the urge to tell Anna about the renovations on Gibson's house.

"I thought—"

"I'm going to be late. Are you sure Hank won't mind me taking all this pie?"

"Looks like a slow night," she said as she wiped her hands on her pink apron. "Actually, you might as well take the whole thing." Anna turned and entered the kitchen. She returned a moment later with the rest of the pie boxed and bagged.

"I can't eat this whole thing," Jaime said, trying to push it away. But the aroma of apples and caramel and Hank's flaky piecrust made her mouth water.

"Nonsense, you'll take it and share it. I'll see you tomorrow," Anna said.

Jaime waved the sacks in her hand and pushed through the door into the warm evening. A couple of gulls sat on the top of her golf cart, but the street was empty. She decided to walk to her parents' home down the street. She was not taking five thousand calories worth of pie back to her cottage.

The evening breeze blew softly against her face as the sun sank lower in the sky. She passed Irene's, a homemade gelato and ice cream hut, and waved at a couple of local artists closing the windows of their kiosks for the night. A few carts were parked in front of the Dugout, the only bar on the island.

Around the corner, a few more carts sat at the township hall, which doubled as a rec center for island kids.

Cindy Ergstrom, Maureen's mother-in-law, managed the center, running basketball and gymnastics camps in the winter and swim lessons in the summer.

Jaime pushed open the front door of her parents' home with her hip and started to call out a hello.

Voices in the hall stopped her.

"It's not just that the place is an eyesore," her father said. "It's dangerous."

"But Jaime needs this project, Mason, and with a new roof and security system it could be good for the whole island. Think about how many tourists walk through the museum at Marblehead every summer or climb to the top of Perry's."

"Even if Emmett is part of the project?"

"He was always a nice boy. A little hard-headed but—"

China banged against the kitchen table and Jaime winced. "He was a menace not a mis-understood boy. He was careless and stupid and should have stayed gone."

She wanted to say something or to do something other than stand in the hallway with pie in her arms. But what? Her father

was determined to either make her forget the
past or bring it up to remind her how dangerous the outside world was. Her mother, on
the other hand, liked to pretend nothing had
happened at all. She didn't want to fight with
them, but she couldn't talk to either of them
when they were like this. Her mother was in
full-on denial mode and her father was still
rampaging because Tom and Rick had sided
against him on the school project. She knew
how the conversation would go, and she didn't
want it, not tonight.

This night she wanted to enjoy a slice of
Hank's pie and be normal. At least as normal
as life had been before all the reunion talk led
to more reminiscing about the past which led
to her questioning everything about her life.
No it wasn't an interesting life, but it was safe.

Jaime backed out of the hall without saying anything, hurried to the diner with both
bags of pie and got into her golf cart. She
turned left on the main road and followed
it until she reached the turnoff for the Deal
house. She stopped the cart for a long moment, considering.

This wasn't about seeing Emmett. They'd
paid for the pie so she might as well deliver
it. Drop off the sack and go home to enjoy
the rest of the quiet Saturday night. Alone.

Jaime sighed. So it wasn't the most exciting life. It was hers and she liked it, damn it. Before she could talk herself out of it Jaime turned up the lane. She parked beneath the maple tree and hurried up the sagging porch steps. She knocked but no one answered. They might be on the back porch or might have taken a walk. She put the sack on a low table between two chairs and turned back to her golf cart.

"Hey."

She started at the sound of Emmett's voice.

"Sorry, didn't mean to frighten you."

"I wasn't scared, not really." She felt silly, holding her hand at her throat, standing so straight she felt as if her spine might never slouch again. "I knocked."

"I was out walking," he said and shoved his hands in his jeans' pockets while he breathed deep and slow.

Not what she needed at that moment. She was acutely aware of the rising and falling of each ridged plane of his abdomen under his thin cotton shirt. She waved toward the door. "I brought your pie. From the diner."

"Thanks. Dad's resting. Do you want to eat?"

"No, I should get home. Busy day tomorrow."

He wrinkled his brow. "It's Sunday. Nothing happens on the island on Sundays until June."

Right, Sunday. Day of rest. Day of absolutely nothing on her calendar because Emmett was right. Until the full summer rush, Sunday on the island meant quiet. She could call her dad to go fishing or maybe have a picnic with Maureen and the kids. Do a little online shopping. All were on her usual list of things to do, but not one seemed remotely exciting. Or even interesting.

"I...right. Sure, I guess."

Emmett motioned her to the swinging bench and handed her a container from the sack. Jaime took a bite and sighed as apples and caramel slid over her tongue. Hank was a genius with sugar. Absolute. Genius.

"God, I'd forgotten what a master Hank is with sugar and eggs," Emmett said as he swallowed.

"Tomorrow morning is his special summertime brunch. Cinnamon rolls, omelets—"

"Stuffed French toast?"

Jaime nodded.

"It's a good thing I'll be swinging a hammer for the next few weeks."

Jaime shot a look at him under her lashes as she took a bite of pie. "Afraid of losing your girlish figure?" She savored another bite on her tongue so she wouldn't wonder what Emmett's definitely-not-girlish abs might taste like. That was a road she would not travel. Not tonight or any other night.

"As any self-respecting man would be when faced with apple caramel pie *and* stuffed French toast."

"In Hank's defense—" She stopped.

Emmett waited a beat. "In Hank's defense…what?"

"He has no defense. Sometimes I wonder if he's on some pharmaceutical company payroll. You know, trying to send us all into sugar comas so we need diabetes prescriptions."

They were quiet for a long moment, Jaime sitting on the swinging bench and Emmett resting his hips against the porch railing. She couldn't read him the way she used to. Didn't know if this was a contemplative mood or just him enjoying a quiet moment. Either way interrupting seemed rude so she waited. Watched the orange streaks in the sky turn to pink and then fade into gray as the first stars in the Big Dipper came into sight.

Emmett finished his pie and leaned forward to toss the bag into a container near the door. His abs rippled with the movement.

Salty, she'd bet they would taste salty.

Except she didn't bet. And she wasn't wondering.

God, grant me the strength to not lick Emmett Deal's abs.

She stood and her arm brushed his. Jaime swallowed and put the fork into the bag and tossed the bag into the container, too.

"Well, enjoy breathing."

Stupid, stupid, stupid. Enjoy breathing? Maybe just grant me the wisdom not to say anything stupid around Emmett in the future.

"I always do."

Jaime opened her mouth but no clever quips came so she turned away. But leaving seemed like a rash thing to do. She didn't need to run from Emmett. He might be built like a god, but he was still just a man. Maybe she should sit down. But if she sat, he might think she wanted to talk and she didn't want to talk.

Except it would be rude to leave without saying anything, and after her last brilliant statement she was a little afraid of what might come out.

"Do you think saving the school is worth it? In your professional opinion, I mean. It's just a brick-and-mortar building with a few pretty windows and an old bell." Jaime couldn't explain why she wanted his opinion; she only knew she did want it.

He was quiet for so long she thought he might not answer.

"Historically speaking, there are better examples of 1920s' architecture out there. Buildings like Union Station in Cincinnati or LeVeque Tower in Columbus. Those buildings haven't been linked to Prohibition, though. If the school administration hadn't allowed the Gullivers to hide their drinks in the basement all those years ago, the winery probably would have folded. If the winery had folded, a lot of people would have been out of jobs. Families would have moved. Other businesses would have closed." He shrugged his shoulders and stayed on his side of the porch. "Chances are if the school didn't offer up the basement Gulliver's Island would be another uninhabited island on the North Coast. I'd say that's reason enough to save it."

"Thanks." She couldn't explain why, but his words eased the worry that had begun creeping in once the trustees had agreed to move forward with the project.

Emmett rested his arm along the seat back, the tips of his fingers centimeters from Jaime's shoulder. "It's going to be okay, in your hands, I mean."

"I'm going to hire some people, that's hardly reclaiming old floors or saving a stained-glass window or three." She crossed her legs, turning slightly toward him.

"Just as important, though." He tapped his fingers against the wooden rail, but his gaze was focused on the door of the house. That made it incredibly silly that her heart began beating in time with his tapping fingers.

"Maybe." Jaime slowed her breathing and willed her heart to go back to its usual rhythm. It wouldn't. Hiring the crews. Writing the checks. Those were the easy jobs. Ten-hour days pulling up rotten floors or knocking down moldy walls would be so much harder than anything Jaime would do for the project. And what the heck was he tapping in time with?

"I didn't mean to step on your toes about the crew. I went to Tom's office because I knew your father wouldn't want my input and it's impossible to catch Rick outside of meal-times. Before I knew it I was offering my crew instead of offering to make some calls."

Her heart seemed to stop for a second, but his fingers continued their rhythmic tapping against the wood. "I called every construction company I could find on Google. All of them turned me down."

Jaime studied Emmett's profile in the

growing darkness. More stars winked out, but they were so far off the main road there were no streetlights to interfere with the brilliantly burning stars. "Renovations are your business. And you did give me the estimate that helped sway Tom and Rick."

"I figured Mason would be the holdout." He stopped tapping his fingertips against the bench.

"My father is nothing if not predictable. He sees the building as a danger to the community."

Emmett snorted. "More like a danger to his authority. He's been trying to keep people away from that old place for as long as I can remember."

"And we've all be trying to get inside."

He did a double eyebrow raise. "Some of us made it in."

"And got twenty hours of public service for the effort."

Emmett shrugged. "It was worth it."

"Always the rebel." Jaime smiled. "I'm glad you're going to be involved with the project. You'll make sure everything is done right."

Jaime stood and her shoulder brushed against his as she took the first step off the porch. She felt the light contact through the thin sleeve of her shirt. It was a light spark, the kind she used to get walking around in her socks in the winter time. She would touch the metal of the fridge door or her desk drawer and get a shock. She'd never enjoyed those sizzles as much as she liked the feel of Emmett's body near hers, though.

He reached out and tugged a lock of her hair. A Canadian Soldier, a tiny insect that came out of the lake during the early summer months, alighted on Emmett's shoulder. Jaime flicked her finger at the mayfly then smoothed the material.

"Have a nice night," she said, her voice sounding rough to her ears.

"You, too."

Neither moved. Emmett tucked the same strand of hair behind her ear or maybe he was caressing it, Jaime couldn't tell. And she told her hand to let go of his shirt three times, but the order seemed to short circuit somewhere between her brain and her hands.

"It was good to see you, Jaime."

Was it her imagination or was his voice slightly more husky than normal?

"I'm sure we'll run into one another a few more times before you leave." No guessing about that, her voice was definitely huskier than normal.

"Probably so. It's only a mile-wide island."

"Two miles across, three miles around," she said, hating the words even as they passed her lips. Emmett knew the size of the island; he hadn't been talking literally. Just making conversation. And when had he stepped closer to her?

No, wait, she was the one doing the stepping because his glutes were still very much attached to the porch railing.

Not smart, Jaime. Step away. Walk away.

But she didn't step back.

Jaime swallowed and so did Emmett. She watched; her attention focused on the way his Adam's apple slid down and then up along the strong column of his throat. He needed a haircut, she decided for at least the tenth time since recognizing him in the diner, but hoped he didn't get one. She liked the way the longer hairs tangled against his neck. Wondered what his hair would feel like now compared to the short spikiness of it when they were kids.

"I should go." She didn't want to, but she should and maybe saying the words aloud would force her feet to obey.

"Me, too."

"But you're already home." This time her feet obeyed and Jaime stepped away from him.

Just then Emmett stepped forward, bringing his chest up hard against hers. His heat seemed to wrap around her and her hands crept over his shoulders. He leaned in, his lips brushing her cheek, singeing her. Jaime gasped at the contact, wanting more and less at the same time.

"We should try that again," he said and didn't wait for her reply. His mouth came down on hers lightly but with purpose. Emmett buried his hands in her hair, holding her where he wanted her, but even if he didn't hold her she wouldn't move. Not ever. Not as long as his mouth was against hers.

Jaime wound her arms around his neck, playing with the long hairs at his nape, thinking how strange it was that his hair was so soft. Softer than her own. Wavy and thick. Good hair, she decided as she slanted her mouth to give him better access.

Emmett adjusted his stance, bringing her body in closer contact with his. His leg wedged between hers and he teased his tongue along the seam of her mouth.

Asking her to let him in. Telling her he wanted more.

She wanted more. Wanted the taste of him on her tongue. So she opened and his tongue dove inside to tangle against hers in the dark cave of her mouth. The thrusts of his tongue licked flames of desire to life in her belly. Jaime went up on her tiptoes, wanting more. Wanting to feel his chest more firmly against hers. Wanting better access to his lips.

Wanting more, period.

"Sweet." His voice was quiet in the dark, but it was enough to bring Jaime down to earth. She pulled back slightly, resting her forehead against his chin. "You taste like the best dessert I've never had."

"Hank's caramel apple pie. A moment on the lips," she said, smiling.

"Mmm. I think it tastes better on you than on the plate."

"This isn't a good idea." She had to put the words out there. Had to at least try because this was crazy. He'd been on the island a couple of days. She was crazy to have kissed him.

Emmett stepped back and put his hands in his back pockets as if he didn't trust himself not to reach out for her again. Part of Jaime wished he would. Part of her wished she had pockets so she wouldn't be so tempted to be the one to do the reaching.

Jaime swallowed. "It really was good to see you. And I do appreciate your help with the start of the school project. We should leave things there, though."

He nodded. "I'll see you around." Jaime

watched him for a long minute and then turned toward her golf cart. She slid onto the smooth leather seat but just sat there for a long moment. Playing the kiss over in her head. Watching Emmett watching her from the porch railing.

She turned the key and stepped on the gas.

"I'll see you Monday," Emmett said, his voice ringing out across the yard.

Jaime swallowed. Monday was entirely too close for comfort.

CHAPTER SEVEN

EMMETT THREADED HIS fingers behind his head and looked out at the lake. He shook his head. What was he thinking? Kissing Jamie was so not in the plan. Kissing Jaime wouldn't resolve any of the feelings that had come rushing back the moment he'd set foot on the island. Impulse had led him into the diner when he got off the ferry instead of going straight to the house; impulse had made him offer to look over the old school.

Instead of going inside the house to check on Gib he sat on the porch swing, pushing it with his foot.

Impulse had also made him pace the almost-wallpaper-less dining room—the only space in the house with room to walk—and then head out the back door. He'd walked the north shore and then taken the beach road back to the house where he'd seen Jaime on the porch and his pulse had thundered to life. His better judgment had encouraged him to turn back toward the beach, but impulse had led him to the porch and made him tuck that wayward strand of hair behind her ear. Made him wonder if she still smelled sweet like berries or if she'd changed not only the way she dressed but her chosen perfume, too.

She'd changed it. Gone was the sweet berry scent he'd dreamed of too many times to count. In its place was a musky, flowery smell that went straight to his groin. She'd grown up. Changed.

Damn it, so had he. All those years ago he'd been bored with island life and followed his impulses wherever they led. Toilet-papering houses, rerouting a few casks of wine into the city water supply. Breaking in to the school so he could arrange his dad's office furniture in the school lobby.

It was impulse that had made him suggest to his friends that they leave the hotel early to catch a baseball game instead of sitting through *Romeo and Juliet* at the theater. Because of him, Jaime had been hurt. Because of him, loud noises made her tense up even on practically crime-free Gulliver's Island. Even when she'd started to feel normal again, the town had kept talking, bringing up the attack, making her relive it. It wasn't their intention to hurt her, he knew that now, but at the time he'd wanted to demand they all leave her alone.

Emmett blew out a breath. She was supposed to be so much more that a glorified secretary at the winery. She should be sifting through rubble on dig sites around the world or teaching at a university. Saving the school was important, but it wasn't the kind of accomplishment he'd wanted for her.

Lightning bugs danced across the lawn as more stars blinked to life in the night sky. In an instant, it went from gunmetal gray to a deep indigo. The fireflies disappeared into the woods and more stars winked to life above. Emmett stepped to the porch railing, watching. Picking out a few constellations.

Starting now, impulse be damned. No more aimless wandering around the island. He was here to do a job, and that job had nothing to do with Jaime and everything to do with his father's health. He sat on the railing, resting his back against a pillar and stretching his legs across the space.

It would be easy. He didn't have to wonder what she tasted like because he knew. He didn't think the scent of musky wildflowers would ever completely leave him, but that was okay, too, because he knew what to expect. No surprises. No wondering.

He would finish the house and his crew would focus on the school and then he would go back to Cincinnati and a life of careful planning and forethought—because when he thought, he made the right decisions. Maybe someday the right decisions would make up for the mistakes he'd made before.

Jaime deserved the right decisions from him. He'd left the island once to save her. He could do it again.

JAIME HIT THE speaker button on her phone and put it on the counter so she could finish getting ready while Maureen told her what an idiot she'd been to kiss Emmett last night. Not that she needed Maureen's input. She'd spent half the night reliving the kiss and the other half reminding herself why it was important to never do that again.

"How was it?"

"What do you mean how was it?"

"I mean I saw you sitting with him at the diner last night, and his hair is the same unruly black and his skin is just beginning to tan and I'm pretty sure he could rock a pole with the guys from Chippendales. So how was it?"

"It was a quick meal with his dad telling old island stories."

"I call bull. What happened after dinner?"

This was not the way this conversation was supposed to go. Steady, married Maureen was supposed to be on the No Kissing Strange Men side of the argument not the He's Kissable Enough for Hollywood side of it. Especially when he was.

Not that Jaime had kissed anyone from Hollywood, but she'd had her share of first and second and last kisses. Usually they didn't leave her so winded.

"It was a kiss." She would not kiss and tell. It was too juvenile.

"Soft lips? Did he do that tasting thing or was it full-on onslaught?"

"Are we adults here or have we reverted back to senior year?"

"I'm a married woman so, of course, I've reverted. Living vicariously through my friends is how I make it through PTA meetings and dinners with the in-laws."

"You and Cindy have the best in-law relationship I've ever seen."

"And I love Clancy to the moon and back, but I'm still alive and Emmett is so the hot guy on the construction calendar." She was quiet for a moment. "And if you're not talking that means it was of the better-than-good kiss category."

It had been good. Better than kissing him in high school. Better than any of the men she'd dated out of obligation over the past few years. Better than being with Byron, the biologist who'd come to the island a few summers ago to study frogs. With all of them it had been easy enough to break things off. To keep her head. To not say something ridiculously stupid such as that "enjoy breathing" comment. Not a single one had made her want to risk showing her scar, and if things had continued another minute last night Emmett would have seen it. Reacted to it.

Looked at her differently. Pity would have replaced the wanting in his eyes, just as it had with Byron. Guilt would have taken his breath away and the ugly red line that curved around her left breast toward her rib cage would have been a living, breathing thing between them.

It was definitely better not to kiss Emmett again.

"I'll bet he's learned a few things since you saw him last."

Heat rushed to Jaime's face even though Maureen couldn't see her. The eyebrow pencil slipped from her fingers. It was as if she could still feel the heat from his thumb caressing her chin, the weight of his head in her hands and the feel of his hair against her palms.

"I've learned a few things since I saw him last." She replaced the pencil in the drawer and picked up her phone, carrying it with her to the bed where she slipped her feet into high-heeled, black-and-white polka-dot sandals.

Maureen knew her better than anyone, on the island or off. She would know there was more to it if Jaime dodged the question. Besides, maybe talking about it would take the gilded edge off the kiss. Really, no man kissed like a god. She'd merely been caught up in the moment, enjoying talking to Emmett again. She hooked the ankle straps on her sandals in place, stood and wobbled. There was a reason she didn't wear heels, but she was not changing them.

"It was different."

"Sigh-worthy different? Because if he's not sigh-worthy, I don't think I want to know."

Jaime smiled. Sigh-worthy was one way to put it. Combustible another. "The I-know-he's-learned-a-few-things different."

"I like that different."

"I stayed up all night because of that different." She picked her bag up off the blue-plaid sofa that reminded her of her grandparents' home in Cleveland and her keys from the table by the entrance. "He made me— No. I let myself get lost in it for a few minutes. I can't explain why," she said as she closed the blue front door.

Jaime paused for a moment on the porch of her bungalow, taking in the quiet island morning while she told Maureen how kissing Emmett was different and the same at the same time. Different in the way it had made her feel as though she'd never been kissed before. The same because it was Emmett and kissing him had always been familiar. Like coming home.

A mockingbird sang from the trees lining the beach road and a few more daffodils had bloomed in her little garden near the front steps.

She started the golf cart, but didn't turn down the lane that would lead to the winery. She sat behind the wheel, waiting for Maureen to say something, anything, that would help her assign Emmett's kiss to the past.

Maureen was silent for a long moment. Finally she whistled over the line.

"I'm not going to fall in love with him again. It was just a kiss."

"Maybe it wouldn't be so bad—"

"Mo—" Jaime said, a warning in her voice.

"So don't fall for him. Just have a little fun for the summer. You know what they say about all work and no play."

"You're not helping, you know." Jaime put her Bluetooth attachment in her ear. Sitting here staring at the trees was getting her nowhere. She'd kissed Emmett, and it had been good. But that didn't change anything. He'd still left all those years ago; he was leaving again in a few weeks and she would stay.

She turned her eyes toward the winery, determined to get some plans on paper for the weddings scheduled later in the summer. Too much of her time the past few days had been taken up by Emmett. She still had a job to do. Three of them, in fact.

"I'm sorry, did you not get the memo that I'm living vicariously through you this summer?"

"Then you better buy a hammer and nails because that's the most action you're going to get."

"Did you time warp to your forties because the last I checked we were both twenty-eight and twenty-eight is definitely Have Fun Time. Kiss a boy. Do something daring."

"I have work to do."

"And I have two kids under the age of eight and another on the way."

"You what?"

"I'm pregnant. I love Clancy and the kids, and I'll love this one, too, but I didn't think I'd be Preggo Girl my whole twenties." She sniffed and even through the cell connection Jaime could hear the brittleness of her voice.

"Maureen, that's great. It's wonderful." And that tightness in her chest wasn't jealousy that her best friend's life was turning out like a made-for-TV movie. It wasn't leftover angst about her own choices. "How far along?"

"Eighteen weeks. And I really am happy. It's wonderful and scary and I hope this one is a little boy." Jaime heard her blow her nose. "And I just spent five minutes facedown in the carpet because of a high school graduation commercial on *Sunday Morning, Cleveland*. But, Jaime, you aren't married and you haven't dated anyone seriously in a long time. I love you and you can tell me I'm completely off the island on this one, but if you don't let go, just a little bit, you're going to be forty-eight and alone instead of twenty-eight and kissing a hot guy at sunset."

She thought over Maureen's words as she sat in her golf cart and stared at the little white cottage with the blue door that didn't really belong to her. The bungalow, like the furnishings inside, belonged to her parents. She never thought about the choices she'd made all those years ago, but maybe it was time. And maybe it was time to relinquish a little bit of the control that made her feel secure. Just for a little while. How much trouble could a few kisses create in the grand scheme of things? At the very least she would have more to put in the What Are You Doing Now column of the reunion questionnaire than her job description.

"So kiss Emmett." The words felt foreign as they slipped past her lips.

"As often as possible," Maureen instructed.

"We're going to celebrate your news over lunch tomorrow, so clear your afternoon."

"We'll toast the kiss while we're toasting the bun in my oven," Maureen agreed.

Jaime disconnected the call and started up the golf cart, mulling over the kiss and Maureen's certainty that Jaime throw caution to the wind. She thought about the future she'd wanted all those years ago. That future had had the career and the man and kids. This future had her living in her parents' rental property, planning weddings and parties. Saving the school was a good addition, though.

She pulled to a stop beneath the sweeping

oak at the winery. Kissing Emmett. Adding fun to her summer. Jaime blew out a breath.

Maybe.

EMMETT WOKE IN the porch swing, sunlight pouring from the sky and a crick in his neck. He could feel pins and needles in his feet when he stood and stretched. Not the way to start another day separating trash from treasure in his dad's living room. He cracked his neck and pulled first one arm and then the other across his body, trying to stretch out the kinks.

The smell of freshly brewed coffee wafted through the open windows and he headed for the kitchen. Most of the coffee mugs had landed in the trash with the rest of the plates and cutlery he'd deemed too dirty to save on that first day so he pulled a foam cup from the plastic bag he'd picked up at the convenience store the day before. The coffeemaker seemed to taunt him, withholding the drink but tempting him with the scent of freshly ground beans and brewing coffee.

Kind of like Jaime. Not that she tempted and teased, not in the least. But the memory of that kiss taunted him. Or maybe haunted him. He could feel her soft lips on his, the scrape of her short nails on the back of his neck and, though there had been a few inches between their bodies, the feel of her hips against his. How she'd shivered when he'd run the back of his hand over her ribs.

He didn't want to be haunted by those memories.

Coming back here was supposed to be simple. Paint a few rooms, pack up the things Gibson wanted to keep and go back to his real life. But the simplicity he wanted grew murkier by the second.

The coffeemaker beeped and he poured a cup, blew on it and sipped. Closed his eyes and sighed. Feeling slightly more awake, he went in search of his father. Gibson was still asleep so Emmett returned to the dining room to finish removing the wallpaper. He switched on the steamer and waited for it to heat, watching a couple of robins chase one another around the mulberry bush outside the bay window.

Jaime had changed and not just in the physical sense. She was more willowy now than she'd been ten years before. Her jawline more defined. She wore her hair shorter, letting the curls bounce around her head. Before the accident she'd been a bright light. After, she'd withdrawn to somewhere he couldn't reach her. Her parents had made it impossible to see her and, as hard as she'd tried to hide it, he'd known she hadn't wanted to see him, either.

She'd blamed him for not being there, for not protecting her all those years ago.

Emmett didn't buy the act she put on for the community. He'd seen the sadness behind her smile and felt the tremors in her hands. Jaime was no longer the fearful, withdrawn girl he'd tried to save by leaving, but she wasn't the audacious girl who'd helped him put a bass booster on the dispatch microphone at the police station, either.

When steam began pulsing into the room from the hand unit, Emmett picked it up and began steaming the walls to loosen the wallpaper glue. It was boring, methodical work, but it would make the rest of the job go faster.

He couldn't stop thinking about her. Wondering how she'd slept. Wondering if the kiss had kept her up or if it hadn't meant a thing to her. A corner of the paper curled up from the wall. Emmett put the steamer back on its hook and gently pulled, tearing a long strip from the wall.

He'd become complacent; that was the trouble.

At first it had been hard not to come back to the island, but he'd made himself a promise and it was one he'd been determined to keep. So when he'd wanted to come back, he would ask his uncle for more shifts. Uncle Donny had always been happy to comply and there was always work to be done on his construction jobs.

Emmett had once confided in his mom during one of their weekly phone calls how hard it was to stay away from the island. The following weekend she and Gibson had showed up at Emmett's apartment with mismatched kitchen fare and a few familiar blankets. His mom had brought him a fern she'd culled from one of her plants. Gradually he missed the island less. His parents had volunteered to come to him on holidays before he could make an excuse not to come to Gulliver.

Emmett readied to pull another strip of paper from the wall but grimaced when the edge of the steamer brushed his finger as he put it down. He shook his hand until the burn lessened and then started removing more paper.

He'd become complacent about not returning to the island. He'd dated a few women and then become complacent about them. The construction work had kept him going, though; redesigning old buildings, bidding for contracts on new builds with his uncle. The first year had been a blur, the second even faster. Time had slowed for a while after his mother died. Now it was ten years later. He was back on the island, kissing Jaime and wondering when he might get her alone again.

That was just stupid. Ten years was plenty of time to get over her hold on him. To have moved on… To have assuaged his guilt for what had happened that night or, at the very least, to have some idea of how to move forward from it…

Kissing Jaime had brought all those old feelings, the non-guilty feelings, back to the surface. Made him wonder.

Made him want.

He pulled the last section of paper from the wall and began collecting the bits of soggy paper scattered around the floor.

That was the most dangerous part of all this. Because he was guilty. She would never have been in that alley if it hadn't been for him. Forgetting that, ignoring it, would be a crime. She deserved better than his actions that night. Deserved better than him, period.

Wanting Jaime was nothing new to Emmett, but he was older now. He could control the attraction. Keep his distance. Figure out a way to help Jaime without endangering the fragile peace he'd made with himself when he'd first decided to never come back.

CHAPTER EIGHT

MONDAY MORNING JAIME decided to take the long way to work. She motored along the beach road, waving at tourists and stopping to chat with any residents already out for the day.

What was she going to do? Thoughts of Emmett took up way too much of her time, and he'd been back for less than a week.

Through initial planning at the winery yesterday she'd caught herself thinking about Emmett's broad shoulders and narrow hips way too often.

Over breakfast this morning she'd forgotten to eat, twice, because she kept envisioning Emmett's strong thighs and flat abs. The third time she'd skipped right over shoulders to relive the feel of his lips on hers, the heat from his hands burning through her T.

Another cart honked, bringing Jaime back to the present. She swerved to her side of the road and shook her head in apology.

Pushing thoughts of Emmett and the kiss

from her mind Jaime continued around beach road and then realized where she was. If she took the next right she would come to the road leading to North Beach and the path that led to Emmett's. Maureen's voice echoed in her mind.

You're going to be forty-eight and alone instead of twenty-eight and kissing a hot guy at sunset.

It had been nice just talking the other night. Having a conversation that hadn't ended with a pitiful look or uncomfortable questions. Instead it had ended in a hot kiss that kept distracting her from...well, everything. Obviously in the past ten years Emmett had gotten to a point that he didn't automatically associate Jaime with victim.

Jaime turned onto the road that would curve around to the north side of the island and then onto the quiet lane that led to the Victorian home where Emmett had grown up. She bit her lip. Her physical reaction hadn't dimmed since he'd been on the island. That could be a problem in Operation Friendly Talk.

The lane curved and she could make out the slate roof of the old home. No turning back now.

Jaime stopped the cart under an old sycamore tree but almost immediately put it into Reverse. Adults who used to date having a conversation was one thing. Female actively seeking out male was something completely different. The kiss had been amazing, but she didn't know what Emmett wanted. Maybe it was just the sunset thing.

Maybe he thought it was a mistake.

"Whatever you're selling, we'll take two." Gibson's voice startled her and Jamie nearly fell out of the open cart. "Gibson Deal," he said, holding out his hand.

"Jaime Brown." He shook her hand but Jaime had an odd feeling the older man wasn't teasing her with the introduction. He didn't seem to recognize her.

Something clicked in her mind and Jaime swallowed. Until a few months ago Gibson was all over the island. Eating at the diner. Taking long walks along the beach road. Before Saturday night, though, Jaime couldn't pinpoint another time she'd seen him since before Christmas. And he'd asked about his pie over and over at dinner. "I'm here to see Emmett."

"Sure, everybody wants to see Emmett." He started inside, carrying a basket with blackberries in his hands. He motioned her to follow. "He lives in Cincinnati most of the time."

The porch steps creaked as they climbed to the front door. Gibson pushed it open and called out, "There's a pretty lady wants to sell us something, boy," before continuing through the dust-caked rooms.

Jaime gasped as she stepped inside, noting the stacks of newspapers on the floor, the jackets hanging on a lampshade and the muted television. The inside of the house was so much worse than the outside. And Emmett still wanted to help with the school?

She shouldn't be here. She stepped back, hoping to leave before she embarrassed herself or Emmett. He wouldn't want her to see this, she knew. She made it to the front door and was about to step out onto the porch when Emmett came through the hall door that led to the dining room. He wore another pair of faded Levi's, these with a hole in the knee, and a crisp green T-shirt that flowed over his form like butter. He held a steamer in one hand and a putty knife in the other and he looked delicious.

"I, uh, thought we could talk." She had no idea about what. The machine in his hand puffed out a trail of steam and Emmett waved it away from his face.

His blue eyes widened for a moment, surprise clear in his expression, and then his gaze shuttered and he was the remote stranger talking about security systems with the trustees a few days before.

"The crew will be at the school after lunch." He looked over his shoulder. "This isn't a great time."

She nodded. "Yeah. I should have called or something. I didn't know."

Emmett disappeared inside the dining room and when he returned the steamer was gone and his hands were in the back pockets of his jeans.

Jaime ordered herself to focus on Emmett's words not his body.

"No one knows. Other than his doctors."

"Dementia?"

"Early onset, but it's moving fast."

She squeezed her eyes closed for a moment, trying to regain her composure. For all her talk about Emmett having no ties to the community, for all the times she'd mentally castigated him for avoiding his family, she knew he loved Gibson. She couldn't imagine going through anything like this with either of her parents.

"I'm sorry. I didn't mean to intrude." She wanted to reach out to him, to comfort him in some way, but touching Emmett never ended well for her so she kept her hands to herself and stayed on her side of the foyer. "I'll go. I just wanted to say, about the other night—"

Gibson came into the foyer, a stack of wet newspapers in his hands. "We're out of sugar."

Emmett looked from Jaime to his father. "Those are newspapers, Dad."

"'Course they're newspapers. I was draining the blackberries."

"They're empty newspapers." Emmett crossed the room to his father, taking the stack of dripping papers from his hands.

"Well, you don't carry wet blackberries over hardwood floors, do you, boy?"

"I saw the blackberries," Jaime confirmed. Emmett turned his attention to her and she felt blood rush to her cheeks. "When Gibson met me at the golf cart he had a basket filled with berries."

"I wanted pie. Blackberry pie with fresh, wild blackberries. We need sugar, and I'm out of cheese, too." Gibson turned to Jaime and smiled. "Well, hi, darlin'. When did you get here?"

"Just a few minutes ago," Jaime said. "How are you, Gibson?"

"Losing my memory, if you want to know

the truth," he said, a wistful expression on his face.

His voice, though, was strong, as she remembered. Maybe it was still the same house she remembered, too, underneath the dust and mess.

"But not today. You gonna get those supplies, boy, or do I have to go myself?" Before Emmett could answer Gibson turned and disappeared through the door to the kitchen.

"I apparently have to go to the grocery store."

"Should you leave him alone with blackberries, a craving for pie and an electric stove?"

"I unplug the appliances every morning. He should be safe." He grinned at her, the smile lopsided and a little sad, and then she did reach out.

"I'm so sorry," she said as she crossed the room and put her arms around Emmett's waist. His body was stiff against hers, his breathing shallow. It was like hugging one of the cannons in the city park. Jaime dropped her arms and stepped back.

"It's not, I think..." He paused, shoved a hand into his almost too long hair and shook his head. "It's why I have to get him to Cincinnati. I've lost enough time with him. I don't want to lose whatever is left. And now

I'm going to go for dairy-free cheese and sugar. Can we talk later?"

She should just say it. Let him off the hook for the school reno that he obviously didn't have time for. Let him take Gibson and leave the island. Why wouldn't he want to get away from a house that she remembered being bright and colorful and filled with life and now was old and dusty and sad? None of this was his fault. She'd decided on that shortcut through the alley in Pittsburgh. The town blamed him for what she did, and she never once stood up for him. Jaime couldn't change the past, but maybe she could make things better now.

"Do you want company?" She knew she should feel guilty for blowing off work, or crazy for wanting to spend more time with Emmett. Still, he'd been her best friend once. And now he was the one hurting. She couldn't leave him alone.

He seemed to weigh his options, standing in the foyer in a faded T and old jeans. All that was missing was the tool belt. "Sure," he said finally. "We're also out of bread and most other necessities."

"Oh." Necessities meant a trip to the mainland. The convenience store on the island was heavy on sugary drinks, lightbulbs and past-the-expiration-date bread. An actual stock-up meant the grocery store in Port Clinton.

Her hands twitched. Silly, because she could leave the island. Anytime she wanted. She just usually didn't want to do so. Just before the holidays she took the ferry over to pick up a shirt for her father. That she had the shirt delivered to the ferry station was beside the point.

"You probably have work, it's no big deal. Dad's blackberry pie craving got me thinking about the peanut butter pie at Big Boy."

Jaime's mouth watered. It had been a long time since she'd had a slice of peanut butter pie. Last night it was apple caramel. Today the promise of peanut butter. She was turning into a pie addict. At least it was pie that had her mouth watering and not Emmett.

"I'm actually waiting for a couple of callbacks, but I have my phone with me," she said. "Let's go."

She could finish her drive and go to the winery where she had nothing to do. Or she could hang out with Emmett for a while longer. What was it Dr. Laurer had said during their sessions? The difference between full-on phobia and simple aversion was a willingness to deal with the fear. It still sounded like hokum, but hokum made more sense than the roller coaster of emotion she'd experienced in the past five minutes. Excitement at seeing Emmett, sadness that he was losing his father, lust at the way he filled out the faded denim and on to nervousness that he would see right through the person she was pretending to be to the scared girl she still was inside.

Jaime decided to focus on the excitement. The "being twenty-eight and unattached with no responsibilities." *Enjoy playing hooky from work,* she ordered herself. *See what happens.*

TEN MINUTES LATER they were on the ferry motoring to the mainland. Emmett congratulated himself on getting Jaime not only out of the house but off the subject of Gibson's condition, as well. He didn't want to talk about the incurable disease he and he father would deal with. He wanted to focus on fixing problems. Finding solutions.

Problem one: Jaime's school project. Solution: call in a few favors and get his guys on the job. Most of them had taken off for the summer hiatus, but a few were still in Cincinnati. They lived for this kind of project. They would have to stay on the mainland, but the ferry system was reliable, if slow.

Problem two: Get Jaime out of Gibson's

house before she— No, scratch that. Jaime being in his childhood home wasn't the problem. Jaime showing up unannounced wasn't the problem, either. Jaime still living on the island, planning parties for the winery when she could be doing so much more? That was the problem. Solution: build her confidence. He could solve that by getting her off the island, at least for this morning. He would figure out the rest as he went along.

Besides, it was nice to be on the ferry with the warm breeze blowing and Jaime sitting beside him. Like old times.

He'd been startled to see her standing just inside the door as she'd done thousands of times when they were kids. Maybe a little embarrassed. Somewhere between his shock at seeing her and realizing he held the wallpaper steamer like some kind of ceremonial staff he'd realized every half-baked idea about changing Jaime's life started with getting off the island. Gibson's love of dairy-free cheese, which the island gas-n-shop didn't carry, was as good an excuse as any he'd come up with over the past couple of hours of reliving a kiss that shouldn't have happened.

A few families sat toward the front of the ferry, but Jaime and Emmett were the only passengers in the rear. Wind whipped through the upper seating area as the boat picked up steam. The captain announced they would be at the dock within a half hour; the same message he'd heard last week. The same message he'd heard countless times over the years. A half hour from either South Bass or Gulliver to the mainland, fifteen minutes to Kelly's.

Jaime mumbled something under her breath and Emmett looked over at her watching the island grow smaller off the bow of the boat. Quiet. Hands clasped.

The captain finished his monologue about life jacket location and not leaning over the high-sided ferry railings.

Her knuckles turned white, but her skin didn't go green as it might before a person became seasick. Not motion sickness, then. Had to be nerves.

"Are you okay?"

"Sure." She cleared her throat. "Just distracted about the school project."

No way. From the white knuckles to the way she kept her gaze trained on the quickly shrinking tree line on the island, this wasn't distraction about work. This was a full-on case of nerves and it stemmed from him. He'd done this. He'd made her afraid.

The sound of Jaime's voice in the diner that first day echoed in his mind. She had been determined, more like the girl he remembered from before the attack. Maybe if he could get her to focus on something more than the island.

"Do you want to talk about window choices or floor stains?"

Jaime had always been a perfectionist, always wanted everything done *this second*. Her attachment to the school was as good a place to start as any other.

"Not especially," she said, keeping her gaze trained on the shrinking shoreline.

"I checked out the basement yesterday, and I didn't see any water or foundation damage."

She nodded and the whiteness at her knuckles lessened. "That's good."

"So we can start demolishing walls this week." He watched her carefully, weighing the tone of his voice with the actual words and feeling completely out of his depth. He didn't have a degree is psychiatry or counseling. Still he plunged forward because the more he didn't talk about the mainland or the ferry, the more relaxed Jaime became. So he talked about the open-concept room and how they would strengthen the staircase to the classroom level.

The stiff line of her shoulders softened, the color came back into her knuckles.

The captain came over the loudspeaker again and Jaime's focus returned to the blip-size island behind them. She swiveled her head as the ferry approached the mainland dock. Gripped her hands tighter in her lap.

This was a mistake. Bringing her here, pretending it was no big deal for her to leave the community she obviously needed for her peace of mind.

"We don't have to leave the ferry. We can stay on board and take the turnaround trip, be back on the island within the hour." He would pick up sugar and milk at the convenience store, it didn't matter. Jaime mattered and this was too much for her. "It's okay."

"You promised pie." She swallowed and her voice sounded tinny, but she flexed her hands and the white left her knuckles. "I'm not afraid. I'm perfectly fine."

"I didn't say you were afraid."

"You implied it," she said defensively.

"You've been white-knuckled for the past twenty minutes. What was I supposed to think?"

"Do you know how many shipwrecks there have been on the Great Lakes? Six thousand—and that is a low estimate—and most are because of collision or ship malfunction not weather."

"So you've been watching the shoreline in case the ferry collides with another boat in the middle of a clear spring morning?" Emmett studied her. "I have to tell you if the boat spontaneously combusts we're going to need more than your mental calculations of the distance between us and the shore."

"I've been thinking about the calls I still need to make when we get back, not doing algebraic equations about Boat One traveling at twenty knots and Boat Two at thirty."

"No, you haven't." He knew the argument was silly, but at least there was life behind those pretty brown eyes again. Flecks of gold flashed as Jaime insisted she'd been thinking about the backlog of work that a half hour before she'd insisted she didn't have.

"Yes, I have."

"For the past two days anytime the school or the reno is brought up you get excited. Not 'jump around on a trampoline' excited but your eyes light up."

"Well excuse me for not jumping for joy that we need a location for the big reunion party and the only possible space needs to have walls knocked down, windows replaced and a new staircase." She stood and started to pace between the aisle of seats while the captain gave the disembarking instructions.

Good, this was good. Get her out of whatever moment she was having. Get her thinking about something else.

"I can't hire painters or interior designers until the walls are down, the windows are up and the whole place is shored up." She flung out her hands, hitting his shoulder as she passed by. This was the Jaime he remembered. Opinionated. Passionate. "We're trying to save a historical landmark. A building with ties to Prohibition and freaking NASCAR, for crying out loud."

"Ah, I don't think any NASCAR drivers are from the island."

"The Gullivers used the school as their holding facility and had the drinks shipped to the mainland. Stock car racing developed out of bootleggers running whiskey across county and state lines back in the day."

"That would link the school to F1 Powerboats."

Jaime shot him an annoyed look. Little flecks of gold stood out in her brown eyes and her curls blew wildly in the wind. "Right, not the point."

The captain slowed the ferry, making a wide turn and then beginning to back toward the dock.

"The point is we're here and you might as

well pick up a case of Pledge and another of Pine-Sol because you're going to need them more than sugar and milk."

Emmett bit back a grin. He'd annoy her right back into her old life if he had to. Distract with little confidence builders; annoy until she didn't remember to be afraid.

This was going to work.

"EVERY MALE HOUSEHOLD needs at least two kinds of steak in the freezer at all times." Emmett held up a package of rib-eye steaks and another of New York strips. "You women have a million different kinds of chocolate for every mood. We men have steak." He put two of each type into the cart then added a package of ground beef.

Jaime rolled her eyes at his broad back, wondering how she'd gone from possible pop-in flirtation to mainland grocery shopping. Things just seemed to happen when Emmett was around. Not that she was complaining. Aside from that little moment on the ferry this was the best day she'd had since…well, definitely since she'd taken on reunion-planning duties.

"I'm just saying a lean, skinless chicken breast wouldn't kill the cholesterol-fest you've got going in that cart." She spotted a rack filled with stuffed shrimp and pretty party foods and pulled a notebook from her bag. Cake and punch, indeed, she decided, making notes for the next party planning meeting with Maureen. "And don't you dare add those mixed vegetables to your cart. The ones in the freezer section are better."

"But I like these."

"But those are loaded with salt and sugar. Drop 'em, buddy." He'd already put packages of frozen twice-baked potatoes and butter noodles in the cart along with a casserole dish that, from the packaging, appeared to be 90 percent cheese product, 5 percent vegetable and 5 percent additives.

"Fine, I'll get the chicken." Emmett put the canned vegetables in the cart and at the end of the aisle picked up a package of legs and then added breading mix and vegetable oil. "We'll fry it up with the twice-bakeds."

"You're messing with me."

"What?" He raised the hands, palms up, and looked at her with a baffled expression on his face.

"Pre-packaged, cheese-slathered and canned vegetables and a cart filled with red meat? Do you even remember the food pyramid?" She put the notebook back in her bag and skewed him with her gaze. Emmett took the canned veggies out of the cart and left them on the rack above the chicken case.

"I thought they decided the pyramid wasn't completely accurate." At the seafood counter he ordered fresh filets of lake perch.

"At least it was a guideline." Not that the way he ate seemed to disagree with him. Possibly it was all the manual labor he did knocking down walls and reroofing houses. Still, cholesterol could be a silent killer. And disagreeing about groceries was better than thinking about the fact that she was about a mile from the dock and that the ferry wouldn't be back for at least an hour.

"Will it make you happy if I pick up some fresh bananas and apples in the produce section?"

"Not completely, but it's a good start." Baby steps, she reminded herself, and unfolded her arms. She wrapped her palms around the cart handle and pushed it while Emmett picked up shrimp and cocktail sauce.

"Great, but first we need to hit the cereal aisle. Dad has a thing for Grape-Nuts."

"Grape-Nuts are very healthy. Don't forget the skim milk."

He picked up a container of chocolate almond milk and then turned into the cereal aisle.

"You forgot the milk."

"No, I didn't." He pointed to the carton of in the cart. "You haven't lived until you've put chocolate milk on cereal."

Jaime just shook her head. What Emmett ate was so not her business. Kissing him on the porch didn't make her his keeper, and even if it did, she shouldn't want to be that keeper. He would leave in a few weeks. Even though she currently felt as if the life she'd chosen was a bad fit, it didn't mean she could leave everything behind. Not after nearly losing it on the ferry ride across the lake.

"Are you sure you want to sell the house?" Jaime didn't know where that question came from.

They turned into the canned soup aisle and Emmett was comparing the labels for the healthy and original versions of chicken noodle soup. He, of course, chose the originals.

"Yeah, seems like the best option. It isn't as if my father is going to wake up one morning and not have dementia, and my life is in Cincinnati now."

"It just seems sudden, to be cutting off all your ties."

"What ties? The island has survived without me for a long time. With Gibson coming with me, there's nothing for me there."

But not visiting the island and having no reason to ever return were two very different things. Weirdly enough, the idea of having no ties to the island made butterflies beat against her belly. Not in a bad way. In a "what would it be like" way. What would it be like to be free? Going wherever she wanted. For a time she'd thought that was what she wanted.

That plan had started to fade in the summer before their senior year. Where the thought of living out of a suitcase had seemed exciting and adventurous before, it had begun to feel intimidating. She couldn't put a finger on why.

Then there was the attack in Pittsburgh and the thought of traveling the world alone became so much more than intimidating. She'd had a full-on panic attack when the acceptance to Ohio State came in the mail. Her mother had found her rocking on her bedroom floor, incoherent. That was when her father had brought up the online degree options. It was the first time she'd felt she was taking back control of her life.

"I think it mostly feels strange that your family won't be in that big house. The island will be different if Gibson isn't taking his afternoon walk around the dock or sitting on the park benches telling stories about everyone."

"He still does that?"

Come to think of it, it had been a long time since Jaime had seen Gibson on one of his afternoon walks. She told Emmett.

"They can't tell me when it started, and since my mom's been gone no one was up here to keep an eye on him or to notice anything off." His voice was hard as he said the words. "He stayed with me over Thanksgiving and I didn't notice anything until he left."

"What happened?"

"There was a pile of newspapers under his bed. Folded and stacked according to section, just the way he's always separated the morning paper. But he had multiple copies for every day. It was weird, but I shrugged it off."

He blamed himself, Jaime realized. Emmett. She wanted to reach out to him, to let him know this wasn't his fault. But he had to know that. How could he blame himself for this kind of diagnosis?

Emmett put three cans of original chicken noodle soup into the cart and then tossed a few cans of corn and green beans in, too.

"You can't want to talk about this."

Actually it was nice, talking about his

problems. Not thinking about what a lunatic she'd been on the ferry. Freaking out as the island got smaller. And for what? She didn't make a daily habit of leaving the island, but it wasn't as though she was mentally incapable of taking a water taxi or a ferry to the mainland now and then. It just seemed silly to put off that kind of carbon footprint when most of her work could be done by phone and email. Plus, it was island custom for each family to rotate picking up groceries and other staples from the mainland; everyone left lists at the community center and Cindy Ergstrom kept a calendar so people knew when their week was coming up.

Her last week had been a few years ago.

What was wrong with her? Not taking a calendar week to pick up other families' groceries wasn't a felony. She was cured of her phobias, damn it. Cured.

"It isn't your fault you know."

"I know. It's my responsibility. He taught me how to fish. How could I not know that my father was human? Not some machine who just happened to know all the right things to do and say as I was growing up? I missed that. I missed figuring out he was a person, not just a dad."

Jaime couldn't stop herself from reaching

for him. She put her arm around his shoulders. "You know now."

"I should have known then. I could have seen it."

"But you couldn't have stopped it."

He reached up, squeezing his hand over hers. "He wouldn't have been alone with it."

"Yeah, he would have been. Even if you'd known, there would have been moments when he was alone with it. When nothing you could say or do would have changed any of it."

That's how it was with her. Everyone was always around. Her father had never left her hospital room after the attack and, once they were back home, Maureen had spent every second with her. And if Maureen wasn't there her mother had been or Emmett was stopping by. From the time she woke up until the time she went to bed, people were there and it was the loneliest feeling she had ever experienced.

"Those first few weeks after the attack I felt so alone."

"But you had your parents and Maureen."

She couldn't believe she was going to do this in the canned fruit aisle. She'd avoided this conversation for ten years, damn it. Why not avoid it for another ten or twenty? It wouldn't change anything that had happened, but she couldn't stand here with Emmett, couldn't see him in pain, and not try to help him. Yeah, he'd walked out on her a long time ago, but before he'd walked he'd tried to be there. Every single day. Those first few days she wouldn't leave her room, but Emmett had kept coming back. Trying to make up for something that wasn't his fault. She hadn't known how to tell him then, but maybe she could now.

"You were there, too, just like Maureen and my parents. And you all were trying to make it go away. My dad by shadowing me on the way to school and back home. My mom by telling me over and over that none of it was my fault. You by constantly trying to do everything for me. God, you tried to do my homework, remember? Maureen tried to help by not talking about it at all."

Jaime put a can of mixed fruit in the cart and Emmett put it right back on the shelf.

"Pears and peaches and cherries in the same container is a crime against fruit," he said.

Jaime put individual cans of each into his cart. Emmett eyed them warily but didn't take them out.

"I wasn't there to stop the attack, but I wanted to be there to help you recover."

"I know. But what nobody understood and

what I couldn't express was that it wasn't your job to fix it. It wasn't my parents' and it wasn't Maureen's. I loved you all for trying, but you couldn't stop me from hearing that man's voice or from feeling his hands on me. Over and over. I was alone in that.

"Your dad's illness isn't exactly the same. I came to terms with what happened to me. I dealt with the pain of it. This isn't something your dad will ever come to terms with, and it's something that he will always be alone with, at least a little. That doesn't make it your fault. Your responsibility from this point forward is to make the most of the time you have with him. Not to fix him."

Emmett was quiet for a long moment and some emotion flashed in the blue depths. She caught anger and guilt but there was more going on and it made her uneasy. "I'm sorry I couldn't help you more," he said.

"I wasn't your responsibility, and you did try. You came to the house. You were at the hospital." His eyes widened. "I asked my dad not to let anyone through. I wanted to separate home from the hospital. I know that doesn't make sense. I thought if I kept the attack in another state that it wouldn't come home with me." She shook her head at how wrong she had been. "But I knew you were there. The nurses told me. One of them even encouraged me to let you through, but I couldn't."

And she wasn't going to tell him why. Not now. Not when she could see how much he hadn't let go of what had happened. All he knew was that she'd gotten a concussion when someone had tried to rob her. He didn't know she'd been scarred, that her attacker had slid his knife into her ribs and then again into her chest. Emmett might never be able to let go if he knew about that.

Or, worse, he would never leave her because he'd feel even more responsible.

Jaime didn't want his pity.

She blew out a breath and put a few ears of sweet corn into his basket. Gibson loved sweet corn.

She didn't want Emmett's guilt.

"Maybe if I had, things would be different, but I couldn't open that door, not back then. I'm telling you now that I'm okay. I really need to you believe that and to forgive yourself."

She wanted him, as much as she'd wanted him in high school. It was different now. She understood what it meant when her hands went clammy and when moisture dampened her panties. She wanted to know what it would be like to give herself to him, knowing what she knew as an adult rather than as a teenager.

Add one more thing to the list she wouldn't tell him, Jaime decided.

CHAPTER NINE

As THEY WAITED in the checkout line, Jaime picked up a magazine and thumbed through it. She talked a good game about dealing with the pain of the attack, but Emmett wanted more for her than to exist in a bubble. He wanted more than that for her. Emmett knew he couldn't make everything the way it had been before, but he could help her get her confidence back. Show her the old Jaime was still in there.

She deserved more than the kind of half life he'd been living since his uncle had given him that first job. Working construction had saved Emmett from the angry boy he'd been. Given him purpose. His uncle had helped him. Now he was in a position to finally help Jaime and he wasn't going to bail.

He also just wanted to be with her. Talking to her. Hearing her laugh. Feeling her skin under his hands. He shouldn't want that, but he did.

That wasn't a conversation he wanted to

have in front of a green-haired grocery clerk with an eyebrow ring, though. Emmett paid for the groceries and loaded the cold bags into the handcart he'd borrowed from the boat.

"I left because of you," he said when they got to the sidewalk that would lead to the restaurant.

Jaime offered him a half smile. "I know."

"You do?"

"I kind of feel like a broken record, but the attack wasn't your fault."

"If I hadn't skipped the play—"

"If I'd stayed with the class. If I hadn't cut through that alley." She grimaced slightly. "How about if that maniac had been on his meds? What if the system hadn't failed him and me in the process? How about letting just a little of that go?" Her words were angry and Emmett couldn't blame her.

What would her life have been like if that night had never happened?

"What happened to me was awful, but the man who attacked me is now in a mental health facility and he can't hurt anyone else."

"I wasn't there. When we got back I saw how you kept to yourself. How you shied away from anyone talking about the trip. They kept talking, even when you wouldn't talk about it."

She shrugged.

"Some of the talk wasn't about you, it was about me. How I was a bad influence on you. How if I'd been more responsible you wouldn't have been hurt."

Her mouth dropped open. "I knew my dad blamed you, but I didn't realize... I thought they were just gossiping about what had happened, not assigning guilty statuses."

"The sentencing report came out the night of the prom. I went into the diner for my mom and they were all talking about it. How he'd gotten what he deserved and on and on. And someone asked when I would wake up and realize my part in all of it." They arrived at Big Boy and placed their orders at the counter. When the server left, he continued. "I knew they would keep talking about it as long as I was around, and I knew you needed to get over it, so I left."

"Oh, Emmett."

"I just wanted you to be the Jaime you were before that night."

"I'll never be that Jaime again. I'm better, and maybe a little worse. I don't like crowds. I like routine a little too much."

"I'm sorry."

She shook her head. "Don't. I'm not mad

at you for that night and I'm not mad at you for leaving."

"I've heard the talk starting up again."

"I know. It started when all the reunion planning began."

"I'm sorry for that, too, then."

She narrowed her brown eyes at him and shook her head. "Stop it. My happiness and peace of mind aren't your problem. I like my life. I like my job. And I'm really going to like this peanut butter pie."

No, Jaime wasn't his problem. She was his responsibility.

"I'd like to see you. You know, when I don't have twenty pounds of groceries to lug around."

Jaime grinned. "I'd like that."

"Good."

THE GENTLY SWAYING swing and colorful petunia blossoms spilling over the flower boxes on her porch welcomed Jaime home. She loved the little house with the peaked, blue roof, wooden shutters and big bay window. More than that, she wanted to crow because she'd done it. Not only gone to the mainland, but grocery shopped and eaten out. She'd showed Emmett that she was damaged but not bleeding and definitely not his obligation.

Maybe, with the past out of the way, she could get back to where she had been before all this reunion nonsense had started.

The butterflies in her stomach beat wildly against her abdomen when she recalled how he'd said he wanted to see her. Gratefully, Jaime collapsed onto the swing, her head hitting the cushion with a thud. She scooted her body up, so she could rest comfortably with her feet at one end and her head at the other. He wanted to see her. She definitely wanted to see him. She kicked her feet lightly against the swing seat in a horizontal victory dance and then lowered one leg to set the swing in motion.

"Focus, Jaime, focus," she said. "Work to be done. You can think about him later."

"Thanks for coming with me today," Emmett's voice startled her into the present. Jaime sat up, her head hitting the arm of the swing. She put her hand to her forehead. That was going to leave a mark.

"What are you doing here?" She rubbed her fingers against her head. And why did it seem quaint and fun that everyone used electric golf carts on the island when really it just made it easier for people to sneak up on you?

"Making sure you got home okay," he said

from the walk. "Nice place." He nodded at the planters on her porch.

"Thank you. I like it. And Gulliver is a two-mile-wide island that I've lived on all my life. I know my way around," Jaime said, this time enjoying the spark of electricity moving between them.

"It's your dad's, right?"

"They decided to stop doing summer rentals a few years ago and I moved in. I pay rent," she said a little too defensively. Especially since her miniscule "rent" was to pay the water and electric bills.

"Nice setup." Emmett stepped up to his side of the railing and, arms crossed at the wrist, rested against it. He motioned with his head at a note stuck between her screen door and the jamb. Jaime stood, snatched it, saw her mother's writing on the outside and stuck it in her pocket.

The house was nice. Just off the town square but nearly half a mile from her parents' overprotective reach. Most of the time. "It works for me. So, what are you doing here?" She crossed to stand on the opposite side of the rail from Emmett.

His heat warmed her arms and made her fingers itch. Coupled with the fact he was at mouth-level with her breasts, Jaime stepped off the porch. Standing next to him didn't stop her raging hormones, though, it only made them worse. Because now she was mouth-level with his pecs.

A small voice cautioned her not to move too quickly. She felt like two different people. One who wanted to wrap herself around his length to see what happened; another who didn't want him to know she'd just been day-dreaming about him. They'd agreed to see one another just a couple of hours before but that didn't mean she had to jump right into forgetting all the reasons whatever this was wouldn't last.

Chief among them: she lived on Gulliver and didn't see that changing anytime soon.

"I thought maybe you could help me with something," Emmett said.

"I knew there would be a catch to helping you grocery shop."

Emmett chuckled. "I need a local cleaning crew to work on the debris at the house and Dad insists we can't use Island Maids. You know anyone?"

"We've used a couple of different compa-nies from Port Clinton at the winery, for big jobs. I'll get you their numbers. Why do you need a cleaning crew?"

"You've seen the interior."

"Yeah, and you keep telling me you're handling it."

"I don't like to get my hands dirty," he said, grinning as he lifted his pristine but callused hands for her inspection. "I figure if a cleaning crew can do the bulk of the actual cleanup I can figure out paint colors and listing prices and help out at the school more."

"No." Jaime shook her head. "You got your crew to come up here, that's enough. Your dad needs your help now."

"I can do both."

"You shouldn't have to do both." She couldn't let him do both. He left all those years ago because of her, she would not let him lose even more precious time.

"Says the woman holding down a full-time job, planning an island-wide reunion and overseeing a huge renovation project."

"Multitasker." She sang the word and batted her eyelashes. Emmett bumped his fist against her shoulder, like a buddy would do, but the fire of awareness that sprang to life again was anything but friend based. So much for taking things slowly. Her body was already off and running.

"I invented that word. House renovator, do-it-yourself television show." He counted off his accomplishments on his fingers as he spoke.

"But this is a volunteer project."

"A volunteer project that is going to pay my company quite well with the added benefit of putting my firm in a good light with the state historical registry. Win and win." He waited a beat. "Plus, if you play your cards right, you might be consulted about paint colors for the interior of the house and for the school. I hear you have an amazing eye for coordinating colors."

"Maureen or Anna?"

"Both, along with Tom in his office the other day. Dad wants the green-navy-peach combination Mom picked for the outside. We compromised on new colors on the inside."

Jaime couldn't decipher the look in Emmett's eyes, but she liked the way it made the blue darken. "I don't know if I have the time," she lied, not wanting him to see how interesting the offer was to her.

"I can only go by the exterior of your house, but I'd say you've got an eye. Plus, the beauty of Victorians is that everyone expects lots of color. I think yellow in the kitchen and dining rooms, but the rest is…murky."

The last thing she needed was another job, but the idea of seeing Emmett every day, of having more conversations the likes of which they'd had today was tempting.

"You could have just called, you know."

"I know. But it's easier for you to turn down dinner on the phone than in person." Emmett pointed to his flat belly.

"I thought this was about paint colors and wall treatments." She raised an eyebrow.

"Just keeping you on your toes. But lunch *was* hours ago."

"And we pigged out on cheeseburgers and pie."

"Technically you ate some of mine. It's been a half hour." His stomach growled as if on cue. Jaime couldn't stop the laughter from bubbling up. Banter. She was bantering. With Emmett Deal. On her front porch. Giant, freaking leap into unfettered adulthood.

Emmett leaned against the railing.

"You're the one who ordered French silk instead of peanut butter. I had to sample. Besides you brought a second piece home."

"Dad ate it."

"In the ten minutes since I left you at the dock I don't think you went home, unloaded the groceries *and* lost your pie to your father." She narrowed her eyes at him. "Are you using me for pie?"

"Or cupcakes. I'm not choosy."

"You know grown-ups eat more than cheeseburgers and desserts."

"Are you going to hassle me about all my favorite foods? I'm a growing boy." Emmett's eyes were wide and he spread his hands out, palms toward the sky.

"You're a sugar-holic."

"I hear they have a meeting for that at the community center."

"I am not taking you to a Sugar Shakers meeting. I don't have a problem."

"Gibson says Hank made meat loaf at lunch today. And after the best cheeseburger on the North Coast you said you wanted to see me."

"In the future."

"It's the future. And Hank always makes enough for lunch and dinner. Plus, it's Monday and that means some kind of fruit upside-down cake."

Jaime's mouth watered. "Last week it was strawberry." Jaime tried to ignore the flip-flopping of her stomach but couldn't quite manage it. It was just dinner. After a full afternoon spent with Emmett. A friendly dinner between two people who used to date but were now working together. Seeing each other. She picked up her bag and started down the steps.

They walked her lane to the beach road, past the ice-cream place and the mini-golf course. Seagulls swooped over the calm waters of the bay looking for dinner. It was peaceful here and for the first time in weeks her life felt as though it fit her.

Only because of the man walking beside her, she knew, but didn't care. Last week the more she'd tried to control her life the more out of control it felt. This week she had no more control but felt as if she was getting a handle on things. Who could be mad about that?

Emmett took her hand and squeezed it as they walked and another piece of the world came into focus.

"I wish I'd come back sooner."

Her heart jolted in her chest. "Because of your dad?"

He nodded. "And other things. I thought I was doing the right thing."

"I don't want to keep having this conversation."

"I know. Last time I'll bring it up."

"I'll hold you to that." She put her free hand on his arm and squeezed. "I'm glad you came back." She needed to break the tension she felt between them. They were just getting their footing, and she selfishly wanted to hold on to the even keel she'd been feeling since they'd left the grocery store. "Because if you weren't here I'd be tearing down moldy walls all by myself."

CHAPTER TEN

TWO DAYS LATER Emmett stepped into the kitchen to find Gibson already there.

"Might not be such a great idea, you working with Jaime on the old school." Gibson sat at the kitchen table stirring a spoon in a mug of hot water. "Everybody's talking about it."

"It isn't as if we're vandalizing the place. The guys and I are already close to finishing the teardown, which means we can start rebuilding soon." Which meant finishing soon. As if that would stop the gossip. Emmett pressed his lips together. Everybody always talked about everything; he should have expected it. Somehow he'd thought no one would notice. Maybe "hoped" was a better word. He'd hoped the islanders would let this one thing slide right past the grapevine. "Maybe everybody should just mind their own business."

Gibson shrugged. "They think they are. Renovated historic building…tourism draw.

That's big for a place like Gulliver. Adding you to the mix just makes it more interesting."

"I'm swinging a hammer and fixing a roof. That's hardly gossip-worthy."

"You have a big business down in Cincinnati, boy. A show on cable." Gibson sat back in his chair and his voice filled with pride. "That's a big deal."

"Let them talk. I'm here to do a job, two jobs now. That's all."

"Sooner or later the talk isn't just going to be about the school. Those dark days will come up again."

Everything came back to the Jaime factor. She'd told him about the renewed talk about her attack. He'd seen the combination of annoyance and fear and he wanted to take both away. He wanted the fun girl he remembered; the girl he'd seen a glimpse of on the porch the other night. He'd be damned if he would run this time; not before he could help her.

"Sooner or later people will stop thinking of me in conjunction with trouble. Until then, all I can do is show them I've changed." Emmett finished his coffee and rinsed the mug in the sink. If they did a good enough job, maybe the talk would stay on the school. Maybe bringing the old school back to life would make up for the water-to-wine incident...for turning the front lobby of the school into his father's office…for borrowing the Gulliver's barge for a keg party that last summer and sinking it when it ran aground on the north side of the island.

There were hundreds of other incidents, mostly small, that he needed to atone for, but the biggest would always be Pittsburgh. Helping with the school renovation might assuage his guilt, but it would surely keep the talk on the future rather than the past.

"You never needed to change, boy." Gibson slowly rose from the table to refill his cup. "I should have reined in your mischievous side, but it was so fun to watch you and your friends plot and plan. You boys weren't doing anything the rest of us didn't think about doing in our younger days. You just got caught a couple of times."

He'd gotten caught almost every time, but Emmett didn't want to go there. He wanted to go to the school and he wanted Gibson to come with him. He had no illusions about his father's diagnosis. This wouldn't stop the dementia, but maybe seeing something other than the peeling paint on these old walls would be good for him. Definitely couldn't be bad.

"If you came with me, we could try to find

remnants of wine casks and whiskey bottles in the basement of the school. See if there are any more stories like the bootlegging one you mentioned the other day." He thought he saw a spark of interest in Gibson's faded blue eyes.

"You know I don't like going places." The old man's voice was gruff.

"We went to the diner the other night."

"That was dinner. Not a day in a strange place." He stirred the water in his cup faster.

"I'll be there. If you need to come home, I'll bring you. No questions asked."

"All the old files are at the township hall, anyway."

"Maybe they missed something. Maybe they didn't. Maybe you could look around the old place and tell me what you know about it."

"I know the same stories you know." But he looked interested. Gibson hunched over the hot water in his mug and inhaled as if he wasn't interested, but his right foot tapped against the tiled floor. He always tapped when he was excited.

"It'll be good for you. When was the last time you took a drive around the island or spent any time away from the house?"

"When I came to see you."

"Definitely too long. The flowers are blooming. An early heat wave is warming up the water."

"You said you were working, not playing in the lake."

"So you'll come?"

"Didn't say that." He sipped from his mug and Emmett winced. Drinking hot water was just strange.

"Then you can go to the community center while the cleaning crew boxes and bags the trash here. Maybe pick up a game of bridge or something." Gibson hated cards. Or, more to the point, he hated any card game that wasn't blackjack. Emmett hoped the threat worked because he had no plans to actually take Gibson to the community center, not when people still didn't know about his diagnosis.

"You play dirty."

"I learned from the best," he said.

"I'll come with you." Gibson poured his water into the sink and turned away from Emmett.

EMMETT STOOD IN the attic at the old school a few hours later. Clancy climbed up behind him along with one of his Cincinnati crew. His old friend had offered to help with some of the demolition. It wasn't intricate work, and they could use an extra pair of hands. All three wore hard hats, face masks and protective glasses. Emmett pointed each to a different area and they began working their way around the underside of the roof, looking for soft spots and damage.

An hour later there was very little floor to be seen, just piles of old drywall and the carcasses of a few dozen mice and hundreds of insects. He could now see that the whole roof would have to be replaced.

"Damn," Clancy said as they looked at the underside of the bowed beam.

"Could be worse," Joe offered. He and Emmett had worked together since Emmett had signed on to work for his uncle.

Emmett left while his men began filling Dumpster containers below.

Gibson sat in a lawn chair outside the building, reading through an old ledger he'd picked up from the boxes stored at the township hall offices. So far he hadn't come inside the building, but Emmett had faith they would get him inside sooner rather than later.

"Dad, find anything interesting in the book?"

Gibson shook his head. "The cost of limestone, which they used on the foundation, but I doubt that will be much help to you fellas."

"Not likely." Emmett handed him a bottle

of water from the cooler and then unscrewed the cap on his own bottle and drank deep. August would bring the real heat, but the attic wasn't well ventilated and he felt as if he'd been in a sauna for the past hour.

Jaime walked around the corner of the school with Tom Gulliver, pointing out members of the crew already working. When she saw Emmett and Gibson she waved and started over to them.

"What did you find in the attic?" she asked.

"Bowed support beam, as I'd thought. We'll be able to fix it."

"What about the budget?" Tom interjected.

"I'll know more after I talk to a couple of suppliers, but we should be within budget."

Tom clapped a hand over Emmett's shoulder. "That's what I like to hear." He said his goodbyes and promised to come by later in the week to check on the progress.

When he was gone Emmett focused on Jaime. "It's a best-case scenario."

"I know." She looked at the old building. "Can't you just see it?"

"See what?" He saw old materials falling into the Dumpster bins; he heard hammers hitting drywall and imagined hearing electric saws and other tools in a few days when the real renovating began. But what he saw was still an old, dysfunctional building with shattered windows and a creaky door hung off a single hinge.

"Kids, running up the two steps with lunch boxes swinging from their hands."

They would have played hide-and-seek out here, built snowmen in the winter. Yeah, he could see it. But that glimpse of the past was dim in comparison with the excitement on Jaime's face. She glowed as she looked at the building. She put her hands into the back pockets of her jeans and the action pushed her breasts forward against the thin cotton of her green T-shirt. She wore a pair of jeweled flip-flops today and her toenails were painted a shell pink with an electric purple flower on each of her big toes.

Gibson cleared his throat behind them. "Did you know the basement walls were made to be about six inches thicker than they needed to be?" He flipped another page in the ledger.

"No, Dad, I didn't know that." Emmett turned to his father.

"Why would they do that?" Jaime stepped up behind Gibson and began reading over his shoulder. The ledger pages listed building supplies and dimensions but there was no further detail that Jaime could see.

Gibson shrugged. "Beats me." He looked at them both with a wry expression on his face. "Just thought it was interesting is all." The older man yawned and Emmett checked the time. Nearly three. They'd been at the site for just over four hours; his father had to be tired. "You know, just because I'm over seventy doesn't mean I know why every decision about this island was made," he said and scratched his cheek, his hand tremoring.

"I should take him home," he said.

"I'll walk. You've got work to do."

"You know, Tom drove me here in his golf cart," Jaime said before Gibson could really dig in his heels. "I could use a ride back to the winery, if you're going that way."

"You know as well as I do the winery isn't on the way home," Gibson said. He folded his arms over his chest, hiding his hands. Emmett had noticed him do that a couple of times and he thought it was a defense mechanism. If Gibson didn't see his hand tremor he could pretend things were normal. "I'll walk."

"So I'll take the long way around. You can tell Jaime more about the school. You know, the story you told me." Emmett herded his father and Jaime toward the golf cart, started it up and turned left on Beach Road.

"I'm pretty sure I told her that story the other night at dinner."

Jaime sat on the rear-facing seat, body turned sideways so she could see Gibson. "I'd like to hear it again. It might help us decide what to do with the interiors."

Gibson started his story and a few minutes later they rolled up to the house. Emmett took Gibson inside while Jaime waited on the porch. The cleaning crew had left a note, detailing their work and telling Emmett they would return the next day. He settled Gibson in his favorite recliner with a bottle of water and the remote control before joining Jaime on the porch.

"He seemed good today," she said, following Emmett out of the house.

"He's tired and his hand started to tremor back at the school."

"What does that mean?"

Emmett pressed his lips together. "According to the doctors, it's just an indicator that he's tired. But every time the tremor starts he loses bits and pieces. Forgets my name. Forgets what he was doing. That kind of thing."

"You should stay then." Jaime put her hand on his arm as Emmett started down the steps.

"He'll probably sleep for the next couple of hours. I'll come back to check on him once we finish the attic." But he looked back at the house that seemed both familiar and completely unknown. He would leave a note, but there was no guarantee Gibson would read it, if he had a spell, and if he woke up and things were normal he'd hate that Emmett left the note at all. "He's had several good days in a row, though. After last night, we have an appointment with his specialist tomorrow. They'll probably adjust his meds a little."

"Is there any chance—?"

"No." Emmett cut her off. He couldn't let himself even think about what-ifs; they weren't possible. "So, the winery?"

She shook her head. "No, I thought maybe it would be simpler to get Gibson home if he thought I needed a ride, too."

"Smart."

She poked her thumb at her chest. "College graduate, press release writer and renovator of old buildings."

"And now herder of old men." Emmett offered a teasing glance in her direction. "Do you even know how to operate a hammer?"

Jaime widened her eyes in mock shock. "Hammers, electric screwdrivers. I can even handle an Allen wrench."

"Then it's about time you pulled your

weight on this project," he said and turned the cart toward the old school.

JAIME SHOULD HAVE taken him seriously. She swung the sledgehammer into the wall again, looking surreptitiously over her shoulder at Emmett working on the other wall. His shirt was soaked through with sweat and his tool belt hung low on his hips. He took another swing and more of the drywall on his side of the room fell to the floor. On their way back from his home, Jaime asked Emmett to stop at her house where she'd picked up work boots and an old shirt to wear.

The first and second floors of the old school still had lathe-and-plaster walls; knocking them down was time-consuming. She looked the part, but her wall was only half done while Emmett was nearing the end of his. He pulled the mask from his face and shook his head when he saw what little progress she had made.

He clucked at her. "And you said you could handle a hammer."

"I said hammer." She straightened her shoulders and hefted the heavy sledgehammer in her hands. "I didn't say thirty-pound rock with a handle attached."

"It's a five pounder, not thirty, Muscles.

And that wall isn't going to move itself," he said. "Aren't we on a schedule?"

Schedule, schmedule, Jaime thought as he knocked another hole in the wall. But she halfheartedly lifted her own hammer. A piece of wall the size of a saucer fell to the ground. At least the hole was getting bigger, even it if was due more to the strength of the hammer than her puny arms. Maybe she should start doing push-ups, or pull-ups, or whatever it was that made the biceps grow stronger.

"What is it that you like so much about knocking down walls?" Her voice was muffled behind the face mask but she knew he could hear her.

Emmett swung his hammer once more before answering, his voice sounding far away, too. "I don't actually like it."

"They why do it?" She turned to him, all pretense at knocking down her side of the wall gone. She wasn't doing much good, anyway.

"Somebody has to." The last section of his wall cracked and, when he pulled on it, came tumbling down. He grunted as he swung the sledgehammer again.

"Come on, I'm serious." He'd always been good with his hands; always had one project or another going in the woodworking shop when they'd been in school. It wasn't a stretch that he would find a job working with his hands. "You have to like something about renovation or you wouldn't do it."

"My uncle built houses." Emmett joined her on her side of the room and swung his hammer into the wall. "He gave me a job after I left the island. I liked the work, but when the economy crashed the real estate market went belly-up. No one was buying new builds. They wanted to renovate what they had. One of the first jobs was this tiny Craftsman home. We blew out the roof, added a bedroom, built up the basement. Nothing sexy about it, but I liked it, turning something that didn't work into something that did." The hammer went straight through the wall. When he pulled it out a hunk of wall fell to the ground. He swung again and another chunk hit the floor. "When he retired a year or so later, I stuck with the restoration."

"So it was chance?" She tried swinging her hammer again but her arms were jellied.

"Chance. Lack of other options." He swung and another chunk of plaster hit the floor. "Do you really want to know this?"

"Yes, I do." She couldn't explain why she wanted to know what was so great about knocking down walls, but his answer seemed like the most important answer she would ever get.

"I like repairing things. Old car engines, flat tires. There is nothing like building a house from nothing." He put down the sledgehammer and crossed the room for a bottle of water from the cooler.

"But breathing life into a place like this is different. Better in some ways because there are memories here. We will probably never know why the builders made the foundation six inches thicker than it needed to be, but we know that they *did*. We know someone thought it was necessary and because they built such a strong foundation the Gullivers were able to use this building for their midnight liquor runs and the Red Cross was able to use the building to fold bandages and sell war bonds." He dribbled the last of the water over his head.

Jaime knew she shouldn't stare. The sane part of her brain insisted she look away but the crazy part—the part she hadn't known still existed until he'd showed up on the island a week ago—wouldn't look away. That part watched his shoulder muscles ripple beneath his T-shirt, made her grip the handle of her hammer tightly in her fingers and forget to breathe when he picked the sledgehammer back up and started to work on another section of the wall.

Jaime swallowed. She'd never been one for masculine displays of strength, but there was something about the way Emmett's hands held the handle… The way he made tiny adjustments that changed how his muscles played under his skin… The way his tool belt hugged his lean hips…and the smell of his sweat in the close room.

All of those things should be completely foreign to her, but they weren't. He smelled like Emmett. His focus was as familiar as her own.

Emmett looked at her from the corner of his eye. "Are you going to help or are you going to watch the show?" A little piece of wall drifted from the ceiling to rest in his hair. It moved.

Jaime shrieked when what looked like a discolored piece of plaster began skittering along Emmett's scalp. He wiped at his hair and the spider settled on the back of his glove. It was big and black and nasty looking, and Jaime knew from a glance it was nonpoisonous, but still it made her skin crawl. Emmett held the beast in her direction and she backed up, tripping over a loose floorboard and landing on her butt in the middle of the room.

Emmett released the spider on the window-sill and turned to her. He pulled the mask and goggles from his face.

"It's just a little jumper," he said.

Jaime didn't care. "I know most of them won't hurt me but they're so...creepy." She shivered and removed her protective gear. "I should get out of here so I don't hold you back."

Emmett held out a hand and helped her to her feet. She dusted off her bottom and tucked her hair behind her ears. He was close. Too close. She knew she should step away from him but she couldn't bring herself to make the move.

"You're not holding me back. That two-foot section of wall you pulled down was really helpful." His blue eyes danced as he teased her.

"Nice. Torment the woman who is donating her time to the project."

"Well, it's good that you're donating or you'd owe me money. The guys I usually hire know how to knock down walls."

"Well, I'm not a guy, in case you didn't notice."

"I noticed." His eyes darkened and he watched her for a long moment, not saying anything. "I've always noticed." Then his mouth was on hers and she couldn't move, not if her life depended on it.

Emmett's hands were soft on her neck, his lips seeking against hers. Jaime felt her arms lift to wind around his neck, and it was as if she were outside her body. She knew she shouldn't kiss him back, but she was powerless not to tilt her head to give his mouth better access. Powerless not to want him.

Rather than step back, she stepped forward and went up on her tiptoes. Her breasts were flat against his chest. His hands bracketed her face, so she couldn't move even if she'd wanted to. She let herself sink into the kiss. Sink into Emmett.

He tasted cool from the water he'd been drinking and the feel of his tongue against the seam of her lips was tempting. She opened, allowing him into her mouth. She sighed and the tiny sound was like a shot in the room.

Emmett stepped back, dropping his hands and looking around as if he didn't understand what had just happened.

"I didn't—"

"Don't," she interrupted. "Don't tell me you're sorry or whatever you were about to just say. I'm sick and tired of you telling me you're sorry."

He turned away from her and ran his hands

through his hair, messing it up. Making him look even more irresistible. Damn him.

"Did you or did you not tell me you wanted to see me just a couple of days ago?"

"That doesn't mean I should—"

"Why not?"

"Because I'm only here for the summer."

"And you think I can't handle that? That I'll break or—what?—fall in love with you?" Jaime shook her head, letting the mad take hold. She pulled on her gear, picked up the sledgehammer and slammed it into the wall, feeling it sink below the surface with a solid smack. It felt good.

"God, you're so conceited. I kissed you as much as you kissed me. Women are allowed to kiss men, you know. We even sometimes have the audacity to start the kiss all on our own."

"Jaime."

"Emmett." She mimicked his tone, wondering why he was so annoyed when he'd started this in the first place. She actively wanted the same things, and it was a little scary, but she wasn't about to turn away from any of it.

Jaime didn't say anything so she marched to his side of the room. "Kiss me."

"No." He shook his head.

"Why not?"

"I don't kiss women who don't know what they want."

"Okay, now you're pissing me off. Since when do I not know what I want?"

Emmett picked up a shovel and began shoveling plaster and dust through the window and into the container below. Jaime moved between Emmett and the window, blocking it.

"I'm serious. Since when do I not know what I want?"

"I don't want to argue with you." He motioned with the shovel and she stepped out of the way.

"Then don't be so hardheaded about a little kiss." Jaime began shoveling plaster and moldings out the window, too. Ten minutes later most of the dross of the walls was off the floor and in the oversize trash container below.

"I liked kissing you." He put his hands in his pockets. "It's familiar, but it's different."

"Then why did you pull away?"

"Because you deserve better than a summer-long fling that wouldn't be half as interesting if it wasn't also our ten-year reunion or if this project wasn't attached."

"I don't know about that. You've always been *interesting.*"

"You, too."

Jaime smiled at that. "I'm not interested in you because of the reunion or because of this project or even because we dated in high school. I'm just interested." She was surprised to find it was the truth. Emmett confused her, intrigued her. What he liked; what he didn't like. Jaime knew she should hold back, and she knew this couldn't lead anywhere, not really. For the first time in a long time, though, she didn't want to think about the what-ifs or the consequences. She just wanted to be normal. To have the kind of life that the people she went to school with talked about in their reunion questionnaires.

Maybe her classmates had a point with their whole partner-by-the-time-I'm-thirty, medical-school, football-playing theories. Kissing Emmett was what she wanted, and for too long Jaime hadn't gone after what she'd really wanted.

She knew kissing Emmett wouldn't solve the problem of her ill-fitting life, and she wasn't sure she clearly understood what would make the fit better. But it felt important for her to figure out what those important things were. Island life. Safety. Emmett. Recklessness. It all meshed together in her mind in a swirl of unformed shapes. She would figure out how it all fit together this time. She would make something pretty out of the mass of emotions and feelings instead of letting them morph into something ugly. Something that held her in place.

"If either of us should be wary of becoming involved it should be me. Islanders love a good gossip and apparently they like a good romance even more. Anna and Ronda keep asking me how things are going."

"With the project?"

"Nope." Jaime shook her head. "I think their interest has zero to do with the school or the reunion and everything to do with you being back in town."

Emmett sat on the window ledge. "I'm sorry."

"I'm not. I don't like being the center of attention, you know that." She sat beside him on an upturned five-gallon bucket. "But I'd rather face the questions about you than face the next few weeks only saying hello as we pass on the street."

Emmett twisted his mouth to the side. "I don't think I'd like only saying hello, either. But if you're going to be here every day, things could get really complicated really fast."

She handed him the shovel she'd dropped to the floor when she'd sat. "Then we uncomplicate it. I think I've already proven I'm a much better planner than actual renovator. I'm turning in my shovel and hammer."

He flicked the brim of her ball cap with his thumb and index finger. "That will definitely speed things up."

She batted her eyelashes at him. "And here I thought you wanted to take things slowly."

"Well, there is twenty-first-century slow and then there is nineteen-twenties slow." A twinkle lit his blue eyes. There was still something he wasn't telling her, something she didn't know, but Jaime pushed that thought out of her head. There was time to figure all of it out.

And maybe, just this once, it would be okay if she didn't examine things so closely.

Maybe, it would be okay to just see where this took them. She leaned forward and brushed her lips across his. "I definitely think twenty-first-century slow is the way to go."

CHAPTER ELEVEN

JAIME LEFT THE job site with the intention of going home, but then made a U-turn to go to Emmett's. He wouldn't be free to check on Gibson for a couple of hours yet.

She stopped the cart on the driveway and hurried up the steps before she could change her mind. Opening the door, she heard the television rumbling from the sitting room. She looked around, noting the non-dust-covered floors and the corners of the room that were free of the stacks of paper. This was the house she remembered; the place she'd felt the most at home outside of her parents' two-story Craftsman home. She peeked around the corner and saw Gibson still sleeping in the chair. The remote sat on the small table beside him along with a bottle of water.

Jaime switched out the unopened bottle with a fresh, cold one from the fridge and added an apple and a banana, just in case he woke up hungry. She turned to the door and then grabbed the notepad from the alcove with the phone and scribbled a quick note.

"An apple a day keeps the doctor away," she wrote. "Jaime." She left the note under the remote and quietly closed the front door.

A few minutes later, she walked through her own front door, thumbing through the mail. There were a few more RSVPs for the reunion in thick envelopes so she knew the invitees had included the questionnaire.

She didn't want to read another listing of the accomplishments of her classmates or others who had graduated before her. Not when she'd done nothing with her life except hide. Jaime left the envelopes on the little table by the door and went into the kitchen to turn on the teakettle. Then she kicked the work boots off her feet in the mudroom off the kitchen and hurried upstairs to shower and change.

Sweat and dust were a good look on Emmett but she had no illusion about how she had to look with plaster in her hair and a fine layer of dust over her skin. She caught a glimpse of herself in the mirror and blanched. The next time they kissed, it wouldn't be through layers of grime, she promised herself, turning the shower to hot as she shed her shirt and jeans.

Twenty minutes later, she felt more human

as she pulled dark capris over her legs and a red T over her head.

"Mom!" She put her hand over her heart and stopped short as she stepped through the kitchen door. Beverly Brown, her mother, sat at the kitchen table, steaming teapot in front of her along with two mugs, spoons and sugar. "What are you doing here?"

"The kettle was whistling like crazy. I thought something might have happened." Her mother's voice was quiet and she frowned in annoyance. "You know better than to leave something on the stove when you're out of the room."

Jaime pushed down her annoyance. Beverly was used to coming and going from her home, but it had been a while since she'd exercised her motherly pop-in rights.

"I helped out at the site this afternoon and needed a shower." She came into the room and sat beside her mother at the table. Beverly wore clam diggers with plain white sneakers on her feet and a bejeweled top in patriotic colors.

"You shouldn't leave things on the stove unattended."

"It was five minutes." Jaime put a tea bag into her cup and bobbed it up and down.

"Why aren't you finishing your flower garden or taking Dad lunch at the station house?"

"Because we came here to see you." Her dad's voice boomed from behind her and Jaime jumped. "I brought a something-upside-down cake from the diner."

Great, a double pop-in with a twist of scare the living crap out of your daughter. At least she looked presentable. "Shouldn't you be patrolling?" she asked and, before he could ask, went to the fridge for a cold soda. She gathered small plates and forks and returned to the table.

"Ernie's on dayshift for the week. His wife's due any day now. Figured it would be simpler for them if he worked days when her sisters or friends would be available in an emergency."

Her father never switched his schedule. "That was nice of you."

"Yeah, well…" He pulled take-out boxes of cake from a bag and Jaime transferred the slices onto plates before passing them around. Beverly refused to eat from take-out containers. Today, apparently, she wasn't eating or drinking at all. The older woman pushed the plate of cake away and while she swooshed the tea bag around in her cup, she didn't drink.

It was weirding Jaime out. Beverly never turned down Hank's desserts and she treated afternoon tea as a full-blown occasion.

"I thought you were just overseeing the renovation."

And there was the shoe Jaime had known would eventually drop. He was still angry about the renovation and her mother was obviously working her way up to some kind of revelation. Jaime pushed her own plate away and sighed.

"I thought maybe I could lend a hand, but I was more hindrance than help." Jaime rolled her shoulders, which were tight even after the hot shower. "I had no idea it was so hard to swing a five-pound hammer at a wall."

"That's man's work, anyway," her mother said.

"Plenty of women renovate buildings, Mom."

"Not my daughter."

"Why don't you just get whatever is really on your mind out there?" She winced. She hadn't intended to say that out loud. Or at all. Her parents were great. A bit overprotective, but couldn't she cut them a little slack?

No. She straightened her shoulders. The time for slack was over. Mason and Beverly had made it easy for her to slip back into island life all those years ago; maybe they made it too easy.

"Emmett Deal was only supposed to consult. Offer a few estimates. You were going to hire local." Mason directed his gaze at Jaime and she didn't see a hint of anything other than disapproval.

"I was. Until every local contractor between here and Cleveland laughed in my ear at the prices we were willing to pay.

"Emmett's here. He has experience and, with his help, we should at least have the ground floor renovated so we can use the building for the reunion. It will be kind of cool to host the reunion in the school that only a few remaining islanders were educated in, don't you think?"

"No, I don't. I think that building is a nuisance, and I think bringing that Deal boy in to renovate is a mistake."

"He'll leave before the project is half over," her mother added.

"Why is it so important to both of you that everyone who is from the island stays on the island? Other people left before Emmett. Other people have made good, solid lives on the mainland—"

"Other people didn't have his responsibilities. Other people didn't leave you to be attacked in some alley—"

"Okay, stop. Both of you, just stop." Jaime gathered the untouched plates and put them in the sink. She needed to keep her hands busy so she could keep her mind focused. "Emmett didn't attack me. Emmett didn't hire the mentally ill person who did attack me. His only crime was going off with his buddies on a school trip. Something you did, Dad, and you, too, Mom. You have to stop blaming him for something he had no control over."

"He should have been there." Her father's voice was quiet in the room. "I should have been there."

"If either of you had been there it's possible you would have been killed. That I would have been killed. I wasn't—"

"He hurt you." Beverly's voice was stringent in the kitchen.

"The attacker hurt me. I shut Emmett out and he left. He's here now to clean up Gib's house for sale and he's offered to help with the school reno, too. And, yes, Emmett will leave the island, and that's okay."

It wasn't dread that he would leave that caused the cold feeling in her belly. Not dread at all.

"His being on the island doesn't mean you

have to go near him. You don't have to see him at all." Beverly clasped her hands under the table.

Jaime rinsed the last cup and set it in the sink. So that was what this was all about. Her parents didn't want her to get involved with Emmett. The school was a cover so they didn't have to come out and say they didn't trust her. Fine. She loved her parents, but Jaime had allowed them to make and influence decisions about her life for too long.

"Maybe I want to see him."

Beverly put her hands to her temples.

Mason shook his head and said derisively, "You went to the mainland with him this week, and then had dinner with him. All the talk is starting up again. Do you really want that?"

"The talk started before he got here, Dad. It was bound to with the reunion. I've heard most of it, been asked questions about it. You know what I realized? People aren't hung up on what happened to me in Pittsburgh. They're interested in the possibility that Emmett and I might start dating or something."

"And that's okay with you?" Beverly sounded incredulous. "To be the center of dirty gossip again?"

No, that part wasn't okay. It was expected

in a town such as this one, however. "I don't want them talking about me, no. But I'd rather they stick with what is real now than all the rumors about what might have happened ten years ago." Jaime dumped her tea and the rest of the pot down the drain. "I've been thinking maybe it wasn't such a good idea to push everyone away back then. It's a small island. People here care about each other. Maybe if I'd been more open about it, things wouldn't have been blown so far out of proportion."

Mason slammed his hand against her wooden table and Jaime jumped. "You were attacked. Mugged." He turned from the table and pointed at the scar hidden beneath the cotton of her T-shirt. "That man cut you and would have done worse if someone hadn't heard your screams for help. You're my daughter and I couldn't protect you."

"You were three hundred miles away. There was nothing you could do to stop it."

"And Emmett Deal was right there and did nothing." Anger seethed between the words Beverly spat into her kitchen.

This was what she hadn't wanted when Emmett came home. For the town to come down on him; place the blame on him once more. She hadn't wanted it back then and she didn't want it now. Because now there was a chance for them. A chance to fix what had gone wrong. She wasn't deluding herself that he would stay on the island, Jaime knew better than that.

"What happened to me wasn't his fault. He was nowhere around when I cut through that alley."

"He should have been. If he'd thought, for one minute, if he'd thought of something other than what he'd wanted—"

"He was eighteen. Away from home for the first time in his life. Clancy and Jason and the rest of the guys didn't want to go to that play. They all skipped it."

"Emmett was the ringleader. He always was."

"That doesn't make him responsible for something he couldn't have known would happen." Jaime reached out to hug her father, who was hunched over the kitchen table he'd refinished the year Jaime had moved into the cottage. "I'm responsible for separating from the group. I'm responsible for not paying attention to my surroundings. The man who attacked me is getting treatment for his disease. You have to let it go, Dad. I'm letting it go."

"You can't just pretend it didn't happen."

Mason stood, brushing her away from him. "You can't pretend you're back in high school."

Jaime gritted her teeth. "I'm not pretending. How could I?" She stomped into the hall and picked up the RSVPs and questionnaires. "For the past few weeks I've looked for a place to hold the reunion. I've stressed out over the number of RSVPs to the weekend events and I've read the answers on every single one of these questionnaires. Do you know what my classmates have been doing while I've been here on the island?"

"You've been doing things, too." Her mom butted in, but Jaime kept talking because if she let either of her parents continue to interrupt her they would never get to the point. She would get tired of arguing, as she'd always done in the past, and nothing would change.

She wanted the change.

"Dad, I write press releases for your best friend's winery. I arrange meetings with suppliers via video chat instead of going in to Cleveland or Detroit or even Napa. I plan parties and events with you, with Mom, and sometimes it's fun and sometimes I want to bang my head against a wall." She shook her head. "Jason tried out for an NFL team and when he didn't make it he went into broadcasting. Pam is on track to become a partner in a huge law firm in Cleveland. Emmett renovates historic buildings and homes around Cincinnati and he's so good at it he's got his own television show, for crying out loud. Maureen and Clancy got married and have two perfect kids and another on the way. I've had exactly one serious relationship since high school and it lasted all of nine weeks."

"What you do is important, too. You'll find your own happiness." Mason leaned his shoulder against the kitchen window.

"Before Tom hired me he used college interns for my job."

"You're better than an intern," her mother insisted.

"No, I'm not. I like my job, I do. But what I've realized is that the job isn't what I want to be doing."

"This is because of Emmett. If he'd never come back here..." Beverly scraped her chair over the kitchen tiles. "He shouldn't have come back and you shouldn't be working with him." She left the room and Jaime could only stare after her. Part of her wanted to chase after her mother, to reassure her. But wasn't that what she had been doing for the past ten years? Going along with what Beverly wanted or what Mason instructed because it was easier than facing what she had become in her life? Alone and lonely. She turned to her father instead.

"This isn't because of Emmett. Not entirely. It's about the reunion and the old school, but mostly it's about me. *Me*, Dad. I want more than to spend my life driving a golf cart around the island or videoconferencing with people in other parts of the world. I want a life."

"You have a life, honey." Mason's voice softened and the annoyed look left his face. He was hearing her. For maybe the first time in her life, her father was listening. The realization pushed Jaime on.

"I don't have the life I want. I don't have the life I'd planned to have. I have the island and I have friends. I know I have you and Mom. I want more than that. I want to love someone and I want to get married and have kids and—"

"And you think Emmett is going to give those things to you? He left, sweetheart, and he never looked back."

"He had his own demons to fight, and I don't know that Emmett will be any of those things to me. But what we had was unfinished and I think I want to see it through."

"He's going to hurt you."

"Dad, I've already been hurt and I let that

hurt dictate too much of my life. If Emmett hurts me, I'll live. You know what? That's the point. I don't want to be afraid. I want to live."

LATE-AFTERNOON SUNLIGHT swept into the second-story room where Emmett worked. A week on the job and his crew had made more progress than he'd hoped.

He wiped his forehead with an already wet hand towel and then pulled the face mask under his chin to breathe in fresh air. The upper level of the old school was taking shape. The old building wasn't air-conditioned, which would have to be changed eventually, but the old windows had been taken out the day before and for the first time a steady breeze blew the mustiness out of the building.

"Hey, shouldn't you be working up there?" Jaime called up from the ground. Today she wore a sun-yellow top and navy pants that reached just past her knees. Jeweled flip-flops adorned her feet.

He saluted her. "Just getting a breath of fresh air, Slave Driver," he retorted. "Come on up and see what we've done."

Jaime's visits were the best parts of his days. In the early mornings he would sit with his dad on the back porch. The bulk of his days were spent sweaty and covered in debris from the building. Evenings were spent having dinner with Jaime or walking the island. Waving to people he'd known all those years ago and feeling as if they accepted him being back. As though maybe a little part of the island missed him.

It was a nice feeling. One he wasn't looking forward to giving up when he returned to Cincinnati.

He met Jaime at the head of the stairs. The main floor was ready for new windows and paint; the upper level would be ready as soon as his guys finishing installing the new roof support beam at the end of the week.

"I'm impressed."

Emmett shrugged. "Well, when you work with the best."

Jaime shook her head. "I'm so glad you aren't the least bit conceited."

Emmett grabbed two bottles of water from the cooler and led the way into one of the classrooms. "Look what we found."

When his crew had pulled off the drywall that morning, they'd found another wall made of old blackboard behind it. The top was dusty and aged but he'd carefully wiped away some of the grime and found names scribbled underneath. Several Gullivers and a few Browns and Blevins. The grandparents and great-grandparents of kids they'd gone to school with.

Jaime traced her hand over the writing.

"Don't touch. We're going to have to be really careful with it."

Jaime pulled back. "That's amazing."

"That's why we restore," he said, excited by the find. In the grand scheme of things it was a blackboard and not worth the fee at the dump. But it would have value to islanders; would connect them more deeply to the school and their history.

He twisted the top off his water bottle. "I called a friend at the Historical Society in Columbus and he's going to come up tomorrow to take pictures. We should save it, don't you think?"

"Can we?" Jaime's eyes widened.

"It's structurally sound. I took off a piece of it and the two-by-fours are solid underneath. The roof didn't leak in this room, so I think we can definitely save it."

He couldn't *not* touch her. He tried, but it seemed so natural to put his hand on the back of her neck. To let it slide to the small of her back.

Jaime stepped into his embrace. "This is going to sound ridiculous, but I never imagined we would find something like this. Also, this might be the stinkiest you've ever been." But she didn't step away from him.

"I'll have to see if I can top the smell tomorrow, then. And I never dreamed we would find this kind of history. I'd hoped for some old car parts or something in the basement. You know, from the bootlegging—"

"You're such a guy."

"Hey, you're the one who compared Gulliver Wines to the birth of NASCAR." She elbowed him. "I figured we might find some old ledgers or maybe an antique desk or podium. Those would have been nice, but this is better. It's a piece of them. A piece of everyone who came before us."

Jaime wiped at a cobweb with her finger and uncovered another scribble on the board. Edward Brown. Her great-grandfather.

Emmett whistled.

"What do you think we should do with this room?" she asked excitedly.

"I think we keep it a classroom. There were a couple of chairs in the basement. We could get era-appropriate desks from antique shops in the area. We should put some kind of protective glass over the wall."

"I think so, too."

He showed her the other rooms, one that

would be completely gutted by the end of the week and the room she'd helped him with that first day, which still needed new drywall and paint.

"I have to get back to the winery," she said when they finished the tour. "Call me if you find any more surprises?"

"Of course. Do you want to come to the house for dinner? We could go over paint samples."

"I knew this visit wasn't just about the blackboard."

"I scratch your back, you scratch mine."

"You haven't scratched my back."

They'd had dinner or lunch together every day since the project had started. He'd grown accustomed to talking with her, telling her about the little finds inside the school such as the old chairs in the basement and the box of ledgers they'd saved from the attic.

She'd helped him convince Gibson to add color to a few of the rooms on the main floor at the house and promised to help them paint the porch. Somewhere along the line asking her opinions had stopped being about building her confidence and started being about discovering her likes and dislikes. Although the bonus of seeing her share her opinions more readily was the kind of bonus money couldn't buy. Dangerous territory, Emmett reminded himself. But he couldn't seem to stop asking. Or flirting at every opportunity. "That scratching thing can be arranged."

Her cheeks pinked at his words, but her voice was confident when she replied, "I expect pie. Fruit-based this time." He walked with her to her golf cart and watched until the cart turned the corner.

She was coming back. Emmett pumped his fist in the air. Jaime was coming back.

That evening, Emmett walked in the front door of his father's house, exhausted. And looked around in shock. The stacks of newspapers were gone, the walls washed. He could see floorboards and not layers of dust and dirt.

"Dad," he called out.

Gibson hollered back from the kitchen. He was looking through boxes and had pictures strewn around the big kitchen table. It had been a couple of days since he'd had an episode, and Emmett couldn't stop the little thread of hope that the new medications the specialist prescribed were doing their job. Maybe he could keep his father with him, at least a little longer.

"This crew you called in from the mainland knows their stuff," he said. "Took them all week, but this house is as clean as when Mary Margaret was here."

Emmett pulled a bottle of water from the fridge. "Jaime's coming over for dinner. We're going to talk about paint colors."

Gibson continued looking through the box. "White. It's a good, solid color for walls. Shows off what you put on 'em."

"People like color now, Dad."

"It's my house and I say white."

"You agreed with her the other night that some yellows or lighter colors would add to the place."

"And now I've changed my mind."

"Why don't we see what Jaime has to say?"

"Whatever," he said. "You ordering from the diner or are we eating bologna sandwiches?"

"I called Anna before I left the school. She's sending the busboy with Salisbury steaks, green beans and dinner rolls."

Gibson whistled. He went to the sink to wash his hands but grabbed the counter, his knuckles turning white with the grip.

Emmett hurried to his side. "What is it? What's wrong?"

Gibson shook his head. "Nothin'. Just a little light-headed." He shook his head and the shock of white hair whipped around. He bent over the sink and his stomach heaved.

This wasn't just light-headedness. Emmett grabbed his truck keys and helped his father to the vehicle. The last ferry would leave in ten minutes and he didn't have time to putter around the island in the golf cart.

Gibson fussed all the way to the dock, telling Emmett he was overreacting. Emmett didn't care. He could deal with the memory losses but whatever this was wasn't about blanking out.

As soon as the truck was secured on board the ferry, Emmett called the diner to cancel Gibson's order, and then texted Jaime that he had to cancel.

They were the only passengers on board and Emmett asked the captain to hurry.

As the ferry neared the mainland Gibson quieted. A few minutes after docking, Emmett pulled to a stop in front of the urgent-care clinic in town.

The on-call doctor, a young man who looked to be about Emmett's age, took Gibson into a treatment room and Emmett followed. "What seems to be the problem?" he asked.

"Nothing," Gibson said.

"He's been diagnosed with dementia and became light-headed at home." Emmett stared hard at Gibson, daring his father to contradict him. "It's early onset, but this hasn't happened before that I know of. A cleaning crew came to the house today and I wasn't there to oversee—"

"I don't need to be 'overseen,'" Gibson interrupted.

Dr. Harrison nodded and began asking questions about diet and medication while a nurse took Gibson's blood pressure and hooked him up to a portable heart monitor.

Fear was a nasty taste in Emmett's mouth, and he choked back the what-ifs that manifested in his mind. What if he took Gibson straight to Cincinnati without fixing up the house first? What if he'd come home at any point in the past couple of years? What if he didn't help with the school project? What if he'd stayed late to work on the upstairs room?

"It looks like he's just overtired," the doctor concluded, interrupting Emmett's thoughts. "I don't see any echoes or arrhythmias on the EKG. He didn't complain of chest or arm pain?"

"No." Emmett and Gibson spoke at the same time.

"You should follow up with the specialist in the next day or so, just to make sure it isn't a reaction to his medication."

"You can talk to me, Doc," Gibson said as he buttoned his plaid shirt and took the alligator clip off his finger. The nurse tried to help but he brushed her hands away.

"Okay, I'll tell you both. You need to take it easy, Mr. Deal. You need to take your meds, eat and get plenty of sleep."

"I've been doing that."

"Then you won't have to change your lifestyle." The doctor turned to Emmett. "You said you were cleaning up his home?"

"Yeah, that's what he said," Gibson muttered. "God forbid I do anything. He threw out all the dishes."

"They were caked in dried oatmeal. I'd have needed a jackhammer to clean them up," Emmett said, frustrated. Gibson needed to let him talk to the doctor, not argue with him about dishes that didn't mean anything.

"Let the cleaning crew do the work," the doctor interrupted. "Light work is okay, but he shouldn't overdo it. I'm sure the specialists have told you about leaving him alone for long periods of time."

"Don't need babysitters," Gibson grumbled.

"They were cleaning people, Dad."

"And I'm not well enough to use a mop and a dust rag?"

"I didn't say that. I thought you wanted to focus on packing, not cleaning."

"Same thing."

Dr. Harrison held up his hands. "In any case, light work—"

"He was going through a box when I got home," Emmett interrupted, feeling like an idiot for fighting with his father in front of this stranger but apparently unable to stop.

"A box of pictures. I don't think looking at a few old four-by-sixes is going to send me to an early grave," Gibson chided. Now that he'd regained his equilibrium he was acting more like himself.

"Going through a box of pictures is fine." Dr. Harrison tore a slip of paper from his pad; he'd written the clinic number on it. "You came over from Gulliver?" Emmett nodded and he continued. "Then you'll be staying on the mainland for the night. Follow up with his regular doctor within a week. Have them call the clinic if they have any questions." He shook Gibson's hand. "Stay out of trouble."

"Don't worry about me, Emmett's the troublemaker."

Emmett laughed. "I have changed my ways." He held up two fingers and placed them against his forehead in a salute. "I'm just a construction worker now."

"I'd believe that with a lot more heart if you'd actually been a Scout," Gibson mumbled.

THE NEXT EVENING Emmett hired the ferry captain to make an after-hours trip to the island. It had taken most of the day but Gibson's doctors were sure exhaustion had caused the episode and not the meds. They were referred to a home health office and he was told a nurse would arrive on the island the following morning to stay with Gibson during the day when Emmett was working.

Emmett couldn't wait to get back on the island and it was an odd feeling. He couldn't remember ever being anxious to be home, not home on the island and not home in Cincinnati. The ferry neared the Gulliver dock and his heartbeat sped up.

He would call Jaime once he got Gibson settled and maybe take a walk around the island and convince her to come with him to Detroit tomorrow to approve tile and hardwood orders from a supplier. It wasn't just a test, Emmett told himself, although he wanted to make sure she didn't have another meltdown like the one she'd had when they'd gone grocery shopping. Mostly he wanted to be with her outside the island.

Gibson joined him at the railing. "You think Hank's making pancakes tomorrow morning?"

"Has there been a morning in the past fifty years when he hasn't made pancakes?"

"Nope."

"Then I guess we'll be having pancakes for breakfast."

"You should call Jaime, since you bailed on her last night."

Emmett blew out a breath. "I didn't bail on her. You were sick."

"I was light-headed and it was so unimportant that the urgent-care doc sent us to a hotel."

"And then we saw your doctor this morning and you have the all clear. And it's thanks to my conversational skills—"

"Your credit card, you mean."

Emmett went on as if he hadn't been interrupted "That we're getting home at all tonight because the ferries stopped running an hour ago."

"You gonna call her tonight?"

"Dad—"

"I don't need a babysitter. I plan to go home and sit in my chair and have a cold Coca-Cola. So you might as well call her." Gibson sat on the hard bench attached to the outside of the pilot room. "Unless you're nervous about seeing her after you stood her up."

"I didn't stand her up and I'm not nervous about Jaime. Jaime's great. She's a friend—"

"One you used to date."

"—that I'm getting reacquainted with. That's all." Maybe if he said that enough he would actually believe it. Or make it true.

"You love her."

"I loved her. Years ago. This is just…" Emmett couldn't put a finger on what, exactly, was going on between them. It wasn't just him trying to fix what had gone wrong all those years ago. And he wasn't trying to recapture the past because there were too many old wounds back there. Building a future was out because she came attached to the island. "We're friends."

"Friends with benefits? I watch the movies, you know. You young people are a lot more at ease with the sexual aspects of relationships than my generation ever was."

"We are not friends with benefits, Dad. And even if we were I wouldn't talk to you about it."

The ferry whistle bellowed into the quiet island evening as the ship docked. Emmett helped his father down the stairs and into the truck and then pulled onto the beach road. A few golf carts were gathered outside the diner, but Jaime's cherry-red model was missing.

"I definitely want pancakes," Gibson said.

"I thought we agreed on pancakes for to-morrow?"

Gibson grunted. "Live a little. I had a big scare last night. I need pancakes to recover."

Emmett bit back a smile. Only Gibson would use exhaustion and dementia as a reason to have pancakes for dinner.

They entered the diner and took a corner booth. Anna brought them mugs of coffee and didn't raise an eyebrow when they placed their order. She was back in a few minutes with two steaming plates.

"You two need whipped cream or anything else?"

Emmett drowned his pancakes in maple syrup and shook his head.

"I could use some bacon," Gibson offered. Anna winked at him and yelled the addition to Hank in the kitchen.

"So, how's the old school coming along?" she asked, her attention on Emmett. Gray eyes twinkling, expression too innocent for that to be an innocent question.

"Coming along. We should be ready for the big reunion weekend unveiling."

"And? How's everything else coming along?"

Emmett chewed another bite and swallowed. "If you mean the house—"

"She means you and Jaime," Gibson offered. He turned to Anna, a big grin on his face. "They're 'friends without benefits,'" he said, making rabbit ears with his fingers as he did so.

Anna nodded and folded her arms over her ample chest. "Really?"

Gibson nodded. "Apparently they haven't gotten the memo that we're all waiting for them to get back together."

"Dad," Emmett warned.

Anna playfully slapped Emmett's shoulder. "Honey, we're just talking."

The bell over the door tinkled as Jaime walked into the restaurant. She spotted them at the table and waved. Emmett motioned her over.

"So, how are things going?" Anna asked when she'd settled in.

The woman was beginning to sound like a broken record, Emmett thought and frowned at her. Gibson cackled as he forked more pancakes into his mouth.

"Things are good, Anna. How about you?"

"Can't complain. Hank's working on a new cake. Red velvet with dark chocolate icing and a raspberry topping. So far it's all sweetness, but he'll figure out the blend. You want pancakes like your friends here?"

"Just iced tea, thanks. And tell Hank I'll be his official taste tester when he's ready."

"I will." Anna waggled her eyebrows at Emmett. "Well, you two keeping things *friendly*," she said and returned to the counter.

Jaime chuckled. "She's so subtle."

"You know?"

"Have you forgotten I've lived on the island for twenty-eight years straight? I know when gossip is happening."

"And you're okay with it?"

She shrugged. "Let's just say I understand it." She turned her attention to Gibson. "How are you doing tonight?"

Gibson launched into a litany of what wasn't wrong with him and what was wrong with Emmett, but thankfully didn't tell Jaime he thought Emmett was still in love with her. Emmett didn't need that kind of trouble. Women like Jaime loved. Men like him left. He wanted to keep a firm line between the two, no matter how friendly they got over the next four weeks.

"So, are you hiring a nurse to come in when you're at the school?"

Emmett nodded. "The doctor's office is

sending a home health aide over tomorrow morning."

"Which I don't need."

Jaime patted the older man's hand. "Maybe it'll put Emmett at ease, though."

Gibson shrugged but then squeezed Jaime's hand. "If it will make things easier on the boy," he said.

The three of them fell into a companionable silence, which was just fine with Emmett. How did Jaime know how to ease the older man's conscience? He was Gibson's son. Why hadn't he thought about using reverse psychology so Gib could keep his illusion of independence? It was another sign of how different they were. Jaime nurtured people, helped them. Emmett ordered people around.

He pushed his plate away. Maybe he could start learning how to nurture, really nurture. Not just to ease his guilt over the past, but so he could build a real relationship with his father.

And maybe, with Jaime, too.

HE WAS SO ADORABLY, uncomfortably cute, Jaime thought. Sitting in the booth at the diner, eating pancakes and looking furtively around the room as if another islander might ask them a question. Or, maybe more to the

point, *the* question. She didn't want to spill
her guts to all and sundry about Emmett or
the school project or her wanting more between them. Besides, the questions weren't
the problem. The caring of the islanders and
even the annoying overprotectiveness of her
own parents weren't the problem, either. It
was the way she'd felt about the questions.

As if, by being curious about her life they
were trying to hold her in the past. Obviously
they weren't trying to do that. At least, Anna
wasn't. Jaime had a feeling her parents would
love it if she forgot about their kitchen conversation. Mason had been abnormally silent
since leaving her kitchen the other day.

Even that she couldn't be angry about. He
knew better than anyone the terrors in the
world. Before settling down on the island he'd
been a marine, and had seen too many terrible things. He never talked about those days,
just as he'd never asked her to talk about the
attack or questioned her need for privacy at
the hospital.

On the other hand Beverly had called,
texted or Facebook-messaged every couple
of hours and Jaime had been tiring of the silly
cat pictures, funny dance videos and birthday
name-games being passed to her in the name

of I'm Not Interfering But You Should Listen To Me Anyway interference.

Jaime finished her drink. "What's next at the school? Can I see the classroom yet?"

Emmett shook his head. "We aren't quite done. The guys will finish the roof this week. I was thinking about playing hooky tomorrow, if you're game?"

Play hooky? With Emmett? She could be game for that. How many times had he asked her that when they were kids? Too many to count and every time she'd joined in. From sneaking to the north side of the island when they were supposed to be cleaning up the park to leaving a scribbled Back in Five Minutes sign on her roadside stand of corn and green beans one summer. She'd returned hours later to find her vegetables gone and a cigar box filled with ones and fives from people who'd stopped.

"I don't have anything pressing on my agenda."

"I need to go to Detroit. Check on those flooring samples for the house and for the school."

"Oh." Going to Detroit for the day. The thought was a lot scary. A lot interesting. Detroit was a long way from Gulliver's Island. It might be a fun way to try out her newfound need for independence, assuming she didn't have a panic attack on the way as she'd had on the way to Port Clinton.

"I could go alone but—" a funny expression clouded Emmett's face for a moment "—I don't want to. We could make a day of it. Borrow Clancy's boat, have Hank make a couple of sandwiches to eat on the way. Come back at night."

"What about the aide for Gibson?"

"She should be here on the first ferry."

"You know I'm sitting right here. You could ask me about the nurse lady."

"Dad," Emmett's voice held a warning. Gibson rolled his eyes and went back to his pancakes.

"It would only take a couple of hours," Emmett told Jaime, "because the supplier isn't all the way up the river. We pick out the flooring, maybe have dinner and come home. Weather reports are clear, so we should have a smooth trip."

Jaime decided to ignore the nerves in her stomach. "Sounds like fun. Let's play hooky."

THE NEXT MORNING Emmett pulled Clancy's boat past the no-wake zone and into the body of the lake before throttling the engine up to fifteen knots. Jaime sat in the cocaptain's seat, watching the island fade into the distance. No white knuckles. No fast breathing. Smile on her face.

All good signs. No—*great* signs because once Emmett approved the flooring samples, the supplier would ship them to the island and the crew could start the last phases of both renovations.

That meant he could get Gibson off the island and into the kind of care facility that he needed.

That also meant leaving the island. For the first time Emmett's gut clenched at the thought. He didn't want to leave, he realized, almost as much as he wanted to go home. Home. Huh.

He leaned back in the captain's chair and stared off briefly into the lake. He'd never thought of Cincinnati as home. It was where he worked. Where he lived. The island was the home he thought of around the holidays or during particularly hot stretches of the summer, but it had stopped being his home. He'd convinced himself he didn't need a home, didn't want a home. Now he had two and he didn't know what to do about either of them. Emmett shook his head. His father might be the one with the dementia diagnosis, but Emmett was the one losing his mind.

CHAPTER TWELVE

JAIME SAT BACK, enjoying the feel of the sun on her face and the wind in her hair. She couldn't remember the last time she'd been on a boat instead of the island ferry, and she was determined to enjoy the day. Once they were past South Bass and the smaller islands the lake opened up. She could see the mainland to her left and to the right the faint outline of Pelee on the Canadian side of Lake Erie.

The nerves she'd experienced when Emmett had mentioned the trip faded as she relaxed against her seat. It was a gorgeous summer day, and she was with Emmett in the middle of a beautiful lake. There was nothing to be afraid of.

They skimmed past a few sailboats and waved to the passengers, but the motor was too noisy to do more than grin at one another as their sunglasses plastered to their faces. Jaime stood, keeping a firm grip on the bar to her left. Once away from the traffic of other boats, Emmett brought the boat to the plane level and throttled down slightly to conserve fuel. It was still too noisy to talk so Jaime settled for taking in the view.

The island had shrunk from the last time she checked, but the fact didn't bother her on this two-seater boat the way it had when they'd been surrounded by people on the ferry. She pointed to a gull swooping down toward the water. The bird caught a small fish in its beak and swept back up into the sky.

Jaime relaxed in her seat, watching the water. Watching Emmett. Watching him watch the water. Mostly watching him. He was at ease out here in a way he wasn't back on Gulliver. Not that he seemed stressed on the island, but there was a guard that always seemed to be up. As when Anna had been talking to him just as Jaime had arrived at the diner. There'd been a tense expression on his face, a tightness to his shoulders.

It could be that he needed time to get used to the differences between the small town where he grew up and the city where he lived now.

Maybe it wasn't her place to analyze him. Maybe she should just enjoy the sun on her face, the warmth of the breeze and shut down a little. Her eyes drifted closed and the next thing Jaime knew the motor was throttled down. She opened her eyes as the boat passed Grosse Isle Township on the Detroit River and all too soon Emmett throttled even lower as they pulled into a marina.

They left the sandwiches in the cooler and called a cab to take them to the flooring outlet. Jaime didn't resist when Emmett put her hand in his. She slid closer to him than necessary as the cab pulled away from the marina, all the while conscious of the connection between them. Felt the shift in his attention from watching the world outside the cab window to him watching her.

"I'm glad you came with me."

"Me, too. I can't believe I fell asleep."

Emmett wove his fingers with hers as the downtown buildings of Detroit showed up on the horizon. "We could go all the way downtown for dinner, since we never got around to those sandwiches."

"Sure," she said before she could think twice. She wasn't that girl, Jaime reminded herself. That girl took for granted her freedoms. The girl she was now understood the responsibilities that came along with making decisions. She could do this. Date Emmett. Spend time with him. Enjoy his company for as long as he was back on Gulliver, and when he left…she would have memories that would keep her warm when the lake froze over.

God grant me the serenity to accept that he is leaving, the courage to sleep with him, anyway, and the wisdom to not fall in love with Emmett Deal again.

EMMETT HELD UP his glass as the sky turned a brilliant pink. Jaime clinked her glass, filled with lemon water, with his and smiled.

"Thanks for dragging me off the island today."

"You seemed willing enough." Emmett signaled the waitress for their check. They were sitting by the window at a restaurant overlooking the Detroit River. In the distance he could see the huge downtown skyscrapers and to the side one of the big casinos loomed in the evening light.

"I don't want to go back, but it isn't fair to your dad for us to stay out all night."

"I'd be more worried about the nurse. Gibson ran off a cleaning crew a couple of years back and from what I've seen he's got the nurses at the urgent care and his doctor's office on the run."

The home health aide was a full-time position, but he still wanted to make it back to the island before dark. Just in case Gibson had a bad night.

"He's harmless."

Emmett wasn't so sure about that. "We should start back soon." Except he didn't want to go back. He wanted to stay in the little bubble they'd created since he'd pulled away from Clancy's dock in the boat. A bubble where only the present mattered. The past was dim behind them, the future a jumble of shadows. There was only him and Jaime and the boat. He thought it would be nice to stay this way awhile.

Maybe forever.

"I have a conference call in the morning." Jaime leaned back in her chair and turned to watch a sailboat on the river. She made no move to gather her things.

"Winery or school?"

"Winery. Sorority party for one of the houses at the University of Toledo. I'm presenting what they can expect if they come to Gulliver."

"And what can they expect?"

"First class all the way. Catered meal in one of the cask rooms, live music and some of the best wine on the North Coast."

"Sounds fancy. Maybe you should have had the reunion there."

"Maybe if you and Jason hadn't routed an entire vintage into the city water system—"

"It was one cask," he said, rolling his eyes.

Jaime went on as if he hadn't spoken, "—when we were seniors, Tom wouldn't have feared another vintage disaster." Jaime shrugged. "And 'nice' is probably a better word for what we offer. I've seen YouTube clips from some of the private parties held at Napa wineries. We pale in comparison."

Emmett slipped his credit card into the rectangular folder the waitress had left on the corner of the table. "To be expected, since Napa is Napa and Gulliver is…not."

Jaime laughed. "That's a nice way to put it."

"Gulliver's not bad, per se. It's just—"

"Not Napa, I get it."

The waitress brought back the slip and his credit card and Emmett took Jaime's hand as they rode the elevator to street level.

"Do you want to walk for a little while?"

"You're sure we have time?"

Emmett checked his watch. A few minutes after six; sundown wasn't for a couple more hours. The wind had kicked up while they were inside, but there was plenty of time so he urged her on to a concrete footpath along the riverbank.

They walked in the growing dusk, watching the water. Mostly, Emmett observed Jaime. Drinking in her calmness. Catching the smell of her perfume on the breeze; the underlying scent that was her teased his nostrils and aroused him. When they reached the end of the walkway, Emmett pulled his cell phone from his pocket to call the cab company. A gust of wind pushed him back a step and for the first time he realized the wind hadn't just ratcheted up a notch. A storm brewed to the west, turning the sky gray and dark.

Jaime's hand squeezed his. "We should have gone straight to the boat."

Emmett hit the call button and relayed their location to the dispatcher. They started walking back down the path and met the cab near the restaurant.

A half hour later they stood on the dock, watching Clancy's boat bob up and down. The marina owner shook his head. "It's not so bad up here, but the river is protected on both sides. The weather service has already issued a small craft advisory for boats out on the lake. It's not safe."

"We have to get home," Emmett said, raising his voice to be heard over the wind.

"You could rent a car, but they've issued tornado watches for the Toledo area."

And they would have to leave Clancy's boat here. Emmett turned to Jaime. "We should wait out the storm, start back as soon as the advisory's lifted."

There was wariness in her gaze. Not wary of him; Emmett was almost sure. Wary of the situation? Maybe. Wary of the storm? Definitely.

"Okay."

"You nervous?"

"To spend the night alone in a strange area with a guy I used to know?" Jaime shook her head and said a sarcastic, "Nah."

"We can get separate rooms."

"You should call the house. I'll deal with the sleeping arrangements."

The nurse told Emmett it had been a quiet afternoon, which was a relief, and agreed to stay with Gibson until they could get back to the island. Gibson, on the other hand, seemed abnormally excited about the possibility of Emmett not being home until morning.

"Don't do anything I wouldn't do."

"Dad, don't go there."

"What? You're dating the girl, right? And you were an item before."

"Jaime and I seeing one another isn't going...doesn't mean..."

"She's good for you, just like Mary Margaret was good for me."

He looked over his shoulder. Jaime stood on the metal steps leading to the dock, with a smile on her face and no worried look. Gibson and Mary Margaret were in sync. Two people with the same likes and a healthy appetite for arguing and making up. Emmett understood the making-up part.

"When you and I go back to Cincinnati, Jaime will still be here. This isn't going anywhere permanent." At least, Emmett didn't think it was. This was only temporary. A way to pass the time over the summer until he could get back to real life.

He looked back at Jaime, talking to one hotel or another. She'd worn khaki Bermuda shorts and a peach-colored top that swung low over her hips today. There was a cutout between her shoulder blades than had been tempting him all day, making what seemed from the front like an innocent T-shirt completely dangerous from the back.

"You keep telling yourself that," Gibson said and clicked off the line.

Emmett barely noticed, he was so caught up in watching Jaime. He couldn't see them from this distance but he knew from the boat ride over that her toes were painted purple with some kind of design etched in silver over her big toes. From her neck to nearly her knees her body was covered but the way the wind blew left little to his imagination. Not that he needed to use much imagination. She hadn't changed so much since high school and he'd known her body by heart back then. Her curly blond hair blew in the wind and her brows scuttled together as she put her hand over her ear so she could hear better. Seeing him, she gave him a thumbs-up sign. His belly clenched at the thought of spending the night with Jaime.

Or maybe spending the night in an adjoining room.

Either way, he knew that bit about getting back to real life was a lie. This was more than passing the time. He only wished he knew how to make her understand that it could only be for the summer. As much as he liked being back on the island, he didn't want to live there long-term. And he'd seen that moment of fear flash in Jaime's brown eyes when she'd realized they couldn't get home tonight.

That flash was all he needed to know he couldn't have her, not really. Jaime's security was on the island and there was nothing he could do to change that fact.

JAIME PRESSED THE end button on her cell phone. For the next few hours she could be anyone she desired and that person wanted to sleep with Emmett. That person, however, wasn't brazen enough to book only one room so she'd found them adjoining rooms in a hotel not far from the marina. Hands shaking, she put her phone in her pocket and waited on the dock as Emmett grabbed the cooler of sandwiches and secured the boat as best he could. Then they were in the cab and all too soon in the lobby of a hotel on the waterfront. Their rooms looked out over the Detroit River. Emmett put his key in one door as she did the same with the other.

"Let me know if you need anything," he said, standing in the doorway.

"I will." She just needed a minute first. A minute to bank a little more courage. A minute to make sure she'd grabbed pretty underwear from her drawer this morning because she was not making love to Emmett wearing grannie panties or a uni-boob sports bra. It would be difficult enough letting him see the scars on her torso.

Jaime pushed her door open and sagged against it, listening to the clang of Emmett's door swinging shut. She didn't have to do this. Serenity prayer or not, she didn't have to offer herself up like some sacrificial virgin who might save her village from the storm gods. She put her room key and purse in the drawer of the bedside table and sat on the edge of the bed.

She didn't have to do this.

She wanted to do this. More than she had wanted anything in so very, very long. For just a second on the dock, panic had clawed at her throat. Being alone on the mainland, in a strange city, brought back the feelings she'd had when she'd woken up in the hospital. As though she was spinning out of control and didn't have any way to bring things back into focus. She pushed the panic down by remembering that she wasn't alone. Emmett had stood beside her in the blowing wind and calmly called the nurse. He hadn't panicked when their plans got blown to hell—literally—by a freak storm. She wouldn't, either. Uncontrolled panic would not rule her life, not any more.

Jaime slipped her feet out of her sandals and checked her undergarments. Light yellow lace. Her favorite matching set.

No one ever saw her undies, but wearing the lacy things made her feel special. Pretty. She bit her lower lip but didn't pull her shirt up to check the scarring. It wasn't as if the marks had changed over the past couple of weeks.

Tonight she would ignore the marks and be normal.

Not scarred.

Normal.

Jaime opened her side of the adjoining doors and knocked.

Emmett opened it. "Everything okay?"

She nodded. "Better than okay, actually. You said to let you know if I needed anything."

He waited a beat and Jaime realized Emmett wasn't going to say anything. She took a deep breath. "I'd like to sleep in this room tonight," she said. "I'd like to sleep in this room with you." Before he could respond, Jaime stepped across the threshold and wound her arms around his neck.

Emmett's lips were warm against hers, his hair soft in her hands, and she took a step forward to press her body against his. Oh, but he felt good. Better than he'd felt against her when they were teenagers. As an eighteen-year-old boy, he'd been thinner, wirier. As a twenty-eight-year-old construction worker his muscles were thicker, more developed. He'd used his time with hammer and saws and whatever other tools he used to create a chiseled physique that made Jaime weak in the knees. Who was she kidding? With his home improvement show, he had to make women all over the country hot for him.

She blew out a breath. No, not thinking about other women. Not thinking at all. She was taking back control.

Since he'd returned home to the island she'd been thinking. About what life was like before the attack; how she'd changed everything post attack. How she wasn't completely sure she liked the life she had now. And now she was thinking more when what she should be doing was feeling. His skin against hers. The heat from his erection against her belly.

From the time she'd heard his voice behind her in the diner she'd wanted him. It was past time she admitted the full truth to herself. Maybe she should tell him, too.

"I want you."

"That's a good place to start," he said, still standing an inch too far from her.

She still wanted Emmett Deal; differently than she had in the past, but just as potently. Rather than feeling as if a bucket of cold water had crashed over her head, the admission was freeing. She wanted Emmett. He obviously wanted her. They were stuck in Detroit for the night…had a fabulous view of the river out the window. Why not indulge?

She closed the distance between them, welcoming the heat emanating from his body to her. It warmed her. Made a heady rush wash over her shoulders to ignite a slow burn in her belly.

Her teeth bumped against his as their tongues tangled together and Jaime smiled, her mouth stretching against his as Emmett licked his tongue against the roof of her mouth. His hands spanned the small of her back, the combination of his fingers and the silk of her top creating a sensual vortex surrounding her abdomen. He bunched the fabric, pulling it up, and a jolt of electricity raced up her spine.

This was what she'd been missing. This was the feeling she had tried to suppress under a life filled with videoconferencing and press release writing. God, how could she have been so stupid?

Emmett pulled away and the absence of his heat made her shiver in the air-conditioned hotel room. He shoved his hand through his hair, mussing it and setting several strands on end. Her hands itched to tame it back into submission. Or maybe muss it even more.

"Exactly where is this heading, Jaime?"

She didn't want to answer the question. Didn't want to think about the options in her answer. For the immediate future this was heading to the big bed behind Emmett. In the long run she wanted whatever this was to head off into a glorious sunset. It was more likely heading to nothing because sooner or later he would leave and she would still be… Jaime pushed the thoughts away.

"I was kind of hoping it would lead to that big bed and the mountain of pillows," she said. She locked her eyes on his, the smoldering blue of his irises almost overpowered by the black depths of his pupils. "This place doesn't have a full bar, and even if it did, I'm not much for public displays of affection, at least not anything more than a kiss."

"We can't turn back, Jaime. Once we take this step, we can't go back to only being friends."

She nodded. "We were never just friends, Emmett. From the second we shared that ice cream sundae at Irene's when we were seven. Through the moment I used my dad's putty container to make a mold of the key to the cask room at the winery." She stepped toward him. "When we spent New Year's inside the old school in senior year. We weren't friends when you offered to help with the renovation and I know that sleeping together doesn't mean we've fully dealt with our shared past, but I don't care. Emmett, I want you and I'm tired of pretending that I don't."

"Jaime," he said and grabbed her hand, pulling her to him.

Jaime was desperate. She wanted Emmett naked and she wanted him clothed all at once. She wanted to taste his lips for five years without coming up for air and she wanted this…this interlude to be over. Over and done with because the overwhelming need to be with him had to lessen once they'd made love. Didn't it? And once the wanting lessened maybe they—no, *she*—maybe she could focus again.

She put her hands on his shoulders, urging him to turn, but when she pushed against his chest he didn't budge. Didn't sink onto the mattress. Didn't even take a step backward. If anything he stepped closer to her. Not a breath of air squeezed between their bodies. Jaime relished his chest rising and falling sporadically as his breathing roughened. When she tried to lift her head to look at him, his hand smoothed against her hair, pressing her lips to his over and over again. Her hands settled at his hips, her thumbs playing with the denim belt loops of his jeans. When her fingers connected with a sliver of abdomen, he sucked in a harsh breath.

Good. She wasn't alone in this all-consuming fire of need.

"This isn't at all what I had planned," he said, finally releasing her head and pulling back a fraction. He rested his forehead against hers as he struggled to catch his breath. She couldn't force her eyes to move the fraction of an inch it would take to look into his deep blue gaze. If she looked she would be lost and she needed just a sliver of control over the situation. Wanting Emmett or not, Jaime wasn't ready to completely let go. Instead, she focused on the zipper of his jeans, wondering if she had the courage to pull it down, down, down.

"What did you have planned?" Talking, talking until she worked up her courage.

"A bed. Flowers. Music in the background."

"You were going to seduce me," she said, laughing because before the weather had kicked up she'd thought seduction was exactly what she wanted. Now she knew differently. She didn't want Emmett to be in control. She wanted him out of control and she wanted to slide along the edge of that control, just for a minute, and then she would take it back. She would return to wearing the same boring shirts and khaki pants and be the good daughter, the good employee. Jaime cut her eyes to his and smiled. "I'd say you're exactly where you want to be, then. This place is primed for seduction."

Emmett grinned back at her as his hands began a wicked trek from the nape of her neck down her back. His fingers grazed her ribs and her abdomen quivered.

A tiny, desperate voice told her to stop playing with fire. To remember what had happened the last time a man had seen her scars. Jaime told that voice to shut up and raised her hands to play with the hair at the nape of Emmett's neck. He wasn't Byron. He knew what had happened all those years ago. Only her parents and doctor knew how badly she'd been scarred, but the rest of the community knew enough.

"There isn't a flower in sight and I can pretty much guarantee that the radio isn't set to slow and sexy anything. That isn't seduction."

His hands inched lower and so oh-so-slowly that Jaime caught her breath. Despite the light silk separating his skin from hers, Jaime swore she could hear a little sizzle at the touch. She planted kisses along his jawline and found his zipper with trembling hands.

"But there is a bed," she said practically. "Isn't a bed the most needed accessory to a seduction?" Her mouth reached his earlobe and she lightly bit down. He sucked in a breath.

"A seduction would include warm, tropical breezes and maybe a palm tree or two to go with the scent of lily or iris."

She could almost imagine it. A tropical beach and a suite with floor-to-ceiling windows. No cell phones, email or computers. Just her and Emmett and more time than they could ever need to explore one another's bodies.

"I like your idea of a seduction scene. Maybe we can make do with—" She pushed against his chest and this time he allowed his legs to collapse onto the soft mattress, pulling her to him so that his face rested between her breasts. "Maybe we should just stop talking."

He chuckled as he played his fingers along her hips, scorching her skin through the thin silk. "Do you know I've been waiting to see you in a summer dress since that first morning at the diner?"

"This isn't a dress. It's a tunic."

"Its long and kind of flowing and I'll take what I can get."

She chucked. The last rays of sunset slanted

through the windows overlooking the lake, catching the raindrops that had blown in with the windstorm and throwing sparkles of light around the room.

"Why?"

He didn't pretend not to understand her question. Now that they were in his room, now that she was in his arms, it was as if all the pretenses they'd been building between them crashed down. "Because I've had entire erotic dreams just about the way your shoulders look when they've been kissed by the sun."

Her breath caught in her chest, heart pounding. "And you said you weren't good with seduction."

He pulled her to the bed, flipped her to her back and laid a scorching kiss on the hollow at the base of her throat. "I said you deserved a good seduction. Slight difference." His hand traced her collarbone and then he buried it in her hair and captured her lips. Jaime opened for him, wrapping her arms around his shoulders and tangling her legs with his.

"Oh, do that kissing thing again."

Emmett pressed another kiss to the hollow at her throat, flicked his thumbs against her breasts and then sucked at the hollow. Every nerve in her body screamed to life. His kisses warmed her skin like hot, tropical sunlight, making her heart beat against her ribs like the crashing waves she thought would be on Emmett's imaginary beach. And, impossible as it was, she thought she might smell lily and orchid instead of the cleaning supplies used in the hotel room. Beyond all of that was Emmett's musky scent. The feel of him touching her breasts, skimming the back of his hand along her belly. Bunching her tunic in his hands and playing along her lower abdomen until he reached the bare skin of her back. It was too much and too little. She wanted to feel his skin against hers; wanted to see the muscles that his clothes only hinted at.

It hadn't been like this before. Certainly they'd turned one another on, but kissing Emmett back then was fun. Exciting, yes, but not unstoppable. Jaime didn't think she would ever be finished kissing him, not this Emmett. This Emmett's touch was made of fire when before his touch had been made of feathers. His hands then had made butterflies beat in her belly. His hands now burned along her skin, starting little fires wherever he touched, making her belly clench and moisture pool between her legs.

"You're wearing entirely too many clothes,"

he said and finally, slowly, began dragging her top over her sensitized skin.

"I thought you said you've been waiting to see me in a dress." She nipped at his lower lip.

"And now I want to see you out of this non-dress top."

"Then maybe you should just unsnap the clasp," she suggested, reaching behind her neck to release the catch.

"Nice." He nodded. "I'll remember that trick for next time."

Inch by inch, he pushed the top to her waist, following the slide of silk with the satin of his kiss. Inch by inch her body went up in flame.

And then he stilled. Sat up. Looked at her as if he'd never seen her before.

"My God," he whispered. And this time when he touched her, his hands were cold on her body. He touched the scar over her left breast, followed it along to her ribs and the crisscrossed scars there.

God, she'd really forgotten. Just for a moment she'd been normal. A woman wanted by a man. How could she have forgotten about the scars? In all the time since Pittsburgh she'd never once forgotten the marks left on her by the man in the alley. Never forgotten the feel of his filthy breath on her face as he muttered, "You'll never forget me." She'd kicked and screamed, using every ounce of strength she had to get him off her and she'd run, straight into a foot patrolman who'd heard her screams and was charging into the alley.

"Jaime." Emmett whispered her name. A cold bucket of water would have had a better effect on her than the sorrow behind his voice filled with quiet agony. "How did I not know about these?"

Jaime sat up, dragging the front of her top back to her neck. She felt like a fool, and not just because of his reaction. For not telling him. The scars had faded from violent purple to red and were not dark, just pinkish lines across her fair skin. Of course he would notice. Of course he wouldn't want her, not now. Her fingers trembled against her neck. Her index finger sought out the mark.

"Not even Mo has really seen them. Only my parents and the doctors."

"No wonder they hold me responsible."

"Stop it, they don't…. It's more that if you aren't responsible and if the man who attacked me is a mental patient who isn't in control of his actions, then it's my fault. They don't want it to be my fault."

"He…he marked you."

"It's not a big deal," she repeated. "They've faded a lot over the years." It wasn't a big deal. In the grand scheme of things it could have been worse.

She lived, and she lived well. Good job. Good friends. That night had changed a lot about her life, but mostly the scars were a reminder of what hadn't happened. She could have not fought back. He could have raped her.

He might have killed her.

"I'm sorry." Emmett kept his hands at his sides, but at least he didn't look past her. Didn't look at her like she was a freak, the way Byron had a few years before. Emmett was still here, and his gaze was anything but pitying. Emmett looked into her eyes, as if searching for something.

"It wasn't your fault."

"I can still be sorry."

"Maybe I don't want your pity." She didn't. Not from Emmett. She wanted the Emmett from two minutes ago. The Emmett who desired her as much as she craved his touch. God, if she could go back in time she would go back to the moment they'd stepped into the hotel room. She would go into the bathroom and use as much makeup as she needed to cover the scars.

She stood, turned her back on him and clasped her clothes to her chest. How could she have forgotten the scars?

"I should go back to my hotel room. The weather should have cleared enough by morning for us to get back to the island."

"Why would you do that?" He marched across the room to stand behind her. In the glass, she saw him reach for her but she side-stepped him. Emmett caught her and turned her to face him. "You think a few scars mean I don't want you? You think I'm that shallow? It isn't the scars. It's that you didn't tell me. How did you…? You changed how you dress so no one would see."

"My dad convinced the investigators to keep the knifing out of the public reports because of my age, so the newspapers all went with the concussion angle. I went along with it because everyone was already treating me so differently. I wasn't just Jaime Brown. I was Attacked by a Mental Patient Brown. I didn't want even more pity."

"That was then. Now it's different."

"Right, because you've seen the scars and all you can think is 'poor, pitiful Jaime.'"

"I don't pity you." Emmett clenched his jaw. "Maybe you could learn to accept empathy, though."

She searched his eyes for several minutes, looking for something—anything—that would prove he pitied her. Sorrow was there. Understanding. But there was no pity.

"Jaime," he said, "I wish I could change it."

She took in a shaky breath. "I wish you would kiss me." She refused to back down. Refused to step away from what she wanted. For too long she'd shied away from things. Tonight was about taking back what was hers and it all started with Emmett.

"I wish I'd never skipped that play."

She ran her finger over his chin. "I want your hands on me."

He clenched and unclenched his hands. "I wish I could have protected you."

She reached behind her neck, again unclasping the halter and letting the top fall to her waist. "I won't break," she said.

She stood in front of him, naked to the waist, daring him to turn away from the moment. Daring herself not to turn away. She took his hand, brought it to her chest and ran his fingertips along the jagged line that crossed to her ribs. Her tummy muscles shook and he sucked in a heavy breath. She dropped her hands from his, but his fingers continued to trace the lines on her skin.

"I still want you, Emmett. The question is do you want me?"

His lips followed his fingers and Jaime

closed her eyes. His lips seemed to sear against the scar.

"More than anything else in my life."

"Then take me," she said, raising her arms to him.

Emmett lifted her and Jamie rested her head against his shoulder for a moment. Then she let out the breath she hadn't realized she'd been holding. He was back. He was here.

He'd seen her and he was still here.

Emmett lowered Jaime to the bed, tracing her collarbone with his tongue, pressing kisses above and below the delicate line as she arched against him. His fingers found her breasts, the rosy tips hard and waiting. He tweaked one as his mouth lowered to taste the other.

Jaime reached between their bodies, the palms of her hands pressing against his belly. Her smooth fingers trailed over the hard muscles of his abdomen as if reading his body. His jeans stopped her progress.

Emmett started to rise, but Jaime stopped him.

"Let me," she said and pushed her hands under the soft denim. No rough cotton from underwear met her hands, just the warm skin of his hips. She slid his jeans over his hips to drop over his ankles and she took in another breath as Emmett kicked them to the floor.

He was thick and enticing and Jaime reached for him, her hand encircling his erection. Emmett groaned when she squeezed her hand around him, loving the feel of his soft skin and the hardness below the surface.

"If you do that again, I can't be held responsible for my reaction," he said before flipping her so that she lay beneath him on the bed. He took her mouth, his tongue plundering the way she wanted him to plunder the rest of her body.

Emmett traced her ribs and abdomen, making Jaime shudder. He kissed the scar once more and then his hands continued their journey over her belly to unsnap the button on her shorts and push them over her hips. Jaime kicked her legs free and sighed when Emmett's fingers walked over her hip and upper thigh to the place where she was wet and waiting for him.

He teased at her lower lips, pressing his finger into her through the thin silk protecting her mound.

"Oh, please. Emmett, please," she whispered against his mouth.

Emmett hooked his index finger through the silk, playing her clitoris with his thumb as he pulled the thin garment from her.

Jamie bit her lip and arched against him.

"More," she said, and then her eyes shot open when he left her completely.

He chuckled. "You're not getting rid of me." He grabbed his jeans from the floor, taking a condom from the back pocket and sheathing himself before pressing her back into the mattress.

Then he was thick inside her, filling her. Jaime arched against him, wanting to take him deeper into her. They made love once as teens, just before the Pittsburgh trip, so kissing him, touching him, was familiar but different. He still knew what she needed before she could say anything. He gripped her hips, pressed farther inside her in a rhythm as old as time and that, too, was familiar.

"Emmett. Emmett," she urged, raking her nails over his back and shoulders. "Now. Now, I need you."

He quickened the pace and, reaching between them, found her hard nub and pressed. It was as if he'd released her from ten years of control. Jaime's muscles tensed and then she was soaring, outside her body but still feeling every tremor his hands brought forth from her.

Jaime lay under Emmett, concentrating on her breathing. In. Out. In. Out. She should feel mortified, letting go the way she had. Saying the things she had. Pleading with Emmett the way she had.

She didn't, because he let go, too. But she did need to talk to him about it, for being with him now was different. Then, she had been head over heels for the bad boy and had gotten her heart broken when he'd left. Now, she was dangerously close to falling for the good man who was only around for the summer. And who would break her heart all over again when he left.

But until he left…

Until then she could enjoy him. Enjoy the person she was when he was around and maybe figure out what she wanted once he was gone again. Jaime turned onto her side, folding her hands beneath her head. She watched him for a long minute. His eyes were closed and his breath rose steadily in his chest. A sheet partially covered his hips.

She wanted him. For as long as she could have him. That was all she knew in this moment and for the first time in years Jaime said the first thing that popped into her mind.

"I want an affair."

CHAPTER THIRTEEN

EMMETT LEANED LOW over the pool table in the darkened back corner of the Dugout and shot the seven ball into the side pocket. It was Friday night, and the bar was filled with islanders looking for a little fun. Emmett didn't want fun. He wanted to know why sleeping with Jaime left him feeling so…off-kilter.

What did it mean that she'd come to him? He'd seen the panic, seen that split second of fear. Twenty minutes later she'd been in his room, telling him she wanted him. Was it to dispel the fear or was it because she'd wanted sex? Somehow neither answer was satisfying.

He took aim at the nine ball but it glanced off the corner and Clancy took over the table.

"So the boat's none the worse for wear."

Clancy had met them at the dock yesterday morning and Emmett, standing by while he checked everything over, had known the boat was undamaged. Clancy was never one to be overly direct, though, so Emmett had let him circle the conversation knowing sooner or later it would end up with Jaime.

He only hoped it didn't also go to the past because that was a whole gray area that he wasn't ready to dissect, not after seeing the scars. Now he understood, completely, why Jaime had shut him out. Why she wouldn't allow him to see her in the hospital. Why, once she was home, they'd gone on multi-couple dates and she'd stopped wearing her favorite dresses. His hands squeezed the pool cue as a fresh wave of guilt washed over him. There was nothing he could do to fix the marks left on her body. No penance that would take it away, no apology to be made.

It sucked.

He had always been able to make up for his mistakes, whether it was by freezing his ass off cleaning up a public beach in the middle of winter or being used as volunteer labor to ready the cask rooms before tourist season began. Hell, there had to be something he could do to make up for not being there all those years ago. He just had to figure out what it was.

"So I heard about your dad. That's rough."

Emmett nodded and took aim after Clancy missed his second shot.

"You're taking him to a facility in Cincinnati?"

"Once we're through painting the house and installing the new kitchen floor."

"You aren't staying, then." Clancy's words were flat.

Emmett straightened, not taking the shot. "Why don't you get to the point?"

Clancy scuffed his booted foot against the floor. "Look, I know we're all adults. We make decisions based on personal morals, but Maureen's pregnant—"

"Congrats, man, I hadn't heard," Emmett interrupted.

Clancy shook his extended hand. "Thanks, this will be number three, and I'm not sure if I'm supposed to be excited or terrified by it. Do you have any idea how expensive college for three kids is going to be? Even if a couple of them decide on community campuses?"

Emmett tossed his cue on the table. Neither of them was any good at the game, anyway. Clancy didn't seem to notice they'd left the corner as Emmett led him to a table near the big oak bar. He ordered a round of bourbon and listened to Clancy ramble on about hand-me-downs and girls versus boys, and a part of him was jealous.

"Anyway, she's pregnant and emotional and she's Jaime's best friend." Clancy had finally gotten to his point, and Emmett didn't like it.

"She's worried about what will happen to Jaime after I'm gone."

"Yeah."

Emmett wished he had an answer to that one, too.

JAIME KNOCKED ON the screen door that led to the kitchen at Maureen and Clancy's. She had a hash-brown casserole in the heat-sealed bag in her hands and she was looking for answers.

Maureen, hands sudsy with dishwater, motioned her inside.

"You slept with him."

"I brought you a casserole."

"A guilt casserole because you slept with him," Maureen said, sliding the bag and casserole dish into her oven.

"I don't feel guilty. I seduced him, he didn't seduce me."

"Then?"

Jaime sat on one of the high stools lining the big island in Maureen's pretty peach kitchen. She rested her chin on her palms and sighed. "Then why do I feel like I've done something wrong?"

Maureen released the drain catch and soapy water began sliding down the drain. "Well, I can only answer for me. But we live in a small town with three churches and everyone on the island goes to one or the other almost every Sunday. Your mother's manners are legendary and your father was a deacon and now he's the chief of police—"

"You forgot ex-marine. And my dad was never overly religious." Jaime popped a cashew into her mouth from the bowl on the counter.

"We live in the Midwest. People don't have to thumb their bibles every Sunday to be religious. Your dad has a code and he instilled that code in you."

"I never had the guilt problem when I slept with Emmett in high school."

"Because you were in love and love trumps guilt when we're kids."

She ate another cashew while Maureen chopped zucchini on the granite countertop. "So how do I get rid of the guilt?"

"Depends." Maureen slid the zucchini into a bowl and set it aside.

"On what?"

"On whether you really feel guilty."

Exasperated, Jaime said, "You just told me I was guilty."

"Yeah, but I'm only basing that on the fact you didn't call me last night when you got stuck on the mainland and you ignored all seven of my texts throughout the day. That's spells guilt to me. Or maybe worry." She began chopping squash.

"Worry."

"About what happens now. What it means that you and Emmett used to be in love, but he left and now he's back. Do you still love him? Does he love you? What happens when he's done with his father's house and you're finished with the school reno?"

Jaime examined that possibility and didn't like it any more than she liked the idea that she felt guilty about sleeping with him because of some latent moral gene she'd never experienced before. It had been her decision, made without the influence of alcohol and because she'd wanted to make love with him. "I don't like any of those possibilities."

"Then don't come to a hormonal, pregnant woman for advice."

Maureen watched her for a long minute. "I love Emmett, you know I do. He was a smart, caring, funny guy who made life on the island tolerable during our teen years when all we wanted was to get off the island. You loved him, as much as I love Clancy. After the attack you shut all of us down and when he left you were lost. I don't want you to get lost again."

"What if I said I finally feel like I've found the person I used to be?"

"Then I'd hug you and cry all over you and we'd go have margaritas on the mainland to celebrate." She rinsed her knife in the sink. "Are you telling me to call in a babysitter?"

"Maybe. Maybe all four of us could go. You and Clancy, me and Emmett."

Maureen's eyes went a little misty. "I've missed you."

"Yeah, me, too." She took a breath. "I'm going to sleep with him again."

"If you're asking my permission, I'm just going to say you should do what you want."

Jaime took three cashews this time and trailed them over the counter. "Am I a fool, Mo?"

"I don't think so. I think you were hurt and you didn't know how to deal with it, and I think Emmett needed to blame someone so he blamed himself. I think I've seen you more excited in the past couple of weeks than in the entire ten years since graduation and…"

She trailed off, focusing her attention on the two remaining squash.

Jaime let her cut for a couple of minutes and then asked, "And?"

Maureen offered her a sad smile. "And I think, whether it's with Emmett or on your own, you're going to leave Gulliver and I'm going to miss the hell out of you."

Jamie came around the corner and hugged her friend, wondering how she got so lucky as to make a friend like Maureen. She pushed Maureen into the chair she'd just vacated and finished chopping the squash before putting it into a bowl and starting on the onion.

"Make me a promise?" Jaime nodded her head and Maureen continued. "This time, when you're doing all the things, make sure you're doing them for you, okay?"

"Promise," she said and crooked her pinkie. Maureen hooked hers through and they shook. Jaime put the veggies into the pot and turned the burner to low before sitting at the counter with her friend. It had been a long time since they'd talked this way, about plans that didn't involve the island. "It isn't just because of the reunion."

"I know."

"I just…reading all those questionnaires

made me realize I haven't done anything. And I want to do things."

"When he leaves, will you?"

"He hasn't asked." Jaime bit her lip. She wanted him to ask; it would make this so much simpler. If he asked, she would go. If he didn't ask…

She didn't want to think about that.

THE FOLLOWING MONDAY Emmett sat next to his father on the bench seat on the second floor of the ferry, staring into the lake. A few gulls followed the boat, hoping the other riders would toss some bread crumbs or leftovers over the side. The late morning was gray and dreary, the light fog from earlier that morning just burning away.

He wasn't sure what to say. After going through the reports from the urgent care center, the specialist had decided the light-headedness was likely a side effect of Gibson's medications and prescribed another pill to help combat it. Emmett also had a list of instructions and orders to maintain the home health aide until they could get Gibson to the care center in Cincinnati.

If they left now, without the house being finished, Gibson could have around-the-clock care within twenty-four hours.

"I'm not leaving yet." The older man folded his arms over his chest. "You and the doc can talk all you want about my diminished capacity and what's best for me. I'm not leaving."

"Dad, we already decided this."

"I'll leave when we're through packing the house. That's my deal with you. I won't argue. I won't fuss. I'll teach that damn parrot at the nursing home how to talk and I'll be happy about it. But I'm not leaving before the house is ready."

"I don't think that's a good idea." The ferry backed up to the dock and passengers who'd brought their cars or golf carts across began to disembark. Emmett waited with Gibson on the upper deck. To get to the medical center they'd borrow a car one of the other islanders had left on the mainland so the work crew could use Emmett's truck. "I know you've had a lot of good days—"

After the other passengers departed, a steward came upstairs to help Emmett get Gibson back to the main floor. He'd insisted he wanted a view and Emmett had caved, but he wasn't caving on this. It was important that his father get the right care.

"This isn't about me, it's about you."

"This is about the fact that you nearly passed out in the kitchen the other day. What if I hadn't been home?" Now his father was just being argumentative. This was completely about Gibson.

"I'd have sat down until I felt better, same as I've done for years."

"You weren't diagnosed with dementia before."

"And you're afraid."

"You're damn right I'm afraid." They reached the golf cart and Emmett fastened his seat belt and Gibson's before starting for the house. "I'm afraid the next time I come home you won't know who I am. I'm afraid the next time your mind blanks you won't come back."

"You're mad."

"Of course I'm mad." Emmett took a corner too fast and the cart swung crazily to the left. He righted it and shot Gibson a look. "I'm pissed off that I left the island all those years ago and not once did you or Mom try to make me come back."

"We did what we thought was best, for you. Just like you're doing what you think is best for me. But it isn't. I need to see the house, as it was, one more time. I need to make sure all the important things are still there for you. I can't just leave a list because I'll forget something, but if I'm there to go through the boxes,

I won't forget. I'll remember." Gibson put his hand on Emmett's arm, urging him to slow down.

Emmett pulled over onto the side of the road.

"I need to remember as much as I can and for as long as I can. Staying here will help me, and once everything is boxed or trashed or given away, I'll go to Cincinnati."

"Dad—"

"I promise, boy."

"Fine, but if you have another spell like the other night we'll talk about this again." They were quiet for a long moment. "Why didn't you call me? Ask me to come back or…" Emmett couldn't finish the thought. Gibson squeezed his hand.

"We did what we thought was best. After Jaime's— After Pittsburgh, you turned yourself inside out trying to make it up. To her, to her dad, to the town. There was nothing you could do. You needed to start over and we knew if you stayed or came back that fresh start would vanish. Once we saw how well you were doing, we knew we'd made the right decision. We came to you, as often as we could, so you could keep that fresh start."

"I could have helped you. I could have—"

"What are you afraid of? And don't say

it's losing me. You have me." He put his hand over Emmett's heart. "Me and your mom, we're right there. We'll always be right there."

Emmett shook his head. "I was complacent before. I let myself get busy with work and for a while I could forget everything that happened back here."

"There's nothing wrong with that. And I wasn't talking about me or what happened all those years ago when I said you were afraid."

"I don't want to talk about it," Emmett said, pulling the cart back onto the narrow road.

"You're afraid of losing Jaime again."

"No, I'm not. She isn't mine. I know that."

"She's yours." Gibson folded his hands on his lap. "She's been yours since you were both seven years old. You only have to look at her to see it."

"I'm not good for her."

"Hogwash. You light her up. She sees you and she wakes up. It's been good to see her waking up these past couple of weeks."

Emmett shook his head. "She needs the island. I want to live away from it."

"I didn't say it would be easy. I just said you work for each other. Despite what happened in the past and in spite of how different you may seem to be on the outside.

Relationships aren't about being the perfect match all the time, you know."

"You and Mom were perfect." Emmett parked the golf cart and helped his father inside.

"Your mom hated—"

"Oh, God, Dad, not this again—" Not now, not when things seemed so normal between them.

"I was a school principal and superintendent in Ohio and I was head over heels in love with your mom, but she made me angrier than any other person in the world."

"All couples fight."

"She was Catholic and I was Protestant."

"Lots of couples are from different religions."

"She was a Democrat, I was a Republican." Gibson sat in his recliner and flicked on the television. "She liked afternoon naps and staying up late. I liked early nights and mornings. We fought about everything."

"And you made up like people in romance novels."

"We did. Because we knew the secret was accepting those differences and loving each other in spite of them. You can have that, you know."

"Sure, Dad." Emmett went into the kitchen

to get a drink and some crackers for his dad. He liked to snack while he watched daytime television.

He and Jaime weren't just different in how they looked at politics. There were fundamental differences. She loved island life, the small-town atmosphere. It was easy for him to fall back into the routine, to get used to people knowing his business before he knew it himself. But already he was eager to get back to Cincinnati. Back to his work.

Emmett took the snacks into the sitting room and once Gibson was settled he left for the school.

There was no getting around the different living situations. No way to make that work. So he would enjoy the time he had on the island and when it was over, he would go back to the anonymous life he'd created.

CHAPTER FOURTEEN

JAIME SPREAD A large blanket over the grass in the town square. The sun was sinking over the tree line and she caught sight of Emmett and Clancy walking toward her through the crowd. Maureen put a couple of big throw pillows on the blanket and arranged a cooler to the side.

All around them islanders were doing the same thing, getting ready for the first Friday night movie in the township square. Once the sun went down, an old movie would be projected onto the side of the convenience store. Things would quiet and for a few minutes the whole town would be transported to whatever story Rick Meter had chosen for the night.

Jaime hoped it wasn't a slasher flick. Rick was known for his gory taste in films.

Emmett and Clancy made it to the blanket just as the streetlights around the park and convenience store shut down. A few stars twinkled in the sky.

Jaime saw her father standing on the sidewalk, arms crossed over his chest. He was still working the evening shift for Ernie, whose wife had still not delivered their first baby. Mason seemed to hesitate and then gave a short wave before continuing on his patrol. Jaime knew it was silly, but she felt relieved. It was a small step, but an important one. Her father was overprotective and a little bit controlling, but he loved her.

She wanted the three of them to get along. For however long Emmett was back.

He sat behind her and she leaned against his chest as the opening credits rolled through. The crowd cheered when Julia Roberts's face came on the screen. The actress wore a wedding dress and was riding a horse through the countryside.

"Damn, no blood and guts tonight," Emmett said.

Jaime shushed him and settled in to the classic movie. She still didn't know where this thing with Emmett was going, but she wasn't as worried. Or guilty. Stressed out. Maureen passed the bowl of caramel popcorn and Jaime took a handful. Emmett took one from her hand and popped it into his mouth.

This afternoon she'd taken her golf cart to the school and watched the guys lay the new flooring on the second level. With the first floor done and the second floor firmly in hand, she knew it was time to finalize planning the reunion.

The painters had finished at his father's house, too. Gibson still didn't like having a nurse on hand all day, every day, but he'd mellowed about it. Last night over dinner he'd been talkative, entertaining them with stories about the old school and the journal he'd found a few years before.

"Is it my imagination or is this kind of fun?" Emmett whispered in her ear.

Jaime looked up at him and grinned. "Fun. Now shut up and watch the movie."

Emmett stole more of her popcorn. It was more than fun. It was just about perfect.

"WHEN ARE YOU and Jaime going to come by the diner on a proper date?" Anna picked up the pillow Maureen had brought and walked with Emmett toward the golf cart.

"We've eaten at the diner plenty of times."

"With your dad or with Maureen and Clancy. I know we're not all that fancy, but Hank serves some of the best food on the island. And we don't get many new couples in. It's fun to watch."

"I'm sorry we haven't made ourselves the main exhibit at Gulliver Zoo," Emmett said, only a little bit sarcastically. He knew Anna was teasing him. Just like Ronda when she asked every time he went into the post office when he'd change his address to Jaime's instead of the old Victorian. Just like the guys at the Dugout who asked why Jaime didn't come in for a drink.

Just as his crew made whistling noises once Jaime left the site in the morning or afternoon.

Frankly, he was tired of being the focus of the little town. This was his relationship, not theirs. He put the blanket in the big tub on the backseat and Anna put the pillow on the seat of Clancy's rig. She patted his arm. "You let me know when I can get the old place decorated for dating instead of morning fill-ups, okay?" She disappeared into the crowd a moment later and Emmett went back to their sitting area.

Clancy finished putting their trash into little bags while Emmett dumped the recyclables into the bins at the edge of the park. Jaime and Maureen had disappeared a while before. They'd gotten off easy, he decided as he gathered another blanket and more pillows to put into the golf carts. Clancy carried the cooler beside him.

"You know I hated this place when we were

growing up. Movies in the park on Fridays. The same fireworks display every July Fourth. The same Easter egg hunt every spring."

"I remember." Emmett put everything away and turned to look for Jaime. She and Maureen were chatting with Ronda on the sidewalk.

"All I wanted to do was leave."

It was what they'd all wanted. Emmett had the feeling it was what every generation that had been raised on the island had wanted. Some of them had taken off and some of them had stayed. He was still arguing with himself about which side he landed on. He'd left, but since he'd returned he felt torn. Holding on to the house made zero sense. Letting it go left an empty hole in his gut.

"Now I can't imagine living anywhere else."

Emmett narrowed his eyes at Clancy. "Is this another of Maureen's Figure Out Emmett directives, like the other night at the bar?"

Clancy frowned, but a faint red shine showed up on his cheeks and forehead.

"Would you please tell your wife to back off?" The real question was, was all of this coming from Maureen or was Jaime behind part of it? She never pushed him about his plans, didn't ask a lot of questions about Cincinnati.

Come to think of it, he never asked about her plans, and he could tell by the look in her eyes sometimes that she was thinking about the future. He had to hope she was envisioning her own future and not a future with him. This whole Makeover Jaime plan wasn't about her riding off into the sunset with him. The plan was intended to show Jaime she could still have the life she'd wanted all those years ago. Fix the past, move on to the next project.

"Nope."

"Why not?"

"You've never lived with a woman, have you?"

Well, his mother, but Emmett had the feeling that wasn't what Clancy meant.

"Look, she's happy, I'm happy," he said. "And when she's pregnant and *unhappy* I do everything I can to bring the happy back."

"And knowing when and if I'm leaving the island will make her happy?"

"Yup."

"I'll let you know when I figure it out."

Jaime and Maureen returned to the carts a few moments later. Nearly everyone had already left for their homes and the lights in the park came back on. Maureen and Clancy left to relieve the babysitter and Emmett turned the cart toward Jaime's house.

Clancy's questions bugged Emmett. He tried to push them away, but couldn't. Maureen wasn't a busybody by nature.

Jaime leaned her head on his shoulder and threaded her fingers with his. "That was fun. I haven't been to a movie in the park in ages."

"Why not?"

She shrugged. "It's mostly couples. Tonight was fun because it was you and me, Clancy and Maureen. I don't like to be a third wheel with them too often."

"They obviously don't mind."

"I know, but they get so little time as a couple, it's not fair to them if I'm always hanging around."

"But it's okay if I'm there, too?"

"Sure."

The reasoning didn't make sense to Emmett. If Jaime felt she intruded on their alone time when she was on her own, why did she feel differently when she was half of another couple? Maureen and Clancy still deserved time without their kids underfoot.

"Is that why she keeps asking me about my plans?"

Jaime stiffened beside him. "She what?"

That was all the answer Emmett needed.

Jaime wanted to know about his plans, and her best friend was trying to help her find the answers she needed. Funny, a few weeks ago that would have ticked him off. Now, he merely wished she had asked him directly. He didn't know how he would answer the question, but at least he could try.

"Not in a direct way. Clancy more or less asked me my intentions a few nights ago and then tonight he couldn't stop talking about how much he loved the island and never wanted to leave. Little things like that."

She sat straighter and pulled her hand from his. "And you think I put them up to it? That I'm…what? Trying to influence you so you'll stay on the island when you so obviously want to leave?"

Emmett shrugged. "Yeah, but it's not a problem for me."

"Oh, well, that's great. It's not a problem for you that I'm using my friends to dig into your life and play games. It's expected because I'm a woman?"

"No," Emmett said slowly. He turned to look at her and froze. Anger emanated from every cell from the hard set of her full mouth to the narrowing of her big, brown eyes. Shoulders tense, her hands were clasped in her lap. "I just… You could have asked me, instead of trying to figure it out through third parties."

"Oh, I could have asked you about your plans and that would have been okay because I'm such an insecure person that you'd overlook it?"

This was not going as he'd expected. Not even a little bit.

"That's great, except we don't talk about the future. We certainly don't bring up the past. We barely talk about the present."

"And you want to?" He pulled to a stop beneath the big oak tree in the corner of her yard.

"Talk about things? Why would I want to do that? Things are going so well with us not talking at all."

Jaime jumped out of the golf cart and stormed up to her front door. She slammed it shut behind her.

JAIME WANTED TO SCREAM. How did a person get to be twenty-eight years old and not know if she could survive on her own?

Jaime buried her hands in her hair and clenched them into fists. She paid her bills, went to work. In theory, she could do all those things any place in the world. She wanted to see what life might offer her outside Gulliver Township.

In reality, she still had moments like the one on the ferry or on the docks in Detroit. Moments when she froze.

She wanted to try, though.

There was a knock at the front door and she opened it, not surprised to find Emmett on the other side.

"You knocked?"

"You were pretty mad when you stormed in here."

"I'm still pretty mad."

"At me?"

"Yeah, at you. You think I'm using my friends to figure out what the future holds between us."

"I didn't say that."

"Don't get all semantical with me. We both know what you meant."

"What I meant was that you could ask me what I'm thinking."

"What are you thinking?" she asked, not really expecting an answer.

"I don't know."

"That went well." She turned away but Emmett's hands on her shoulders turned her back.

"I really don't know. I like being with you,

Jaime. I like being on the island and I like getting to know my dad better. And I miss Cincinnati."

As the truth went, it hurt a little less than she'd expected. He didn't know what he wanted. Neither did she.

"I haven't asked because I wasn't sure I wanted to know. But what do you want, Jaime?"

She swallowed and focused her gaze on his Adam's apple. If she looked into those clear, blue eyes she would tell him whatever she thought he wanted to hear. She didn't want to do that. She wanted to tell him what she wanted.

If she could only figure out what that was in the next thirty seconds.

"I told you mine."

"You said you don't know," she said, stalling for time, hoping against hope for the epiphany that would tell her what to do. She turned and began pacing the living room. Stay on the island, alone. Leave the island, alone. Leave the island, with Emmett.

This was the scariest part of all. If she didn't know what she wanted, if she didn't have control over what she wanted, how would she know if what she decided was her decision or someone else's? How could she know she wouldn't wake up someday with another wasted decade spent turning herself inside out because of what another person wanted?

"It's a little freaky, not knowing. I don't like it," she finally said. He put his hand on her shoulder, but the touch wasn't comforting. It made her burn, and she needed to not burn. She needed to be levelheaded. She pretended to straight magazines on the coffee table, putting it between them like a shield. Emmett stayed on his side. "A lot freaky."

Stay, go. One of the answers was right but all she could think about was getting lost in Emmett again. Getting lost in the feel of him because when she stopped thinking there was always a single moment when she thought she knew what she wanted.

"It's okay not to know," he said. "I can help you figure it out, it's the least I can do."

Jaime's skin went cold. The least he could do. It always came back to this with Emmett. She spoke through her teeth. "I know what I want. I want you to leave." And she stormed down the hall to her bedroom.

CHAPTER FIFTEEN

EMMETT CAUGHT HIS foot between the door to her bedroom and the frame just before it slammed shut. He wasn't going down this way, and he wasn't going to let Jaime get away with it, either. She must feel something for him. Otherwise she wouldn't be running so hard.

He didn't understand his own feelings, but he wasn't running from them. Or questioning the motives of the person he cared about. And he did care, damn it.

Impatiently, he pushed the thoughts aside. This was about Jaime's feelings, not his. Stepping inside her bedroom, Emmett cleared his throat. "You haven't answered my question yet."

"Yes, I did. I said I wanted you to leave." Jaime whirled, anger, surprise and wanting warring together on her face. The combination was enchanting.

"You lied." She couldn't want him to leave,

not really. "What do you want? Just tell me so we can figure it out."

A flurry of emotions crossed her face but the most clear was panic. He hated himself for making her feel that.

"You made it clear from the beginning you weren't staying. At what point did you decide 'poor, helpless Jaime' needed 'big, strong Emmett' to fix her world?" She picked his shirt up off the chair and threw it at his head. "My world was just fine until you came back here, and it will be just fine when you leave again." She tossed his wallet to him from the dresser. "You left that here last night. Until you do leave I think it's better that we keep our distance. I don't want you to get confused about the differences between attraction and responsibility again."

Was that what he had been doing? Mistaking his responsibility for what happened all those years ago with the attraction he felt for her now? The argument didn't seem so important all of a sudden.

"I know the difference between responsibility and attraction." He threw the T back on the bed and tossed his wallet onto the dresser. "I don't feel responsible for your happiness, Jaime. I'm attracted to it," he said, advancing toward her with purpose in every stride.

"We'll get to that later. Right now I have another question."

For a split second fear shone in her eyes. As quickly as it came, it was gone. Replaced by an emotion he couldn't decipher. Instead of retreating from him, she stepped forward.

"What's that?"

He traced a line down the side of her crewnecked T, watched her nipples peak as his finger glided between her breasts, and felt her stomach muscles clench under the thin cotton when both his hands came to rest at her waist. He kept his thumbs moving in a circular pattern on the soft skin on either side of her belly button.

Her eyes closed briefly and she inhaled a harsh breath through her nose, exhaling out her mouth. "You said…you had…a question." The words were shaky, her voice husky.

Question. What question? All he could think about was the twinkling blue stone in her belly button ring. How it had winked at him that day in Detroit. The body jewelry was new. It was strange how she covered her body from neck to ankle with her clothes but underneath she wore things made to make a man crazy.

He wanted to ask her why, when she covered up so much of her body, she bothered with pretty jewelry that no one could see. More than that he wanted to kiss his way to the stone and listen to her sigh as his kisses went lower, slower.

"How slow do you want me to go?"

No answer, only the nodding of her head. Emmett smiled. For the first time, he was going to enjoy Jaime from the tip of her toes to the crown of her head.

"Then we'll take things slow this time."

Without asking, he lifted her in his arms and laid her gently on the bed. Slowly, he unfastened one sandal and then the next, freeing her pretty pink toenails. He dropped the shoes and headed farther north.

Her hands found his shoulders, urging him up. He resisted.

He flicked open the clasp of her skirt, pulling it down over her hips and depositing it with her shoes on the floor.

A purple silk thong was the only thing between his mouth and her soft mound. He breathed lightly and watched the purple darken with moisture.

She moaned.

His hands found the bottom of her shirt and pushed it up over her breasts. A matching lace-and-silk bra hid her breasts from him. He smiled. It would be gone soon enough.

Rising from the bed, she pulled her shirt over her head and tossed it to one side. "When you said 'slow,' I didn't think you meant remedial," she said and reached for his shirt.

She wanted to speed things up, but he didn't want another fast-and-furious mating with her. He let her strip him of his shirt and jeans, but stopped her before she could reach inside his boxers. A few touches of her hand and all his willpower would go out the window.

"Not so fast. We're going slow, remember?"

She leaned back against the pillows, smiled and said, "What if I don't like it slow?"

Moving quickly, he entered the bathroom, grabbed the belt off her satin robe and returned to the room. He held it like a lasso. "I don't think you have much choice."

"You think I'm scared of a flimsy piece of material?" she asked, excitement lighting her eyes. "You don't scare me, Emmett."

He chuckled, grabbed both her wrists and tied them to the headboard. "Maybe I should." He traced two fingers down her rib cage, watching her skin quiver beneath his touch. "Now, where were we?"

Her hips bucked slightly. So that was what she wanted. Not quite yet.

With a flick of his thumb, he opened her

bra and traced the lace edges across her sensitive nipples. She gasped with pleasure, her head rocking back against the pillows. For several moments he allowed only the lace to touch her heated skin. When she was writhing uncontrollably beneath his hands, Emmett replaced the lace with his hands, rolling her nipples between his thumb and forefinger.

"Oh, God." The words were barely a whisper from her throat. "Emmett," she sighed. She strained against the belt, but he didn't release her.

He trailed kisses down her chest and over her stomach, his hands never leaving her breasts. When he reached the thin purple silk covering her, he bit at the covering. His tongue teasing her wet lips with the fabric.

She moved her hips, wanting a more thorough touch and not able to get it with her panties still in place.

He looked up, met her eyes and smiled.

"Please?" The words were a question as much as a plea, and he was happy to oblige.

Quickly he pulled the panties from her and began again his trail of torture down her chest and stomach until his lips reached her.

Damn. She was so hot and wet, he thought he would die. Pulling her folds gently apart, he found her clitoris with his tongue and began to slowly pulse against it. She moaned deep in her throat, her hips moving of their own volition now.

She was close. So damn close. Emmett wanted to feel her come around him and he made his move. Aligning their bodies, he thrust deep inside her.

Her eyes widened, pupils dilated. She pulled against her binding again, but he only smiled. "Just feel it," he instructed. "Let everything else fade to black."

When she sank back into the pillows again, he began to move inside her. Going deeper with every stroke. She whimpered when he placed his lips on hers, matching the stroke with his tongue in her mouth.

Her body tightened around him, the muscles in her torso freezing for a few seconds as her inner muscles began pulsating around him, and he pulled his head back to watch her climax.

Eyes closed, the only sign of her orgasm was the relaxed muscles of her face. "Ahhhh," was the only sound that escaped her mouth. Her climax reached, Emmett galloped ahead to his own.

EMMETT STOOD IN the kitchen doorway at Jaime's house, jeans covering his legs but unbuttoned. He wasn't wearing a shirt. He really should be wearing a shirt, Jaime thought helplessly. *I can't have a rational conversation with him not wearing a shirt.* Half the female population would jump on him looking fresh off the sex train. She had to have a rational conversation because they couldn't keep swinging around the going/staying, together/not together conversation, not if she was to keep her sanity. She needed to make a decision.

The muscles in her belly clenched as she waited for leftover pasta and sauce to warm in the microwave.

"You're wearing my shirt," he said as he pushed off the door and padded across the tiled floor to the fridge where he grabbed a bottle of water and cracked it open. "Looks good on you."

Jaime looked down. The old Reds T-shirt reached to midthigh, effectively covering her and yet leaving her strangely open to him. She didn't think she'd ever worn a man's shirt—at least not in his presence—in her life. The few relationships she'd allowed hadn't called for a lot of shared clothing. Or even very much sex, which was odd since she couldn't seem to get enough of sex with Emmett. Maybe there was something to that whole mated-for-life thing that penguins had. He reached around her waist, pulling her back to his chest and nuzzling her neck.

Only, relationships were about more than sex. She shook herself. She would not get sucked right back into bed with him.

"I'm hungry."

"Me, too." He pressed his mouth to her neck and sucked gently. "You taste perfect."

"Not that kind of hungry." She swatted playfully at his hands as the nervousness faded away. The microwave dinged and she opened the door to bring out bowls of warm food. Her tummy growled, an echoing growl sounding from behind her.

She straightened her shoulders and stepped away from him. "Dinner, Emmett."

"Whatever you say, Jaime." He clipped his words and grinned.

His voice should really not sound that good when he spoke her name, she decided, and tried to push him toward the counter. When he only stood behind her, watching closely, Jaime flicked her hands at him.

"What? Sit. I'm starving."

Emmett pulled out a chair, waiting for her to take a seat and then pushed her closer to the table. Jaime laid a napkin across her lap, forked up some alfredo and sighed as the taste of butter, rich cream and cheese woke her taste buds. She closed her eyes and leaned against the chair back. He bit off a hunk of garlic bread and then dug in to his plate as if he couldn't eat fast enough.

She took another bite, enjoying the moment. One she wanted to repeat as often as possible before said man went back to Cincinnati.

The clock on the stove ticked, but the house was quiet. Too quiet. "What's going on with the reno?"

"You've been there every day."

Jaime pressed her lips together. "It's called conversation. People who date talk. They don't just jump one another's bones."

"They do in the beginning."

"Well, if you need an extra body to hammer at something, I'll have time after Monday," she said primly.

"I've seen the way you swing a hammer, remember? We have a schedule to keep."

"Then a paintbrush or window cleaner."

"Maybe we should keep your home improvement skills relegated to the bedroom." His gaze went dark and his nostrils flared.

Her throat tightened. Conversation, she reminded herself. Not just jumping bones.

"I should probably warn you I'm allergic to some cleaning supplies."

"Really?" He reached across the table to caress the back of her hand.

"And I, uh, don't do bathrooms."

"Anything else?"

"I'm pretty good in the kitchen." It was exciting, teasing with him this way. So much better than thinking about what might happen at some unknown point in the future. She would do everything she could to keep everything right here.

He tutted his tongue against his teeth. "Then we are doomed, Jaime Brown, because I'm terrible in the kitchen," he teased.

Jaime sat back, pushed her plate away and leaned her head against the chair. Emmett ate the way he did everything else: with purpose. He swished a bit of bread over his plate, soaking up some of the sauce. Took a bite. Twirled long strands of pasta over his fork. Ate. He twirled his fork around again but a long piece of fettucine hung down. He put the noodles in his mouth and sucked on the trailing piece until it disappeared into his mouth. Jaime giggled.

"I don't think I've seen anyone over age ten do that."

He shrugged. "What's the point in eating

good food if you can't also enjoy the moment? You should try it."

Jaime rolled her eyes at him.

"Scared?"

"Just because I don't want to get sauce all over this fine example of baseball apparel doesn't mean I'm scared."

"It's just a harmless noodle." He picked another long noodle from his plate and sucked it between his lips, eyes twinkling. "Come on."

Emmett reached across the table and twirled some noodles around Jaime's fork. He held it up, long, flat noodles hanging down.

He waggled his brows.

Jaime straightened her spine. It had been a long time since she slurped noodles. She took the fork and breathed in, feeling the thin pieces slide between her lips and into her mouth. She giggled again.

"Tastes better that way, right?"

"I think it's more that the fun adds a certain zing to the sauce and cheese."

She locked eyes with Emmett over the table. Picked one more noodle from her plate and tilted her head to dangle it over her mouth. She felt self-conscious until his eyes darkened and his breathing grew rapid. Jaime sucked the noodle into her mouth. "Delicious."

Jaime picked up the empty plates and

rinsed them in the sink. Emmett met her at the counter, put his arms around her waist and pulled her against him.

"So your best room is the kitchen, hmm?"

Her head relaxed against his muscled chest. How could he do this to her? This kind of physical reaction was supposed to wear off after a few dates, but her attraction to Emmett seemed to be growing by infinite amounts every second and she didn't know how to keep those feelings in check.

It scared her how quickly she'd fallen back in love with him.

Maybe it was more to the point that it scared her how easy it was to admit that she still loved him. Had never really stopped. It was different when they were younger. There had been no gray in her world. Now there was her job and the project at the school. And under it a growing unease with the choices she'd made all those years ago. Then there was him. The boy she'd loved had grown into a man she loved. A man who lived four hundred miles away and was determined to return to his life there. She couldn't impulsively throw away the life she'd built here. This was home. The only safe place she'd ever known.

She leaned her head against Emmett's

shoulder. She traced her index finger over his forearm, liking the feel of his arms around her.

Jaime let a little more gray into her black-and-white world.

Because being in Emmett's arms felt safer than the island ever had.

CHAPTER SIXTEEN

THE NEXT THREE weeks flew by in a flurry of making love, renovating the old school and spending nearly every waking moment with Jaime.

Emmett cast his reel out into the lake. They were on the north side of the island, a picnic basket filled with sandwiches and drinks on the rocky beach behind them. After nearly blowing it that night at Jaime's they'd come to an uneasy truce. He didn't ask Jaime what she wanted and she didn't ask him when he was leaving.

He still hadn't decided.

He didn't think she had, either.

He did know one thing: he loved her. Gibson was right. He'd been in love with Jaime since before high school, even when he was convinced he was bad for her.

A light breeze blew in from the lake, lifting the skirt of Jaime's summer dress as the sun began to set in the west. This was one of the changes he hadn't really expected. As Jaime became more confident in her decisions and more comfortable in her skin she'd changed the way she dressed. Again. Now she wore maxi skirts and summer dresses, and her trash bin overflowed with their mail-order delivery boxes. Today her tanned legs seemed to stretch forever below the midlength skirt that swirled above her knees. She wore another pair of jeweled flip-flops on her feet. A silver chain circled one of her narrow ankles. He let his gaze wander back up her body. She wore a white blouse that showed off strong shoulders while still hiding the scar he'd traced with his tongue the night before.

He loved her and he wanted to be with her.

A few lightning bugs flickered between the shore and the tree line. As the sun sank farther into the lake more firefly lights flickered, flying in little circles around a fallen tree near the rocky shore. He hadn't see this many lightning bugs in…he didn't know how long.

Emmett secured his pole between two rocks and caught Jaime's hand in his. "Come on, we're going to catch a lightning bug."

She looked past him to the bugs flying through the air and broke into a smile. Together they chased fireflies, capturing one and then another in their hands and then opening their closed palms to let them find their way back to the tree line. Finally, Jaime collapsed on the small strip of sand, breathing hard.

"I haven't chased lightning bugs since we were kids."

"Me, either."

Emmett sat beside her and then, because it seemed like the thing to do, lay back on the sand to watch the evening stars twinkle to life. "It's evening."

"What?" Jaime's voice sounded far away so he turned his head. She was right there. Close enough to touch. Caress. Kiss.

But he didn't because he wanted this moment. Lying on the sand, breathing heavily with lightning bugs and stars twinkling in the dwindling light.

"You said it was afternoon. I think that was a couple of hours ago." The first streaks of pink and orange crossed the sky as the sun sank a little farther to the west.

"I didn't realize you were keeping time."

"I'm not, not really. But we should probably start back soon. The aide asked to have the night off."

"Sure."

They stood but before Emmett could gather their things his fishing pole bent hard toward the lake. He lunged for it and caught the pole between his hands just before it would have gone sailing into the murky water.

Something had caught on his hook and Emmett began reeling in the line. Whatever it was, it was heavy. The pole bent but didn't break. Jaime cheered and put her own pole down to help him. She ducked under his arm and grabbed the pole so he could concentrate on reeling in whatever was on the line. Together they worked until a fish the size of Emmett's fist popped out of the water, hooked.

"All that work for a two-pounder," he said, unhooking the fish's mouth and tossing it back into the water.

"It's a crime. Almost as big a crime as this: I hate fishing." She watched him closely for a moment and Emmett tried to read her expression. Kidding? Serious? It was so hard to tell when she went all doe-eyed on him.

"You hate fishing?"

"With a passion."

"Then why are we fishing?"

She shrugged. "You seemed really excited about it. It's a Sunday afternoon. I had nothing better to do."

He pulled her to him. "Nothing better to do?"

"Not when you're out here on the north side

of the island. If I hadn't come, I'd've been all alone on the south side. Probably knitting on my front porch."

"Are you still trying to figure out that booty pattern for Maureen?"

"The last one was good."

"It was supposed to be a hat, right?"

"Obviously."

Emmett hugged her close, liking how she felt in his arms. "You do realize knitted hats are supposed to fit to the head, not just flop over like a blanket?"

She narrowed her eyes at him. "Are you questioning my abilities as best friend of the mother?"

"No, I'm saying outright that you're a terrible knitter."

"And you're a horrible fisherman."

"I never said I was good at it. I said I liked it."

"You like me."

"Yes, I do."

"Then you might want to come with me." She waggled her eyebrows at him.

"What did you have in mind?"

"Not a two-pound guppy," she said and slipped out of his arms. Emmett watched her tiptoe over the rocky shore to the tree line and then disappear into the wooded area.

He tossed both fishing poles onto the picnic blanket and hurried after her. Whatever she wanted was all right with him.

THE INTERCOM ON Jaime's desk buzzed early Wednesday morning and before she could answer, her father walked through the office door.

"Jaime," he said in his gruff voice and then sat in the chair opposite her desk.

"Hi, Dad."

"I think we should talk. Your mother is worried."

Jaime steepled her hands and leaned back in her chair. It had been weeks since their last talk and Jaime still didn't know what they had to say. Mason and Beverly were intent on placing blame. She wanted to move past blame to new territory.

"I don't want to fight with you, Dad."

"I don't want to fight with you, either, kiddo." Mason played with the ball cap in his hands. The police department insignia flattened and rounded as he moved the hat around for a few moments. "When you got hurt, I blamed myself. By the time I got to the hospital you were out of surgery and you looked so small in that bed. I couldn't blame myself and be the strong father you needed. At least,

I didn't think I could. So I looked for someone else to blame. There was the man who attacked you, but even after you came home and were safe I was so angry and you were so quiet. You didn't want to see Emmett, not right away, and I used that to focus the rest of my anger. Because if you were upset with him he must have done something wrong."

"He didn't, Dad. He didn't do anything."

Mason lifted one shoulder. "When he left and you shrank back into yourself, I convinced myself I was right. Right to have placed that blame on him. Right to have made it hard for him to see you. Right to keep you both apart as much as I could. Then he came back this summer and all that anger, all that guilt, came crashing back."

"Dad." Jaime came around the desk to sit next to her father. "You weren't to blame any more than Emmett was."

"I should have protected you more, taught you more about how to protect yourself." He patted her hand and whispered, "I'm sorry I failed you."

"You didn't fail me," Jaime said after a minute. "You protected me. You taught me to scream and to fight. And when that man was on me...that's what I did. I yelled and kicked and screamed and, when I could, I ran."

"I don't want you to leave."

Jaime sat back in her chair. "Where is this coming from?"

Mason offered her a watery smile. "From watching you over the past few weeks. You don't belong here, not anymore. I want you to stay. It's why I agreed to come to your house with your mom that day. I—we—both want you close because even though you're an adult, you're still our little girl. You will be the six-year-old I walked to first grade for the rest of your life. But you have to go, and if you go with Emmett, that's okay with me. And I'll make sure it's okay with your mom, too. It'll take a while, but she'll come around."

"Dad, I haven't made a decision about what I'm going to do."

"Yes, you have. You just haven't known how to tell him. Or me. Or anyone else. You should go, sweetheart, and when you come back, don't stay too long."

Fear was a cold, clammy thing climbing from her belly into her chest. "What if he doesn't want me to go with him?"

"Then go on your own. You need to start building your life, Jaime, and the life you need isn't on Gulliver."

He left, but Jaime stayed in the chair on the other side of her desk. A few papers were scattered on the surface, and there were files in the drawers, but when she looked at the space that's all there was. Files and papers. She'd never put personal pictures on her desk, just the portraits of the Marblehead Lighthouse.

"I want Emmett," she said to the room. "I want Emmett and I'll figure the rest out as I go."

There was something she had to do before she talked to him, though. Jaime pushed up out of the chair and moved to the other side of her desk. She booted up her computer, and sat before opening a fresh document.

"Dear Tom…" She began the letter of resignation.

EMMETT HAD SIGNED the contract to list Gibson's house and faxed it back to the real-estate agent on the mainland before he could change his mind. After touring the renovated home, the Realtor had suggested an asking price and Emmett had worked hard to convince himself selling was the right thing to do.

What he wanted was to not sell. To keep the house. To keep some kind of tie to Gulliver and Jaime.

That was silly when he already knew he didn't want to live on the island full-time, not even if that meant having Jaime in his life full-time. As much as he'd enjoyed the past few weeks, as at home as he had felt, there was something missing. Working with his crew, working up bids for new projects down south, he finally realized he missed the life he'd built while he was running from the past.

While he'd been avoiding Gulliver's Island and Jaime, Emmett had found something he liked about himself. He'd become a man who liked to play, but who understood the value of a hard day's work.

He went up the stairs to the second floor and looked into the classroom. Yesterday he'd put the glass sheeting over the blackboard wall. Ten small desks lined the floor along with a larger teacher's desk at the head of the room. It looked ready for school to start and it seemed sad to him that no kids would come to this room to learn. At least, not reading, writing or arithmetic. Instead when they came some would find a piece of their personal history in the names on the blackboard.

Back downstairs, Emmett gave the guys the rest of the day off. His crew would go back to Cincinnati in another couple of days, leaving the school to him. When the building was empty, he called Jaime and then carried the heavy picnic basket upstairs. He pushed the desks out of the way and set finger sandwiches, fruit and a bottle of wine on the floor.

This project was her idea, he thought, so celebrating the project with her would be the perfect ending.

And maybe a new beginning for the two of them.

"Emmett?" she called from the front door.

Emmett leaned over the newly installed railing and motioned her up the stairs. Light sparkled in through the stained-glass windows, turning her blond hair pink when she stepped onto the stairs.

Jaime gasped when she saw the room.

"It's perfect," she said, running her fingers along the glass until she found the name of her great-grandfather. Then she stopped short when she saw two more names in the bottom corner. "Emmett." She whispered his name.

"And Jaime." He took her hand. "I thought your name should be added to the list, since the building wouldn't exist without your interference."

"And without your adept use of a sledgehammer."

"Plus, our names just kind of sound good together, don't you think?"

She smiled at him and the smile turned to a grin when she noticed the picnic spread out on the floor. "We've tried this picnic thing a few times now. Last time you caught a fish and distracted me."

"In case you haven't noticed, we are nowhere near open water."

"But we are in the public building."

"A public building that isn't open to the public. Yet," he said, popping the top on the wine.

Jaime sipped from her glass. "Before you get too far into this whole scene, there's something I want to tell you."

"You've been secretly plotting with your father to tear down the building despite my amazing work."

"I'm leaving the island."

Emmett's breath caught in his chest.

"For work."

The banging in his chest eased a bit.

"I've realized I want more than the little life I've been allowing myself. This morning I wrote my letter of resignation and turned it in before I could overthink it. It's time to make some new plans that aren't tied to me living in my parents' cottage or working for my father's best friend." She looked at him and her big, brown eyes softened. "I want—"

"Wow." Part of Emmett wanted to celebrate, to cheer her on. He'd done it. When he'd arrived on the island there was only a tiny spark of the old Jaime. Now he could see the girl she used to be in almost everything she did. So why did he feel as if he had to watch what he said? "What will you do?"

"I have a little money saved, and Tom will give me a good reference. And I've recently found that although I kind of suck at the whole hammering thing, I'm really good at picking paints and floor treatments." She moved to sit next to him. He thought for a second she might say something more, but then she kissed him. "I don't know. I'll figure it out. My parents are thinking of turning the cottage back into a rental property."

"You should keep it."

"It was never really mine, I just paid the utilities." Jaime shook her head. "I want a place of my own—that I choose. Not a place that is given to me."

"I signed a contract to sell my dad's house today," Emmett said. "The real-estate agent thinks it will go fast. Maybe be turned into a bed-and-breakfast…maybe stay a single-family home."

"And you're telling me…?"

Because he wanted to be with her and, if she said the same thing, he would keep her with him. He would keep her by his side, and she wouldn't be free to experience the new places she'd just talked about. He wanted her, but he wanted her to be free. "Because my leaving the island might be sooner rather than later."

"Maureen and my father both told me, in so many words," Jaime continued but she wouldn't meet his gaze, "that they knew I would leave the island. I thought they were just trying to… I don't know, build up my confidence or something. But I think I might. Maybe take some classes at Bowling Green or the U of Toledo."

Emmett swallowed; glad for the dim light in the room so she couldn't see what he was positive was a bleak expression. This was what he'd wanted; what he'd been planning for all summer. So why did it feel so…wrong?

"When do you leave?" she finally asked.

"Soon. The final building inspection will be soon, and my dad finally has all the bits and bobs he wants to bring to Cincinnati with him cataloged and boxed."

"Then we should make the most of to-night." She planted a firm kiss on his jaw. "Do you realize we are completely alone in a building where generations of island kids have, uh, not attended classes?"

"I believe we were one of those couples not studying science or math, a long time ago."

"We were, but I think I'd like to replace the memory of dust and cobwebs with this memory of good wine, clean floors and—" she pointed to the sleeping bag he'd put in the corner earlier in the afternoon "—a bed-like surface."

"What the lady wants…" Emmett said, turning to her before he could make the fatal mistake of asking her to come to Cincinnati with him. Jaime needed to make her own decisions free from the influence of him, from the pain of her past or the good intentions of her family.

What he wanted was her, just Jaime. What he knew couldn't do was ask her to come with him.

CHAPTER SEVENTEEN

"YOU KNOW, I really like doing this," Jaime whispered, snuggling against Emmett under the lightweight sleeping bag. Moonlight shone through the newly installed windows and the classroom smelled like fresh paint.

Not the most romantic smell, Jaime thought, but somehow she knew it would be an erotic scent for the rest of her life.

"Good," Emmett said, his lips caressing the tender skin at her hairline. "Because I don't plan to move for a while."

"I'd say we have a solid six hours before the cleaning company shows up to do a final check of the main floor before the inspection." Jaime laughed and flipped so her backside pressed against Emmett's stomach. She felt his muscles clench against her and smiled. She wriggled a little closer.

They'd talked a little about him leaving, about her leaving, but not enough. And too much. She should have said she wanted to go with him, but at the last minute she didn't know how to tell him what she wanted without pressuring him to say yes. The reunion was in another week. She wanted to ask him to stay, just for the party.

She wanted him to leave because the longer he stayed the harder it was going to be to let him go. And she had to let him go. She knew she could build a life off the island, figure out her job situation and then come to terms with loving Emmett when he didn't love her back.

As boring and as unremarkable as life would be without him, she could build something good. Wait! She already had.

Jaime looked around the classroom that felt as if students had just left for the summer. She'd done this. Saved Gulliver School. There was paperwork to be done and the Historical Society to convince, but the trustees were happy, even her father, thanks to the state-of-the-art security system that she'd made sure to turn off for the night.

Emmett's breath sighed over her hair as he slipped into sleep. Jaime shifted inside the sleeping bag until her breasts were pressed against his chest. She pushed a lock of hair behind his ear. Emmett shifted but didn't wake.

"I love you again," she whispered. "I think I always have." Even when she'd hated him for leaving, even when she'd freaked out because he'd come back.

Jaime reached behind her to unzip the sleeping bag and then slipped out of it. Naked, she walked across the room to stand to the side of the window. She looked out on the open space below. It was late enough no one would be out walking, but she wasn't prepared to go full-frontal on the island. Jaime touched the scar that Emmett had kissed at least a hundred times over the summer. It didn't seem as angry lately. She looked over her shoulder.

Emmett lay on his back, his arms thrown over his head.

Jaime heard a shuffle downstairs and froze momentarily. She tiptoed to the door and stuck her head around the doorjamb. One of her father's patrolmen had walked through the front door and was shining his flashlight around the cavernous room below. He checked the alarm system box by the door and muttered under his breath before activating it. Then he shut the door and the mechanical voice began counting down.

"Emmett?" Jaime hurried to his side and pushed against his shoulder. "Emmett, we need to get out of here."

"What?"

"Ernie—patrolman during normal sleeping hours?—just left. And he activated the alarm."

"But I called Dispatch to tell them it wouldn't be set tonight because of the drying paint."

Jaime pulled her capris over her legs and shoved her feel into her sandals as she pulled her pink tank top over her head. "Well, he didn't get the memo, and if we're not out the front door in the next thirty seconds we're going to wake the whole island."

Emmett wiped the sleep from his eyes. "We can't get all this cleaned up in thirty seconds."

"Nope, but you can get dressed and we can get out of here before we get caught."

"Or we could throw caution to the wind and take our chances." His gaze took on a wicked gleam. Jaime threw his jeans and shirt at him.

"I spent considerable time this summer convincing my father a security system would keep the kids on this island from vandalizing the school."

"We weren't vandalizing. We were christening." He pulled his clothes on and threw the sleeping bag over his shoulder.

"To-may-to, to-mah-to."

Jaime picked up her bag but left the hamper of picnic supplies on the floor. There was no time to retrieve all the paraphernalia from their picnic; she would take care of it in the morning.

As they reached the bottom of the stairs the mechanical voice said, "Thirteen."

Jaime started for the front door but Emmett stopped her.

"What if Ernie stayed behind?"

"Back door." Jaime pivoted. "Or you could throw yourself on the mercy of the court. Last time you got caught here it was twenty hours of community service in the freezing cold. No chance of frostbite in the summer."

Emmett put his hand at the small of her back and urged her forward. "Last time I was eighteen and rebellious. I don't think people are as lenient with twenty-eight-year-old breakers-and-enterers."

"Maybe you forgot your hammer?"

"Maybe I thought nailing the hot island girl was worth the risk?"

They made it to through the back door as the mechanical voice said, "Five."

Jaime giggled. "Are we completely nuts?"

"Nah. We're just having fun. Remembering old times."

They looked around the corner. Jaime didn't see the police cruiser so they continued to Emmett's golf cart, parked under the maple tree.

"It's been a long time since I could think about the old times without automatically going to Pittsburgh."

He secured the sleeping bag to the backseat with the belt and started the cart, heading toward her house.

"I can understand that."

Jaime leaned her head against his shoulder.

"Sometimes it's good to remember," Emmett replied.

Jaime relaxed against him. "I'm glad you came back this summer. Are you going to stay for the reunion?"

"I'm glad I came back, too." He took her hand in his. "Think I can find a date? I've heard horror stories about the desperate singles at high school reunions."

"I think that can definitely be arranged."

BANGING ON THE front door woke Emmett the morning of the reunion. The inspection had gone off without a hitch the day before, and most of Gibson's things were already boxed and ready to move. There was no reason for anyone to pound on the door at this hour.

Jaime said something unintelligible, turned over and went back to sleep, but the banging continued. He grabbed his jeans from the floor and pulled them on as he took the steps two at a time. He stubbed his toe on the fancy little table beside Jaime's sofa and cursed. Loudly.

He should be used to her weird placement of random tables by now, but somehow her decorator items of choice kept surprising him.

He opened the door to find Clancy on the other side. "I have to make a run to the mainland for the party, and I'm going to need help getting everything back."

"I'm not on the prom committee," Emmett said, dragging his shirt over his head.

"It's a reunion, not the prom, and we're going after actual alcohol not near-beer."

"And?"

"And Ernie's at the station house, the other guys have to work and the people coming in to help with the reunion haven't gotten to the island yet. You're it, buddy."

Emmett groaned. He didn't want to go on a beer run at six o'clock in the morning. He was too old for such crap. But he pulled Jaime's door shut behind him and texted her that he'd be back in a little while.

This was the problem with small towns. People expected you to join in and be part of the group. He looked back, picturing Jaime on the bed. Somehow the thought of returning to the city wasn't so appealing.

It took most of the boat ride to the mainland for Emmett to clear his head. A boat ride filled with Clancy muttering about the merits of kegs versus cans and boxed wine versus bottled. Emmett reminded him that Tom was providing all the wine, which cheered Clancy up significantly. Until he realized there was still the kegs-versus-cans debate to be won.

"Kegs require disposable cups."

"Cans require recycling," Clancy said.

"Just trying to help."

They arrived at Clancy's slip and borrowed a golf cart from the marina owner. At the liquor store Clancy finally decided on bottles and cans because the owner was out of disposable cups. They loaded the boat and were about to shove off when Emmett's phone rang. It was the real-estate agent.

"The couple we showed the house to earlier this week loved it," she said. "They've come in ten thousand dollars above asking."

Emmett blinked. Ten thousand above asking was huge; it would give his dad a bigger cushion once they moved him in to the assisted-living facility. He motioned to Clancy to cut the engine.

"Why so high?"

"They want to turn it in to a bed-and-breakfast. They saw the renovated school and talked with Tom Gulliver about tourism potential. It's a good offer." She chattered on and Emmett began to pace.

He didn't want strangers sleeping in his home, not if they weren't going to live there. Not if they had no connection to the island or the house.

Emmett felt like a kid who didn't want to share his toys. As much as he had enjoyed being back on the island this summer he didn't want to live here permanently. He didn't want strangers sleeping in his bedroom or scuffing the floors he'd laid the weekend before. He wanted to see a family there, little kids tracking mud over the area rugs and banging pots and pans on the tiled floor in the kitchen.

That was ridiculous, really. It shouldn't matter who bought the home as long as the offer was good and it would help Gibson. Who might live in the house once they were gone, though, did matter. The old place deserved better than that. It deserved to be loved and cared for, not slept in and forgotten about.

Ten minutes later he sat across from the agent talking about escrow and closing costs and firming up a closing date. She slid the contract across the desk and Emmett stared at it for a long time. From the moment they'd received Gibson's diagnosis it seemed natural to sell the house and move his father to Cincinnati. His father might not be ready to leave the island but he was prepared.

What if he kept it? Other islanders used family homes as rental properties. The Victorian would be perfect as a long-term rental. Of course that didn't solve the problem of random people coming and going over the summer months, but he could screen the renters. Add one more job to the list of things he had to do: keep his business running smoothly, make sure the network was happy with the show, keep rebuilding his relationship with Gibson.

And in the middle of that was Jaime. Who'd as much as told him she would follow him and he'd balked; talked over her and around her until she'd dropped the subject.

Because he didn't want her to follow him. Her parents had made it easy for her to move into the cottage and to get her degree online. To go to work for Tom at the winery and never leave the island. They had done those things out of fear. Wasn't his asking Jaime to come with him the same? She'd slid from living at home with her parents to living basically rent-free in their summer cottage.

Following him to Cincinnati, as much as he wanted her there, wasn't so different.

Emmett knew what he wanted. He wanted Jaime.

As much as she had blossomed over these past weeks the reasons for the cracks in her foundation hadn't changed. She needed to figure out what she wanted, away from the influence of the island or the simplicity of sparking up an old romance.

Following him to Cincinnati was the equivalent of using spackling to cover a fist-size hole in the wall. The more intensive way was to cut a new square of drywall to fill the hole. Jaime needed to find her own square of drywall.

Emmett's heart pounded as he put pen to paper. It was time to make the break from the island, for Jaime's sake as well as his own.

He had to sell the house.

PAM, THE VALEDICTORIAN of their class, gestured wildly as her story heated up. "So the judge warns the defense to keep his client quiet or face contempt charges. And the defendant says, 'I'm already in contempt,' and the judge just shut him down. Sent the defendant back to holding, and called a recess. Monday morning we start again."

Jaime watched her, entranced. Gone was the Minnie Mouse voice she remembered and in its place the strong, sure voice of a practiced attorney. She felt badly for making fun of her with Maureen during their planning session. Pam wasn't bragging for attention. She was excited, passionate. She deserved to become a partner in that law firm.

Jason deserved the award he was up for with the sports network.

She excused herself, needing a break from the brilliance of her classmates. They'd done things, and knowing she hadn't made her feel small.

"Great job on the party, Jaime," Clara stopped her at the bottom of the steps leading to the upstairs. "I didn't think you could do it."

"Maureen helped." But she stood taller because she'd wielded a sledgehammer and picked out the stained glass. Planned the reunion party. Maybe her life wasn't what she wanted it to be, but maybe this was the start of something new.

"And Emmett. But my spies tell me you had the vision for this place. You convinced the trustees."

"Well—"

Clara leaned against the banister. "I kind of hoped the reunion would be a flop."

Jaime's mouth gaped. She wanted to be angry with Clara, but she couldn't. If Clara hadn't dumped the reunion in her lap at the last moment, she might not have noticed how lackluster her life was. As much as she didn't like the jealousy she felt listening to her old friends talk about their new lives she knew that jealousy was pushing her to move out of her comfort zone.

"Sorry to disappoint," she said.

Clara waved a hand. "Oh, it's not a disappointment. I'm proud to be a member of our class. As much hell as we raised back then, two of our classmates brought this old building back to life." She raised her wineglass in a toast. "Congratulations. See you around." She joined Jason's group at the bar.

Jaime climbed the stairs and settled near the top, watching through the pickets. The reunion crowd meandered around the main floor of Gulliver School like a river. People inspected the new stained glass she'd convinced Emmett was worth the extra money and then walked past the two display cases with original building pictures and a brief history of the school Maureen had put together earlier that week.

People talked and laughed and got a little misty-eyed when they saw old sweethearts.

Jason flirted with Clara, whose husband looked completely bored. Pam told a few more classmates about her latest case in Cleveland. Her parents were holding court with Tom near the front door. Her mother still hadn't spoken to her but Mason raised his glass in her direction earlier, saluting her work on the school. It was the best compliment she could remember him paying her.

"You've got a great view up here," said Anna as she sat beside Jaime on the stairs.

"Just admiring the view," she said. It wasn't a lie. The room looked great. Anna didn't have to know the view she couldn't keep her eyes off of was Emmett.

"You did a good job. On both projects," she said.

"Both?"

"The school looks good. And I never thought we'd see Emmett Deal spend more than a day or two on the island."

Jaime blinked. "That wasn't about me—" at least, it wasn't all about her "—old buildings are his specialty."

Anna stood. "Sure. And he had to do this one because there are a shortage of old buildings in Cincinnati." She continued down the stairs and joined Pam's group near the display cases.

He'd stayed this long because of her. Not because of the school, and not because of his father. Because of her.

Emmett stood at the bar with Clancy and a few other athletes from their years at Gulliver High. This was her small world, and she loved it. She loved that Maureen was still her best friend, that she could tell the day by what Hank cooked at the diner, and she loved that Emmett let himself become a piece of it again. An important piece from her past; the piece that had made her really look at her present and future. But he was leaving and she was…not going to cry about it.

She didn't want to leave. This was home, whether Emmett was here or not. Telling him about quitting her job, talking in the abstract with Maureen and her dad…it was just talk. Her small life wasn't the prison she'd thought it to be at the beginning of the summer. She'd find a way to make it fit: school or a job off the island, but keeping her roots firmly planted.

She would find a new job; maybe open a business of her own. Maybe take some classes and figure out what she really wanted to do with her life.

Heading up the school reno project had been good; maybe she could look into historical preservation. She'd healed a lot since Emmett had returned; maybe she would look into counseling or a volunteer program for battered women.

For the rest of this night, though, she was going to pretend. Pretend there was a future with Emmett because she didn't want anything to ruin this night. She might not have enough to fill in the whole reunion questionnaire, but the answers she had were solid now.

Maureen waved to her from the corner and Jaime left her place on the stairs to grab a ginger ale from the bar.

"Great party." Maureen sipped the ginger ale. "And I know this is the baby talking, but if one more person tells me I look great pregnant I'm going to throw up on them."

"Your baby bump is beautiful."

"Yeah, well, I don't know why this one waited for the second trimester to start making itself known. I'm supposed to be fat and happy at this point not nauseated and miserable."

"Did you check out the room upstairs?"

"Nice try on the subject change. I'm not done whining." Maureen took another sip and nodded her head toward Emmett and the men at the bar. "Did you tell him you're going yet?"

Jaime nodded. "The day I turned in my resignation but, Mo—"

"Clancy said Emmett met with the real-estate agent when they were picking up the drinks this morning."

Jaime nodded and ignored the pain in her chest. He was leaving, sooner rather than later.

"So when he goes…"

"I won't go with him."

Maureen bumped her shoulder against Jaime's. "Why not?"

The music died down and when Jaime looked over her shoulder Emmett offered a grin.

"He hasn't asked," she said before she could convince herself not to say the words. "I want to do more with my life than plan parties for the winery or hostess another reunion, but I'm not sure following Emmett to Cincinnati is the answer. I need to know what I want first."

Maureen looked as if she might say something more but before she could Emmett tapped Jaime's shoulder.

Maureen cleared her throat. "I'm, uh, going to go find my husband."

When they were alone on the patio, he pulled a sheet of paper out of his back pocket and handed it to her. Jaime unfolded it. It was a copy of the seller's contract for his father's house.

"I got an offer on the house. Ten grand above asking."

Her heart beat a painful tattoo in her chest. The "sooner" was here. "I heard. Congratulations."

"I almost turned down the offer and took the house off the market."

"Why?"

"Because you love the island."

Her thundering heartbeat slowed.

The DJ put on a slow song that pulsed in the night air, but it was as if they were in their own bubble on the patio. His voice was quiet, comforting, but the words were cold against her skin. "I left the island so you could move on, get things back in order, go to school and follow your dreams. When I came back you were still here."

"What does that have to do with selling your father's house? Or not selling it?" Jaime crossed her arms and her fingers sought out the scars for the first time in weeks.

"I thought maybe I should keep it, give it to you to turn into some kind of business. You said you needed a job." He offered her a grin that might have made her knees go weak if he'd said something else. Anything else.

"Is that what all of this—" she motioned to the school "—has been about? Giving me something to do? Was renovating me part of the job you took on with the remodel at Gibson's and the renovation here?"

"No," he said, but something flashed in the depths of his blue, blue eyes and Jaime knew he was lying. Wings of regret beat against the walls of her stomach and she felt the urge to throw up. He'd planned everything. Weaseled his way into the school job, seduced her with peanut butter pie and good sex and a host of little projects that had made her feel useful again.

The whole time he'd seen her as if she were some broken toy left on a playground...

Jaime shook her head. "I never asked you to change anything about your life. I never put what happened to me on your shoulders. It's past time you stopped playing the martyr in this little scenario of yours. I don't need your help." She circled her hands between them. "Damn it, Emmett, I was the one who was attacked. I see what happened to me every day in the mirror and, yeah, I got a little complacent and let my fears about that night have too much control. But you're the one who can't seem to let it go."

"Because you haven't dealt with what happened."

"So you were going to give me your father's house because I hadn't dealt with the past to your satisfaction, but now you're going to go ahead and sell it because…" She dragged out the last word.

Emmett shifted from foot to foot and shoved his hands into his pockets. A few people pushed past them on their way to the line of golf carts in the school parking lot. Once they were alone again Emmett said, "Because you need a clean break from the island."

"And you owning property here would… what? Leave me wandering the island alone, pining for my one true love until you decide to take another trip down memory lane?" Jaime spat the words at him, wanting to hurt him the way he was hurting her. Why not just sell the house and leave the island? Why make his actions about her? She'd never once asked him to change anything. Never asked him to stay here.

"I just want you to be able to move on," he said after a long moment.

"The sad thing is that I have. I'll own that it took me ten years to do it, and I will probably never like large crowds or strange places, and I don't have the rest of my life mapped out, but I'm not hiding on the island any longer. And I don't need to be rescued."

Jaime folded the paper and handed it back to Emmett.

"I don't need to be rescued," she said and walked away.

Broken, but feeling as though she'd finally found herself.

CHAPTER EIGHTEEN

EMMETT LET THE screen door slam shut behind him. Gibson sat in the familiar green recliner in the living room, television muted, reading a tabloid.

Emmett was an idiot. He'd said it all wrong. Made it sound as though he still viewed her as the broken girl from Pittsburgh.

"Your mom was right, these stories are hilarious," Gibson said, launching into a rant about Hollywood drama. The grandfather clock chimed ten and he looked at Emmett. "You're home early."

Emmett shrugged. "There's only so long anyone can talk up the old times."

This summer was such a screwed-up mess. He'd corrected his relationship with his father, for however long it lasted. He'd cleaned up the old house and sold it. Renovated the old school, which would be a coup for his business. Lost the girl who'd made him reconsider leaving the island. Emmett blew out a breath.

"I realize I've been telling you what we're going to do instead of asking what you want."

"And now you're asking?"

Emmett nodded. "If you want to stay here I'll figure out a way to make it happen, at least for a while."

"Thank you, boy." Gibson reached across the space between them, hand tremoring. This time, though, Emmett realized the tremor wasn't a signal of a break but of gratitude. "I don't want that for you. Figuring out nursing schedules for me, wondering if I've taken my meds or eaten dinner. I'll go to Cincinnati, to that care center."

"Dad—"

"No, it's what is best, in the long run, for both of us." He was quiet for a long moment. "Why didn't you go to Jaime's?"

Emmett thought about ignoring the question. "If I'm going to talk about this, I need a drink," he said and went into the kitchen. The only drinks in the fridge were nonalcoholic. Emmett sighed. He chose a Coke and returned to the living room. Emmett told his father about the offer on the house and Jaime walking out on him, and then he went further, telling Gibson why he'd stayed away.

"You're dumber about women than I was at your age."

Emmett groaned.

"I didn't ask your mom to marry me. I told her she was going to marry me because I had a college degree and a solid career and I could provide for her. I figured, what with women's lib and all, she'd like that Darwin-esque approach of family building."

Emmett blinked. "You used survival of the fittest as a reason for Mom to marry you?"

Gibson shrugged. "Seemed like a good idea at the time because that meant I could hold on to all the cards. I didn't have to admit that she made me stronger when she was around and weaker when she wasn't. That's what love is, you know."

"Stronger or weaker?"

"Both. Loving another person makes you stronger. Makes you fight for what you want." Gibson tapped his fingers on the chair arm. "And it makes you weak, makes you put someone else's needs ahead of your own. Makes you think about what that person wants instead of what you want."

"What did Mom say when you told her your Darwin theory?"

"She told me that if she just wanted a man who would keep her in the lap of luxury with nannies for her children and diamonds for every finger she'd go after one of the Gullivers and wouldn't give me a second thought. She had her eye on Tom's older brother for a while."

Emmett choked on his drink. Tom Gulliver's brother was bald, boring and rooted for Michigan. He couldn't imagine Mary Margaret, who lived and died with the Buckeyes, having a casual date with a Wolverine much less marry one.

"But you got her back."

"Yep. Groveling was involved. I told you, love makes you weak."

"Care to elaborate on that?"

Gibson shrugged. "I seem to have forgotten." But there was a look in his eyes that told Emmett he remembered. Maybe that was one memory, one story, it would be okay for Gibson to keep just to himself. They fell into silence, watching the dark sky outside the living-room windows.

"How long do we have to vacate?"

"Thirty days."

"Plenty of time for groveling," his father suggested.

Emmett drummed his fingers on the chair arm. It made the most sense. "Being an adult sucks," he said.

"Boy, that is one thing you've got right. And growing older is right behind it on the suck-o-meter."

A little while later Gibson trudged up the stairs to his bedroom, leaving Emmett alone in the living room. The muted television glowed in the darkness and a tabloid lay beside his dad's chair.

He wadded the contract into a little ball and tossed it into the empty trash can beside the entertainment center. Selling the house made the most sense, but he didn't want to. He didn't want to cut this string to his past, not anymore. He didn't want to pretend the island was just the place he was from. It was more than that. Gulliver Island was part of him, just as Jaime was.

He stood, stepped up to the big picture window and leaned his shoulder against the frame.

He wanted Jaime, but there was no way, after tonight, she would come with him. Staying on the island or leaving had to be completely up to her.

JAIME DROPPED ANOTHER empty bottle into the barrel trash can and looked around the room. Her head hurt from a night spent tossing and turning in a bed that was cold without Emmett beside her. And that was ridiculous since he'd barely been sleeping there off and on for a month. How could she become so accustomed to him being back in her life so quickly? Love didn't make sense. She tossed another five bottles into the big trash can in the corner, hearing them clack together as they landed in the bottom.

She would call the cleaning crew later this morning. After hearing the gossips at the diner this morning, she'd wanted to see the place for herself. The rumor mill had Ernie calling in for reinforcements sometime around midnight, and insisted the school looked like something out of a horror movie. All in all, though, it wasn't so bad. Leftover cans and bottles littered the tables and floor, but there was no real damage. The windows still sparkled and the floor wasn't scuffed.

Leave it to "the class" to have a reunion that had to be one of the most peaceful in island history. She sat on one of the high-backed chairs and looked around. Right there on the staircase was where she'd first realized she wasn't over Emmett. Working the sledgehammer with him upstairs was when she'd decided she wanted more. They'd made love in the blackboard room just a few nights ago and he'd ruined all of it on the patio just a few hours before.

She wanted to be loved, and she deserved that. She deserved more than a guy hell-bent on fixing her. This wasn't an episode of freaking *One Tree Hill* or something. She stood, picked up a stack of disposable wineglasses and threw it into the trash can.

The front door opened and Maureen and Clancy walked in. Clancy surveyed the room, nodding his head.

"I thought it would be worse," he said, bending to pick up a couple of beer bottles from the floor.

"Island Maids will have this place looking less like a kegger within an hour or so," Maureen added, her attention focused on Jaime instead of the mess surrounding them. "How are you this morning?"

Jaime shrugged. She didn't want to talk about last night. Over the past eight hours she'd gone over and over every moment of the summer, trying to figure out when Emmett had decided she needed saving. It could have been when she'd panicked in Detroit or when she'd hesitated about going to the mainland the first time, but an ugly voice in her head insisted it was that first day in the diner. He'd seen her on the island and decided if he hadn't been able to save her ten years before he would do it now.

She sighed. "I'm fine, really. Just…" What?

Maureen pushed Clancy toward the back door.

"I'll just go check the yard," he said.

When they were alone Maureen said, "I tried to give you guys some room but I heard a little bit of what he said."

Jaime nodded as she picked up another bottle and threw it in the trash. "Upset" covered it, but what she felt was more than that. She turned away from her friend to pick up more of the party trash. Maureen followed, pushing the trash can while Jaime threw the remnants of the party inside.

She stupidly thought she and Emmett were building something real or at least were on the same page, but he'd only been after assuaging his conscience. Under the sorrow and pain was anger. How dare he think he was responsible for her happiness?

"I'm pissed off," she finally said. "Pissed off just about covers it." Jaime cleared a section of one table and then sat at the corner, putting her chin in her hands. "I quit my job, Mo. Not for him but because I wanted more. He made me want more, and I feel like now he's saying it isn't enough for me to just want more. He wants plans in place and contingencies."

"Does he, really?"

Jaime blew out a breath. "What I know is he might as well have been playing Barbie's Dream House with me all summer. Everything he did was to assuage his guilt over what happened to me all those years ago. Am I really so broken that he thinks he has to fix me?"

"Maybe in the beginning." Maureen took a seat, reached across the table and squeezed her hand. "It never bothered me that you preferred to hang out on the island because it made it more special when Clancy and I would leave the island. And your mom and dad were scared for you. They wanted you to be safe, and the safest place they knew—any of us knows—is right here."

"I know. But I'm not eighteen years old. I'm twenty-eight and I don't need that now. I need…"

"More?"

"Yeah." Jaime reached for an empty bottle on the table and began peeling off the label. "I want more than this tiny life that I convinced myself was all I could handle."

"You want Emmett."

"I do. I want the man who made me forget my inhibitions in Detroit and the guy who took me on a picnic on the north shore. I want the guy who is rebuilding a relationship with his father. Not the one who still blames himself for my getting hurt ten years ago."

"Then maybe you need to tell him what you want."

Jaime shook her head. "I don't know how. I don't even know what I want. I only know what I don't want."

Clancy brought two unopened bottles of tepid water to their table, bent to kiss Maureen's cheek and then disappeared upstairs. "I can get my own water, pregnant or not," she said when he was gone. "I've been pregnant three times now and it's not until week thirty-seven or so that I don't want to get off the couch. Him bringing me a bottle of water doesn't mean he thinks I can't get my own or that I'm not smart enough to hydrate. It means he's thinking about me. Caring about me. It's one of those little ways he shows me he loves me."

Jaime frowned. "Bringing you a bottle of water isn't the same as pretending to need my input on a renovation."

"True. But loving someone and accepting love from someone is as much about recognizing their faults as it is about celebrating their accomplishments." Maureen was quiet for a long moment. "What is it that you want?"

A corner of her nail polish flaked away from her thumb and Jaime kept scratching until the entire nail was free of color.

"I'd like to go to opening night of the next big blockbuster with my best friend, who deserves a girls' night off this damn island."

"I'll hold you to that, and I want popcorn with extra butter and the biggest soda they have, and you're paying."

"Done." Jaime smiled.

"Jaime. What is it that you really want?" Maureen prompted.

Jaime sighed. Somehow saying she wanted more than the island seemed like a betrayal of the very people who had been her refuge for the past decade. If she wanted to take another step forward she had to start somewhere. "I want to renovate another historical building." She took a breath. "I want my mom to accept that I really am okay and I'd love it if my dad forgave Emmett because none of this was Emmett's fault."

"And Emmett? What about him?"

Jaime chewed on her lower lip and began picking at the polish on her index finger. "I want him most of all."

Maureen put her hands over Jaime's, stilling them. "Then you're going to have to tell him what you don't want as stridently as you tell him what you do want because men, the good ones, are hardwired to protect, even when we don't think we need it."

"He wants to protect me."

"That isn't a bad thing."

"What if all he wants is to protect me?"

"I don't think you have to worry about that." Maureen squeezed her hand again. "One way or the other, though, you'll know. Then you can figure out what you want, in addition to the man, and move forward with your life." Maureen took a paper napkin from the holder on the table. "And I'm going to miss you like crazy."

Clancy and Maureen left a few minutes later and Jaime looked around the room once more. She stood, trailing her fingers along the leading of the stained glass and then over the smooth wood of the banister.

She followed the upstairs hall to the classroom to stand in front of the glass-covered blackboard. In the far corner Emmett had written their names and that night they'd made love in the sleeping bag on the floor... She crouched to look at them.

She wanted more nights like the one spent in this room. More afternoons spent in the lazy sunshine.

She wanted him, period.

There was every chance he didn't want her, not really.

Jaime stood, running her hands over the long skirt of her dress. Whether he did or he didn't, she was tired of wondering and there was one guaranteed way to find out what it was Emmett wanted out of life.

IT TOOK A week before Jaime was ready to leave. A week of packing the things she wanted to take with her and deciding what to do with the things she no longer needed. She retrieved the world atlas Emmett had given her that one Valentine's Day. She hauled her suitcase to the car, locking it in the trunk along with a few boxes of the things she wanted to have with her.

Just in case.

Then she put the atlas on the passenger seat and slid in behind the wheel. Two minutes later she stopped at the diner. Anna met her at the door with a to-go cup of coffee and Maureen pulled her into another hug.

A warm feeling began in her belly and moved up to her chest. Something that felt oddly enough like hope. "Am I crazy?"

"For being in love with Emmett Deal and wanting to be wherever he is?" Maureen shook her head. "Only as crazy as I am for loving Clancy and wanting the same thing."

Clancy met them at the door. "Let me know if I need to come down there and kick his ass for you," he said, chucking her under her chin.

"Call me the second this one goes into labor. And I want godparent privileges on this one just like the other two," Jaime said before getting into her car.

She drove onto the dock and then the ferry. Gripped the steering wheel when the boat began the crossing to the mainland and the breeze hit her face through the open window. Jaime blew out a breath.

Chances were this trip was not going to end the way she wanted it to, but at least she would know.

As least she was going after what she wanted. Emmett.

CHAPTER NINETEEN

EMMETT HUNG UP the phone and turned back to the open suitcase on his bed. Joe would handle the crews for the rest of the week and after that they would figure something out. Either Jaime would be here with him or he would be there with her.

Assuming, of course, she didn't call him ten kinds of a jerk and kick him out of her cute little cottage on the island. He'd known before he hit Dayton the day after the reunion that leaving the island without her was a mistake, but he'd been too bullheaded to turn the car around and tell her what he really wanted.

Her.

He'd started to call her once after Gibson had been settled in the assisted-living facility but decided over-the-phone was not the way to start the groveling his dad had assured him would win Jamie over.

Emmett zipped the case. He opened the front door and froze.

Jaime stood there, wearing old jeans and a

bright red T-shirt, holding the atlas he'd given her all those years ago to her chest.

God, she looked good. Emmett just stared for a long moment, taking in her mop of curls, her long, long legs.

"I thought I might find you here," she said, but didn't move to enter the house.

Emmett raised his arm slightly. "I was just on my way out."

"I'm glad I caught you," she finally said, and even her voice didn't give him a clue what she was thinking. "I would have been here sooner but I took a wrong turn, crossed the river and couldn't find my way out of Kentucky."

Emmett shook his head, trying to clear it. He'd had a speech in mind, reasons for her to leave the island and reasons for him to return, but he'd expected to have four hours to figure out the exact words. Now all he could think about was how good she looked standing on his doorstep in the afternoon sunlight with the sun making her hair shine gold.

"How did you get here?"

"I used my maps," she said, tapping her finger against the cover of the atlas. "Can I come in?"

He motioned her inside and then realized he was still holding the stupid suitcase and standing by the door. He set the case on the floor and when Jaime sat on the cream-colored sofa he took the adjacent chair.

"I'm not going to say I'm sorry for selling the house."

Not the way to start this groveling thing, E. So not the way.

He fisted his hand and squeezed. "I want to say I'm sorry for all of it. Joining in the school project and taking you outside your comfort zone. I'd like to say it was all unconscious, but I've gotten pretty good at figuring out what people need and making sure they get it."

Nice, Emmett, dig that hole a little deeper.

"I just wanted to help."

"I know." Jaime shook her head and sighed out a heavy breath. "The point isn't what you did or didn't do, it's the way you did it. Was all of that—the trip to Detroit and asking my opinion on everything—about me or was it about you?"

Emmett decided to go for honesty since he apparently sucked at the groveling thing. "Both. In the diner that first day I caught a glimpse of the pre-attack Jaime and I couldn't let her go. Not again. And, like I said, I've gotten pretty good at fixing problems for people. Changing tires, hiring people who are down on their luck. I thought maybe I could repair what I couldn't fix then. I'm sorry."

Jaime watched him for a long moment. "I don't want your apology."

"Then what do you want?" Emmett shoved his hand through his hair.

Jaime folded her arms over her chest then stood to look out the window. "I love the island. I love the comfort of knowing every face I see. I love the quietness of the mornings and the stillness of the evenings. I like that every Thursday is meat loaf and mashed potatoes at the diner and that anytime I have a craving for yellow perch I can grab a sandwich on the dock.

"Maureen is the best friend I've ever had... and before this summer I've never felt out of place there, but now I do. I feel like I'm supposed to be somewhere or doing something else. You all have *lives*. I want to find that for myself."

Something like hope seemed to squeeze the breath from Emmett's lungs. He stepped across the floor to stand beside Jaime at the window. Before he could, she moved out of his reach.

"Part of that is you. When you came back I took a hard look at what I'd been doing with my life. I didn't like what I saw. I want more."

"This life you want…" Emmett knew he shouldn't ask the question, not when he was 99 percent sure he knew the answer, but he couldn't stop the words from spilling from his mouth. "Is it on the island?"

She reached out her hand to run her fingers along his cheek and it was the sweetest touch he could ever remember receiving. "The life I want isn't about holding on to the past, it's about letting go to live in the present."

He captured her hand, feeling the burn of her skin against his and hoping he could figure out a way to let her go. "Then stay."

JAIME DRAGGED IN an unsteady breath. She wanted to stay. She'd been afraid he would tell her to go on with her life away from Cincinnati. Away from him. But there were still things he didn't know. Things he should know before she told him everything she wanted.

"I never told you I went to therapy, did I?" She wanted to tell him this without looking at him, but that was a cop-out. So she settled on the sofa and folded her hands in her lap. "I'm going to go a little farther back first.

"I skipped out on the college experience because my mom couldn't deal with me being out of her sight. I took that job with the winery because my dad convinced Tom Gulliver a professional PR person would be better than an intern. I didn't talk to anyone about what happened to me for five years…"

She told him about Byron and about starting therapy to try to get off the island. About never setting foot off the island once the therapist told her she was cured.

"And then Clara dumped the reunion project on Maureen and me, and Tom said they wouldn't open the winery for the big party. People started talking about it all again. The craziness of our class…and all those stories eventually wound around to Pittsburgh."

"And then I came back."

"Not before I decided a big project would take the focus off me. That's where the reno idea developed. And then you came back to town."

"And I came to your rescue and mucked all those plans up."

"No, you made me see that all the plans I'd made were just like the white noise machines that help insomniacs sleep. At the reunion you said I had to figure out what I wanted, and you implied that you having a tie to the island would muddy the waters for me."

"I was—"

Jaime interrupted him. She had to get this out, all of it, or she would never know for sure if he wanted her or if he wanted to fix her. "I want more than the life I've been leading and I'm going to go after it before it's too late."

This time Emmett watched her for a long moment, as if calculating what to say. Or maybe just how to say it. "What is it that you want?"

She wanted Emmett, of that Jaime was certain.

She wanted her parents to let go of their guilt over what had happened to her.

She wanted to walk down a crowded city street with no fear about the people surrounding her.

Mostly, she wanted Emmett.

"I don't want you to want me because you feel guilty about what happened. I can't change choosing to walk through that alley, or the fact that a mentally ill man attacked me. I can only change my reaction to those things. And I choose not to be afraid. I'm going to choose to move forward." *And I'm going to love you*. She couldn't say those words, though. She'd told him she loved him when he was sleeping. Thought it that day on the north shore. A part of him loved her, too, but she was afraid that part of him was smaller than the part of him that felt guilty about an event that wasn't his doing.

"I want you to be happy, and if that happiness comes from the island, then you should stay."

Emmett's voice was raw and it took all Jaime's strength to stay seated on the couch.

"My happiness does come from the island. It's where my friends are, where my parents live. And as frustrating as they are, I love them. The island is who I've been for the past twenty-eight years." She couldn't sit still, not with Emmett studying her like one of the frogs in biology lab. "But I haven't been happy here for a long time. I've been content, and that's okay, but it isn't happy. I want happy."

She looked at him, and the look on his face stopped her from saying more. His expression was stark, the tan he'd picked up working on the school diminished.

"I want happy, too."

"Then you should go where you're happy, Emmett."

"I'm already here."

"Emmett—"

"Where you are, that's where I'm happiest," he said, moving closer to her, the words seemingly ripped from his throat. "Not because I think you need fixing, but because you're home."

Her heart seemed to pause for a moment and the world seemed to stop spinning. For a long moment there was only her, Emmett and the stillness of his house.

"My father wants Cincinnati, I think, to make it easier on me. I was leaving today to go after you and to bring you home with me. Figure out your life here. Figure it out with me. I love you."

Jaime's heart seemed to stop completely. He'd never said those words to her, not before the attack and certainly not since he'd been back.

Pulling her to her feet, he gripped her hands in his and she felt the familiar sizzle that always seem to burn to life when he touched her.

He put his finger to her lips. "Do you want to be with me?"

Jaime's first instinct was to explain but Emmett narrowed his eyes at her so she simply said, "Yes."

Jaime put her hands on his face, holding him in place; making him look at her. "I love you, too. I want to be with you. On Gulliver. Off Gulliver. I don't care as long as you're there." She leaned her forehead against his chin and sighed. There would be obstacles, no matter where they lived, but he loved her. That seemed like the perfect place to start.

Lifting her chin, he pressed his lips to hers and Jaime wound her arms around his neck.

"I don't know what the future holds. I do know that I love you," she said, "and I know I want to be with you."

"We'll figure it out. No. You. You'll figure it out. You're a smart, talented, capable woman."

"I hear there is a construction company here that specializes in restoring old homes. The owner of it likes to show off his muscles on television now and then. You think maybe he'd hire a girl who has zero skill with a sledgehammer but knows how to match flooring and paint samples?"

"He'd be a fool not to."

She smiled and hugged him close. "We make a good team."

His arms slid around her waist, holding her to him. "We make the best team."

Emmett kissed her again, and this time Jaime thought she felt a promise for the future in the way his body melded with hers. A future that was bright, indeed.

Six Months Later

JAIME TRACED HER fingers over the names on the chalkboard. Her name. Emmett's. All the people who had come before. She took a deep breath as Maureen poked her head around the door.

"They're ready when you are. And Emmett looks like he might throw up. Or faint. Don't worry, Clancy has smelling salts and he brought a couple of throw-up bags, just in case."

Jaime motioned her into the room on the second floor of the old school. "Do I look okay?"

Maureen threw her arms around Jaime, careful not to wrinkle the white satin dress she wore or to knock the veil askew. "You look better than okay. You're stunning. I'm so glad you guys came back here to get married."

So was Jaime. They considered a church near Cincinnati, but it didn't feel right. "Tom actually said he'd let us use the winery for the wedding and reception."

"He wasn't afraid of another prank?"

Jaime grinned. "I think my dad had a little to do with it. But getting married here, where we started, it fit."

Maureen stepped back, and Jaime fought

the urge to fidget. Not because of the scars that were completely hidden beneath layers of satin and lace. Because of the belly bump Emmett swore wasn't quite visible yet. Jaime disagreed and so did most of her pants, but so far no one here had guessed.

"You ready?" Maureen asked.

Everything she wanted.

After today everything she ever wanted would be hers. Emmett. The island. The life they were building in Cincinnati.

She took a deep breath. "I'm ready," she said.

Mason stood outside the door, waiting, and Jaime stayed just inside the room. It was silly, she knew, they lived together, after all, but she didn't want Emmett to see her just yet.

Maureen waited at the top of the stairs for a moment as Ronda started the wedding music. Once she was halfway down the stairs, Jaime stepped out onto the landing, and slowly walked to the head of the stairs.

The butterflies in her stomach calmed when she met Emmett's gaze across the expanse of the room. Sunlight shone through the stained-glass windows and sparkled across the hardwood floors.

"You look beautiful, baby," her father said as he patted her hand.

"Thanks, Dad," she whispered.

Gibson sat with his nurse on one side and Jaime's mother on the other. Getting him here had been a struggle, but when he smiled at her from the front row another burst of happiness hit her.

Mason squeezed her arm and they started down the stairs.

Everyone she loved was inside this building. And the one she loved most stood near the windows, waiting.

Everything had changed so quickly, and yet it seemed to have taken forever to get to this point.

Ten years after that trip to Pittsburgh, Jaime had finally come home.

* * * * *

LARGER-PRINT BOOKS!

GET 2 FREE LARGER-PRINT NOVELS PLUS
2 FREE GIFTS!

✦ HARLEQUIN®

Romance

From the Heart, For the Heart

YES! Please send me 2 FREE LARGER-PRINT Harlequin® Romance novels and my 2 FREE gifts (gifts are worth about $10). After receiving them, if I don't wish to receive any more books, I can return the shipping statement marked "cancel." If I don't cancel, I will receive 4 brand-new novels every month and be billed just $5.09 per book in the U.S. or $5.49 per book in Canada. That's a savings of at least 15% off the cover price! It's quite a bargain! Shipping and handling is just 50¢ per book in the U.S. and 75¢ per book in Canada.* I understand that accepting the 2 free books and gifts places me under no obligation to buy anything. I can always return a shipment and cancel at any time. Even if I never buy another book, the two free books and gifts are mine to keep forever.

119/319 HDN GHWC

Name	(PLEASE PRINT)

Address		Apt. #

City	State/Prov.	Zip/Postal Code

Signature (if under 18, a parent or guardian must sign)

Mail to the **Reader Service:**
IN U.S.A.: P.O. Box 1867, Buffalo, NY 14240-1867
IN CANADA: P.O. Box 609, Fort Erie, Ontario L2A 5X3

Want to try two free books from another line?
Call 1-800-873-8635 or visit www.ReaderService.com.

* Terms and prices subject to change without notice. Prices do not include applicable taxes. Sales tax applicable in N.Y. Canadian residents will be charged applicable taxes. Offer not valid in Quebec. This offer is limited to one order per household. Not valid for current subscribers to Harlequin Romance Larger-Print books. All orders subject to credit approval. Credit or debit balances in a customer's account(s) may be offset by any other outstanding balance owed by or to the customer. Please allow 4 to 6 weeks for delivery. Offer available while quantities last.

Your Privacy—The Reader Service is committed to protecting your privacy. Our Privacy Policy is available online at www.ReaderService.com or upon request from the Reader Service.

We make a portion of our mailing list available to reputable third parties that offer products we believe may interest you. If you prefer that we not exchange your name with third parties, or if you wish to clarify or modify your communication preferences, please visit us at www.ReaderService.com/consumerchoice or write to us at Reader Service Preference Service, P.O. Box 9062, Buffalo, NY 14240-9062. Include your complete name and address.

HRLP15

LARGER-PRINT BOOKS!

READERSERVICE.COM

Manage your account online!

- Review your order history
- Manage your payments
- Update your address

> ### We've designed the Reader Service website just for you.

Enjoy all the features!

- Discover new series available to you, and read excerpts from any series.
- Respond to mailings and special monthly offers.
- Connect with favorite authors at the blog.
- Browse the Bonus Bucks catalog and online-only exculsives.
- Share your feedback.

Visit us at:

ReaderService.com